Also by John Owens

Pursuit

YOSEMITE SUMMER

JOHN C. OWENS

LifeRich
PUBLISHING

LifeRich Publishing is a registered trademark of The Reader's Digest Association, Inc.

LifeRich Publishing books may be ordered through booksellers or by contacting:

LifeRich Publishing
1663 Liberty Drive
Bloomington, IN 47403
www.liferichpublishing.com
844-686-9607

Because of the dynamic nature of the Internet, any web addresses or links contained in this book may have changed since publication and may no longer be valid. The views expressed in this work are solely those of the author and do not necessarily reflect the views of the publisher, and the publisher hereby disclaims any responsibility for them.

Any people depicted in stock imagery provided by Getty Images are models, and such images are being used for illustrative purposes only.
Certain stock imagery © Getty Images.

ISBN: 978-1-4897-3341-2 (sc)
ISBN: 978-1-4897-3340-5 (hc)
ISBN: 978-1-4897-3342-9 (e)

Library of Congress Control Number: 2021900942

Print information available on the last page.

LifeRich Publishing rev. date: 04/13/2021

For we wrestle not against flesh and blood, but against
principalities, against powers, against the rulers of the darkness
of this world, against spiritual wickedness in high places.
—Ephesians 6:12 (King James Version)

Acknowledgment

My sincere gratitude and thanks to Becky A. DePaulis for all her assistance in editing and proofreading this book.

Contents

Chapter 1

WALKING THE DOG

August 2020.

Heinrich Mueller knelt down and unclipped his dog's leash. "Go get 'em, Wolfgang!" He smiled as his dog chased a rabbit into the underbrush. Both animals quickly disappeared. Wolfgang's bark echoed through the hot summer-evening air.

Heinrich stood on the hillside near the edge of the forest while patiently waiting for the dog to return. Wolfie was getting older now. *Just like me*, he thought. *Older and slower.* This brought a twinge of sadness to the old German. He surveyed the landscape, and it stirred memories of his boyhood in the Bavarian Alps. But here in the American West, the mountains looked more chiseled and seemed to stretch forever. After sixty years, he was still awed by their grandeur.

After five minutes, Heinrich harrumphed. *I hope he didn't catch that rabbit. It's much too late to bathe that dog.*

After ten minutes, worry stirred in his gut. *This is too long.*

A few moments more and he stepped into the brush after his old hound. On a late, summer evening like this, darkness fell quickly in these mountains. The last thing Heinrich wanted to do was stumble home in the dark over the uneven, stone-filled pathways.

"Wolfie!" Heinrich called to the dog as he left the path and trudged through the waist-high weeds. Up ahead he could see a clearing in the trees. *Ah, I know this area.* The memory came suddenly of the strangely dressed young man he had encountered earlier on his walk. The young man had asked if Heinrich had seen a boy and girl walking this path together.

Heinrich had laughed to himself. *He must be a jealous boyfriend.* Heinrich simply answered, "No."

The young man thanked Heinrich and walked on, but not before turning back after several steps. "Mister, I wouldn't go into the woods tonight. There is something evil in motion here."

Heinrich had stroked his chin and nodded thoughtfully, thanking the boy. He laughed to himself.

At just this moment, whimpering caught his attention in the deep grass off to his left. He walked toward the noise. When he pushed back the grass, Wolfgang lay there writhing in agony. The dog's cries were weakening, and the dog began to shake.

Heinrich lifted his dog up in his arms. He turned to run, but he stumbled over a large limb, then fell, sprawling awkwardly. Wolfie tumbled from his arms and his glasses flew into the weeds.

As Heinrich groped around for his glasses, the limb began to move toward him.

He got to his feet and bent over to recover his inert companion when a loud rattling noise froze him in place. Heinrich looked behind to see a monstrously large rattlesnake strike him on the back of his thigh. The pain from the bite was excruciating. He fell to his knees. As he tried to get up, the snake struck him again on the back of his neck. Then on the abdomen. Now shaking, Heinrich lurched to his feet. The snake struck again and again.

Heinrich peered into the clearing. The dark shadows of men moved slowly around and around in the torchlight. A tall man in a hooded robe stood in the center while holding something shiny high above his head. Heinrich's mind was growing foggy. The lights and the low, guttural chant took Heinrich back to his time as a Hitler Youth. Terror gripped Heinrich as a scene from the grand night spectacle at Nuremburg assaulted his memory. The old man, confused and swaying now, looked down and saw he wore his old SS uniform. Heinrich Mueller managed to raise his arm. As he collapsed over his dead dog, he croaked out, "Seig heil."

Chapter 2

CAMP SEQUOIA

Earlier that day.

The morning sun sent rays streaming over the tops of the pine trees and through the big window in the administrative cabin. It was a sunny but cool morning in the Sierra Nevada, and there was just the barest hint of color change on some of the trees. Aspen leaves rippled in a gentle, morning breeze. The sound of campers' laughter and their shuffling feet on the trails as they headed to breakfast broke the silence of the wilderness. The camp bell rang out its morning salute, and aromas from the camp kitchen wafted in the window.

Sam and Dave Maxwell sat on a long, brown, leather couch in the Camp Sequoia office with camp director Pastor Winston Adamson and their lifelong friend, director-in-training Logan Williams.

"Well, gentlemen, I guess I can leave tonight's program in your capable hands." Mr. Adamson looked at the three young men. "After I finish up handling some correspondence, I'll be leaving for Reno. It's time to do some fundraising at our sponsoring churches. I'll be gone a few days, so if you need anything"—he looked between the young men—"Logan here will help you out. Right, Logan?"

Logan nodded and smiled. The camp director got up, shook all three young men's hands, then went into his office.

Logan smiled at his buddies, the twins. "Guys, you know I'll help anyway I can, but remember Mr. Adamson says we are *really* low on funds, so—"

Sam interrupted. "We understand, and we shouldn't need a penny. In fact, we've got tonight all planned out and ready to go. You wanna hear about it?"

"No. Surprise me. Mr. Adamson trusts you. That's good enough. You know where to find me if you need me." Logan patted a clipboard stacked with invoices in his lap. "I've got enough to keep me busy here, and I know you two well enough to guess you've got something special up your sleeves. I'm looking forward to it." Logan stood, turned, and walked over to his desk in the reception area.

Sam muttered to himself, "It'll be a hot time in the old camp tonight."

His brother elbowed him and shook his head.

Dave waited until he shut the door after they left, then looked at his twin brother. "Sam, I know you want to make this a night to remember, but I'm wondering if performing *Elijah and the Prophets of Ba'al* will scare the bejabbers out of the younger campers—especially with what you've got planned."

"Brother, chill out. Everything's fine. It'll be an evening they'll never forget! I've got it all under control. Ron and Dooley are hooking up a water line in the trees near Elijah's altar, and Leonard is hanging the wires to bring down 'fire from heaven' as we sit here. Believe me: nothing will go wrong. Nothing *can* go wrong. Relax."

Dave looked his twin in the eye. "I hope you're right."

"Quit worrying and enjoy the ride."

Dave got up to leave. "I've got to get fitted for my costume. See you at dinner."

"Don't forget to wear that big, old, bushy, red beard tonight, Elijah."

Dave laughed and left.

Sam smiled and went to check on his work crews. He found Dooley sitting on the canteen porch drinking a soda. "Is the water piping all set?" Dooley was in his late teens and was well-known to be skilled at avoiding work.

Dooley swallowed the rest with a gulp and said, "Yep. Done a while ago."

"Any problems?"

"Nope. How difficult can gluing big plastic pipe together be?"

"You do understand how important the water sequence is to the production, right?"

"Production? Now it's a production." Dooley smiled. "Don't worry, boss. We've got everything covered. Ron thought we should camouflage the pipe run with hunters' camo netting, so we did."

"Excellent, Dooley. Where in the world did you get that bottle of Jolt? I thought they quit making it years ago."

"Uh, the canteen girls found a case back in canteen storage and saved me a six-pack."

"It must be ten years old."

"Tastes fine to me."

Sam shook his head. "Okay. Dooley, don't forget your costume fitting."

"Got it. Later." Dooley raised the bottle and gave Sam a big grin.

Sam jogged to the outdoor amphitheater that also functioned as a chapel for Camp Sequoia. Looking down at the "stage" area, he felt a deep love for the camp. He'd attended Camp Sequoia for just over twenty years—since he was seven years old. The camp experience had played a formative role in his Christian life. Now he enjoyed the privilege of serving as a counselor for teen campers. Sam hoped he could influence other campers in the way that the Sequoia staff had influenced him.

Leonard perched high on a ladder, attaching wires running from a pile of stones to a rudimentary platform in the trees. The highlight of the evening's show would come when Leonard launched a series of flaming papier-mâché balls down the wires, incinerating "Elijah's sacrifice."

"How's it going, Leonard?"

"Right well, Mr. Maxwell. Almost done."

"Looks good. Make double sure the wires are secure, okay?"

"They're all set, Sam, but the wire we *were* going to use was gone. Calvin used it to repair the boundary fence last week. When I explained we had planned to use it to run papier-mâché balls down as part of the show, he gave me this." He held the wooden spool of wire for Sam to see. "He said it should work for hanging the paper balls."

"Gee, that looks pretty thin compared to the old wire."

"Yeah, it's a bit thinner, but I checked online and it *says* that this wire is even stronger than the old one. Seems the Chinese wire manufacturers are doing a bang-up job. Besides, you can hardly see these."

"That's true. Well, I guess it'll be okay."

"No problems, amigo."

"You have your safety harness? It wouldn't do to have you fall out of the tree."

"Yup, and I made a ghillie suit out of some old camo cloth, vines, and twigs, so I'll be invisible among the foliage tonight."

"Great! See you later—or maybe I won't."

Leonard laughed, nodded, and turned to finish his job. Sam walked up the amphitheater steps, back toward central camp. He was thinking ahead to tonight's show. A cool gust of wind rustled the trees above, sending a chill up his arms. He stopped and looked back at the stage. Everything appeared to be coming along fine.

* * *

Over in the "Lydia" section of the High School girls' camp, Dani Maxwell and her friends lay in their bunks chatting about high school girl things: boys, clothes, boys, the upcoming school year, boys, and tonight's campfire.

"I've been saving these new jeans for tonight," said Toni. She hopped up and down on one leg trying to force her way into a pair of faded pants with jagged, thready slits across the front of each leg without ripping them further.

Dani laughed and grinned.

Leah opined, "Geez, those are almost a pair of pants."

"They look like you picked them out of a Dumpster." Dani tugged at a loose thread. Everyone laughed, including Judy, a camper from a nearby town who stood at the mirror. "I have a pair of black yoga pants you could wear tonight."

"No, thanks. I'm not going Goth, and I don't like yoga." Toni wrinkled her nose.

"Besides Dixon might like the Goth look," Judy persisted, prompting another round of laughter and o-o-oh's.

"Dixon? Really?" Toni laughed.

"Toni's got her eye on Dixon," said Dani.

"Dixon? Willie? Who next? Like I'm her social secretary?" Judy protested with a big smile.

"Let's get a move on it." Leah moved toward the door. "I'm starving."

The girls headed off to dinner.

* * *

Sam and Dave sat at a long table in the chow hall with the counselor staff. "Now right after Dave yells, 'Yo, Israelites, kill 'em. Kill all the prophets of Ba'al,' then Dawson, you and your crew will run out from the woods at me hollering, 'Down with Ba'al,' and swinging your swords. Just don't hit me too hard. I'll be ready with this big blood packet that I'll smash on my head."

The table erupted in general laughter.

Chapter 3

SHOWTIME

Sam peeked out from between the makeshift curtains to see the split log benches filling fast and people milling around behind them. He turned to his twin and scratched his head. "Dave, does your wig itch? Mine is driving me nuts."

"No, not really, but it is pretty warm."

"Geez." Sam attempted to resettle his black, oiled wig on his head. "I look more like Elvis than a Ba'aliac, or is it Ba'alian priest?"

Music then filled the night and the curtains parted. An offstage narrator began to tell the story of Elijah the Tishbite and the 450 prophets of Ba'al. There were two piles of stones on the makeshift stage. One was piled roughly, and the other was neatly arranged with a black, shiny, steel barbeque grate on top. Surrounding the latter were four characters dressed in loincloths and tan bodysuits. Crude red slashes representing self-administered lacerations covered their arms and legs. These gleamed in the spotlight. They wailed and writhed in a supposedly pagan dance.

Sam minced out onto the stage, with his nose high up in the air. Boos and hisses cascaded down from the crowd of campers as he joined his group of supplicants. He urged them to dance faster and slash themselves again and again. Sam wore a dark-blue robe adorned with the moon, stars, and skulls. Dave stalked in from the opposite side of the stage. Portraying the prophet Elijah, he wore a goatskin robe and a wild reddish wig and beard. The crowd roared its approval. Elijah raised his staff above his head in both hands and shouted to the priests of Ba'al, "Call out louder! Perhaps Ba'al is on vacation or in the bathroom!"

Laughter erupted from the crowd.

"Enough of this sacrilege!" cried Elijah loudly. He continued to look upward and pointed his staff at the tree overhead, signaling Leonard to be ready to light the paper balls. "Water! Water!" Elijah yelled.

Several would-be Israelites carried buckets on to the stage and appeared to douse Elijah's altar.

The wind was picking up as the narrator continued the story, and Sam watched the tree limbs sway. He brushed away some water that had dripped off his wig and onto his face, then looked up at the water line. A steady drip was quickly becoming a flow of water. Straining, he could see where the water pipe had begun to come apart above his head.

The narration built toward the climactic scene as Sam yelled, "Noooooo!"

Dave smiled. Sam was overplaying it a bit, so Dave called out loudly, "Hear me, Oh Lord, hear me that this people may know." That signaled Leonard to light the papier mâché balls and send them down the wires. As they came sliding down, a gust of wind hit the fireballs, causing two of the wires to snap. Burning balls dropped on the grass near the stage, setting the dry grass instantly aflame.

The crowd screamed and ran helter-skelter from the theater.

Dave yelled, "Water! Sam, turn on the water!" but Ron had already opened the valve.

A torrent of water jetted out the broken line well short of the fire, splashing Sam. Sam took off his robe to beat out the flames. Others followed suit, while Dave and two counselors fought the fire with scenery placards. Ron had climbed onto Dooley's shoulders, reconnecting the pipe. Water now gushed to the blaze, quickly extinguishing it.

"Anyone hurt?" Dave scanned the theater. He caught sight of his sister Dani and her friends exiting the back of the theater, presumably heading toward their cabin.

Sam's leg hair was singed, and Dooley had a small, reddened area on the back of his left hand from the fire, but otherwise, everyone was unscathed.

At this moment, Mary Beth Moody, the girls' head counselor, came trotting up to Sam and Dave with Logan in tow. Logan grinned, "I don't remember the story ending quite that way."

Mary Beth, clearly agitated, interrupted Logan. "What were you thinking? Fire? Water? People could've been burned alive—or drowned."

Sam pulled the now drenched and smoke scented wig from his head. "No one was hurt, Mary Beth, and the only thing burned was a bushel or two of weeds."

"That's not the point."

"Well then, what is the point? Did any of the campers get hurt? Did someone have a heart attack?"

"Rhonda Binkey twisted her ankle, and Cathy Waite tore out the elbow in her sweater."

"You *know* Binkey is always hurt. She can't walk to chow without falling down. And I'll personally buy Cathy a new sweater."

Attempting to head off a full-blown argument, Dave stepped in between the two. "Mary Beth is right, Sam." Dave looked from Mary Beth to Logan. "We goofed up. But even when everything went wrong, no real damage was done so we should just—"

Dani had come running up. She was out of breath and pulled at Dave's sleeve. She gasped, "I need to talk to you two. Now!"

Mary Beth Moody looked at the girl. "What is it, Dani?"

"Family business, Mary Beth. Personal."

"Oh."

Logan took Mary Beth by the arm and steered her away. "Take care of this business with your sister, guys. Come see me later. No harm done. Heck, this might even save us a few bucks on lawn maintenance. We'll need to figure how to uh, spin this for Mr. Adamson." He turned and sauntered away, chuckling with Mary Beth in tow, still sputtering.

Sam and Dave walked offstage with Dani. "What is it, sis?" Dave looked at his sister, eyes radiating concern. Dani was ten years younger than Sam and Dave, and they had always looked out for their little sister.

"It's Toni. She went off with a boy. He does odd jobs around the camp. They left before the show and she hasn't come back."

"Okay." Sam stomped on a smoldering leaf. "And you want to know how to tell her what a thrilling performance she missed?"

"Come on, Sam. I'm serious. She could get sent home."

"Okay. Okay. What's his name?"

"Dixon."

Dave looked exasperated, "First or last?

"Not sure. He just goes by Dixon."

"A one-namer—like Bono or Rinaldo," wisecracked Sam.

"Sam, are you gonna help me or not?" Dani's eyes filled with tears.

"Of course. What does he look like? Do you know where they were going?"

"He's almost as tall as you. He says he's in college. He's probably seven or eight years younger than you. He has brown hair and I'm not sure about his eye color, but I know they were dark. Oh, and he has a tattoo on his forearm. It's a pitchfork, but it's embellished like some kind of symbol. I don't know where they were going. Toni was acting all mysterious, but this guy, he's—he's kinda weird."

"In what way?" Dave rubbed his chin.

"I don't know. He just seemed weird to me. He was always talking about magic."

Sam turned to Dave. "You go talk with Logan. I'll take a walk and look for these two. They are probably down by the lake—making out." He grinned.

Dani started to cry softly. Dave took her elbow and steered her back toward her cabin. "Dani, you didn't do anything wrong. You don't need to cry. Sam will find them and get her back to the cabin by bed check. He knows every make-out spot within ten miles of here."

"It's my fault, Dave. I introduced them."

"Oh."

She didn't see him look away. His little sister was taking this seriously.

Chapter 4

SEARCHIN'

Sam headed back to his cabin and put on a pair of jeans and a T-shirt. It was getting chilly so he went to grab a jacket but stopped and grabbed his damp, smoky, priestly robe instead. *Smells like smoke. A little damp. Maybe that's a good thing. It'll add a bit of gravitas.* He laughed to himself. Sam grabbed his long stick he had used as a staff in the play, threw the gown around his shoulders like a cape, and headed off to find the lovebirds.

As he topped a nearby hill, an old man walking his dog approached.

"Good evening, sir. Have you seen a boy and girl out walking this way?"

"No." The old man smiled and stared at the costume.

Sam turned theatrically to him, warning him of dangers in the night in a theatrically somber tone.

Sam then proceeded to the camp lake, which was really a good-sized pond. A cordoned-off section served as the camp's swimming area. It was formed from an impoundment of a large feeder creek to the Merced River and replete with small coves and reedy expanses. Finding no one, Sam turned and headed away into the fields along a path bordering the creek.

The sky was nearly completely dark now, but Sam knew this area well; besides, he had a strong flashlight. As he walked on, he occasionally called out, "Toni," but didn't receive an answer. A dog barked then yelped a few times in the distance. Then silence again.

Sam walked along the path near the edge of the old woods, swinging his light this way and that, occasionally looking into the trees. He knew the path ahead bordered a drop-off of about six to eight feet on his left so he took extra care hugging the opposite edge of the trail. Through the night silence, Sam stopped to listen several times as he thought he heard what sounded like the murmuring of voices emanating from the woods. He headed off the path through the waist-high weeds toward the noise and a stand of old trees.

Lights shimmered in the distance through the trunks and Sam beelined toward it. He turned off his light, bent over, and crept closer. *They might be poachers.* As he approached, torches flickered, and Sam strained to make out the words of a low-pitched chant. *Sounds like a foreign language. Kind of like a Gregorian chant, but coarser.*

A flash of light came from a clearing ahead. He stopped and stared. *What in the world is going on?* The old man he'd met on the ridge suddenly stood up from the weeds beyond the clearing. The man shouted something incomprehensible, and just as suddenly, he fell back down. Sam watched, transfixed with horror as hooded figures walked slowly around a tall, pale man wearing a cloak and standing beside the large pile of rocks. He held a long, black knife high above his head.

On this makeshift altar was a young woman about his sister Dani's age. *That's Toni.*

Horror-struck, he opened his mouth to call out a warning to the girl, but a hand clapped it shut from behind. He struggled to move, but a pair of strong arms held him fast.

A voice whispered in his ear, "Quiet now. It's too late for the girl. Their guardian knows you're here and he's coming for you. Don't move. Stay silent." The arms let him go slowly, and the man came around to face him. "Sam, go back the way you came, right now. I can hold the beast at bay while you retreat. Quickly. Go now."

"What? Who are you?" Sam blurted.

There was a rustling in the brush, a loud rattling, and then a hissing noise.

"Not now. Go!" the man whispered urgently. "And don't speak. Run!"

Sam tore back through the weeds toward the path. Behind him the noise increased, followed by more loud rattling. A loud female scream echoed through the night air, and Sam felt every hair on his arms stand up.

He ran in terror as loud scuffling noises followed from where he had just been. Like a modern-day Lot, Sam didn't stop to turn and look. *A rattlesnake? Man, it must be a giant!*

A series of loud thumps suddenly erupted from behind, and then all noise stopped. As he neared the trail, he remembered the drop-off ahead and fumbled to turn on his flashlight. He shook it and flicked at the switch while he ran. A blue flash lit the area, causing him to turn as he ran. He was suddenly aware that he was sailing through the air. Pain lanced through his leg as it gave way under him. He hit the ground rolling awkwardly. Everything went black as his head hit a rock.

Chapter 5

RUMINATIONS

Dave was peeved with Sam. Despite Sam's assurances everything was under control, things fell apart, and this time it was fortunate that no one was seriously burned—or worse. Dave's hopes of spending next summer as director-in-training now seemed dashed. He cleaned himself up and sat down to read a bit to relax his mind. After an hour and a half, Sam still hadn't returned. *He probably knows I'm angry.* Dave quickly scribbled a note and tossed it onto Sam's pillow. *Wake me when you get in. We need to talk.* He then climbed into bed and picked up the book he was currently reading, Frank Peretti's *Illusion*. Within a few minutes, his eyes grew heavy and he dozed off.

Early morning sunshine awakened Dave, and the first thing he did was look over to Sam's bed. *He didn't even wake me up.* Anger surged through Dave. Then he realized that Sam's bed was undisturbed since last night and his note remained right where Dave had dropped it. He felt his stomach tighten. He rubbed his face and got up. He walked around the cabin and looked into the bathroom in a cursory search for Sam, but no dice. Had Sam not come home? *Hmmm. This isn't like Sam. He didn't even seem upset or concerned last evening. Where is he?*

Dave went to breakfast and looked for Dani. She sat alone at a table nursing a frown, her food untouched.

She looked up as Dave approached. "I thought Sam was going to find Toni."

"Dani, Sam didn't come back last night. I don't know where he is, and I see you don't either."

Dani shook her head.

"Did Toni make it back?"

"No, but Edie, our counselor, just poked her head through the doorway and said, 'Good night.' I don't think she even looked in to check anyone."

"That's not going to go well for Edie if Toni doesn't turn up soon."

"I'm not worried about Edie, Dave. That's on her."

"Sure. I'm just sayin'. Right now, I'm worried about Sam and Toni. I should go and see Logan. I know we're friends, but in his position here at camp, he needs to know about all of this. Then I'm going to hunt for Sam—and Toni."

"You don't think anything happened to them, do you?"

"I seriously doubt it, honey. Toni made a bad choice, but we'll find her. I just don't get Sam. I can't see any reason he'd stay out all night." Dave paused. "You said this Dixon was weird. Did he strike you as violent?"

"Not that I ever noticed. He was just strange. Like I said, all he talked about was magic and spells and sacrifices. He reminded me of one of those *Dungeons & Dragons* freaks, you know LARPers, but he creeped me out. I got the impression he wasn't talking about a game." Dani shuddered and stared up at her brother. "Dave, you don't think they'll tell Toni's parents, do you?"

"Dani, wouldn't you want to know if your daughter had gone missing? And this is a major liability issue for the camp."

Dani nodded. "Guess so. It's just—it's just that it took me almost two years of coaxing to get Toni to even consider coming here, and her parents didn't seem too keen on the idea either."

"Dani, Toni is old enough to understand camp rules. I can't promise anything. We'll have to see how things play out. Don't get any ideas about being a hero and go looking yourself. You hear me?"

"Yes." Dani's cabinmates began to filter in. When several approached the table, Dave made his exit.

Chapter 6

UH-OH

Logan swiveled in his chair and looked at Dave. A big grin covered his face. "Well, that was quite a show, buddy."

"Yeah, guess so."

"No, I mean it. Before the fireworks, the audience was transfixed. You know it's really hard to bring Bible stories to life for kids nowadays. Everyone wants action. They expect the Terminator or Iron Man shooting up the town. No attention spans. You know what I mean?"

"Yeah, I do."

"Well, you had it nailed."

"Actually, it was Sam who came up with the program. I just wrote some of the narration." Dave cleared his throat. "Logan, there's something I need to tell you."

"Another play idea?" Logan noticed that Dave's somber expression had not changed.

"No, nothing like that. Toni LaRusso was apparently out all of last night."

"Gee whiz, she knows our rules. When did you find this out?"

"A few minutes ago. But there's more. That's what Dani was concerned about when she came running up to talk to us."

"Didn't she say it was family business?"

Dave shrugged. "Yes. But at that time, Toni had just wandered off with your handy boy, Dixon, and—"

"Who?"

"You know, I guess he's a young guy who helps old Calvin the caretaker."

Dave and Logan stared at each other in confusion.

"We have no handyman's helper, Dave. And there is no one here, camper or worker, named Dixon."

"Well, that's not all. Dani asked if we would go find Toni before curfew, and Sam agreed to do it."

"Okay?" Logan raked his hand through his hair and leaned forward.

"Sam hasn't come back all night, either."

"Huh? Dave, you don't think he's with Toni, do you?"

Dave looked incredulous. "No, certainly not. He's nearly ten years older. Logan, you've known Sam all your life. I'm worried about him."

"Of course. Hey, you got any of that 'twin' connection thing going on that Sam talks about?"

"Logan, that's not real. That's just Sam being Sam." Dave shook his head and scowled.

"Okay, okay. Guess we better organize a search party." Logan pressed his palms on his forehead. "Can you start on that while I notify the sheriff and call Toni's parents? Let me get things rolling. We'll meet in, say, twenty minutes at the bell pole."

"Sure, see you then." Dave's heart dropped to his stomach as he left the office to gather the troops.

Puzzled looks from the counselors greeted Dave as they assembled at the pole following Logan's cryptic PA announcement.

Ron was the first to speak as the crowd quieted. "What's up?"

"Sorry to interrupt your day, but we've got an issue. A camper, Toni LaRusso, didn't return to her cabin last night, so we have to consider her missing." Dave noticed Edie Moran looking at her feet and reddening. "Logan is speaking with the sheriff and Toni's parents right now. He asked me to get some search parties organized. Also, Sam is missing."

"Is Sam with her?"

"No, he went out last night to find her. She had ducked out of last night's program with a boy named Dixon. Does anybody know him?"

There was a collective reply of nos and head shaking, but one counselor spoke up. "Maybe. Last week there was a young man walking toward the girls' side carrying a plunger. I asked him who he was and what he was doing. He mumbled something about being sent over to fix the plumbing in the girls' shower. I thought it strange that he carried a plunger but figured that maybe Calvin had hired him so I let it go."

"What did he look like?"

"He had on a very old, holey, green Camp Sequoia T-shirt and jeans. I'd say he was about six feet tall with brown hair and dark, kind of raccoon eyes. Maybe twenty years old or so. He looked normal—other than the plunger."

A ripple of laughter went through the group.

"Any tattoos?"

"Didn't see any."

"Okay. Let's make arrangements to cover our campers, check our cabins, and meet back here in fifteen minutes. No time to lose."

Logan approached as the counselors walked off.

"Sheriff Tate didn't sound all that interested, but he said he'd send out a couple deputies to help with the search. He said, and I quote, 'This seems to be a rather common occurrence at church camps around here.'"

"That's an odd thing to say. What about Toni's parents? Bet they are mad as heck."

"Her father was furious. They are coming up later today to get Toni, and her dad made some threats about suing the camp."

"That figures."

Two sheriff's patrol cars pulled up, disgorging Sheriff Tate, who seemed to have changed his mind about coming out, and two deputies. Search teams were organized and deployed to assigned areas from the large wall map of the camp and surrounding area. The sheriff sat in the cruiser as his two deputies joined the hunt. Logan and Dave stayed at the office to coordinate the counselors' search.

Dave was fretting after an hour and a half passed with no reports. He paced around Logan's desk.

"Dave, I've got my two-way radio. Let's sit out on the porch for a few minutes."

They had just sat down when a third sheriff's cruiser drove up and a deputy exited his vehicle. He pulled the sheriff aside and spoke to him. The sheriff then walked quickly to his car and drove off. The deputy seemed to be in no hurry as he stood leaning against his patrol car and took a few drags on a cigarette. He had just dropped the cigarette butt on the ground to grind it out when the Logan's walkie-talkie crackled.

"Home base. Dooley here. We found Sam. We're gonna need an ambulance, Logan."

Dave lurched forward, grabbing the microphone. "Thank God he's alive! Is he hurt bad, Dooley? Let me talk to him."

"He's unconscious, Dave. His leg looks sort of bent and swollen. I think it's broken. He's breathing, his pulse is strong, but there's a cut on the left side of his head. Looks like it has bled quite a bit and his scalp is pretty swollen. We haven't been able to wake him up."

Logan picked up the phone and dialed 911.

Dave walked toward the large wall map. "Where are you?"

"We are along the stream just east of the old German's property. I can see a road across the stream, but I don't know its name."

Dave was standing in front of the map now. "I know where that is. About half a mile north of our swimming lake, right?"

"Yeah, that sounds right."

Logan relayed this information to the dispatcher. He hung up. "They know where he is and are on their way."

"Dave, I'm sorry. I think he must have fallen from the ledge in the dark. His flashlight batteries are dead." Dooley's voice cracked with emotion.

"Thanks, Dooley."

Logan took the mic. "Any sign of Toni?"

"Nope, not here. We'll stay with Sam until the ambulance takes him, then we can rejoin the hunt for Toni."

"Okay."

The deputy walked into the office and listened as the scene unfolded. He'd had the good sense not to interrupt, but now he asked, "Someone hurt? You found them then?" He had an odd look on his face.

Logan filled in the officer as Dave ran out the door to his cabin for his car keys. "I'm going to the hospital, Logan."

Logan gave Dave a thumbs-up. "See you there."

As Dave pulled out of the lot, the deputy walked back to his cruiser and spoke into his hand-held mic. A frown creased his face as he looked over the top of his car.

Chapter 7

ANTHROPOLOGICAL FINDS

The waiting room at the hospital ER was empty when Dave arrived. There was one ambulance in the bay, parked with the door open. He saw some blood on the floor of the rig and a pile of bloody gauze pads in the corner. Dave approached the desk and the clerk greeted him.

"I think they just brought my brother in. Sam Maxwell. Can I see him?"

The secretary punched a button on her intercom and spoke to a nurse. "The brother of the last ambulance patient is out here … Un-huh. Okay." Nodding to Dave, she said, "Have a seat. His nurse will be out in a moment."

Fifteen minutes later, a young lady in scrubs walked out and directly up to Dave. She had a surprised look on her face. "Well, I can see you are Mr. Maxwell's brother."

"How is he? He's going to live, right? Can I see him?"

"I'll take you back for a minute. He's in serious condition. He's unconscious and his leg is broken. Orthopedics is on their way down right now. Our neurosurgeon has already checked him. We need to get our CT scan results before neuro can say anything. Let's go back. Do you know what happened to him?"

"No, I was told he'd fallen off a ledge. They said he'd hit his head and injured his leg when he fell. He was out there all night."

"That's the story we got from rescue."

Sheriff Tate came through the swinging doors into the nurses' station, a deputy in tow. "How is he?" he asked while looking at the nurse.

"Too early to say for sure, Sheriff. He might need surgery on the leg. Ortho is looking at him now. Neurosurgery has seen him, and they are waiting for the CT result."

"Can I talk to him?"

"No, he's unconscious."

Dave cut in, "I'm Dave Maxwell, Sam's brother. He's my twin. Has anyone found the girl, Sheriff?"

"Sorry to meet like this, Mr. Maxwell. No word on the girl yet. Do you know anything about an elderly German man who lived in the area?"

"I know of a Mr. Mueller. But no, I don't know him personally. You said 'lived.'"

"He's dead. The searchers found him about a quarter mile from your brother, along with his dog. The dog was also dead. They both had what looked like numerous snakebites. It's odd because the fang marks were at least four inches apart."

"Must have been one heckuva big snake."

"Sure was. We're assuming that's what killed them, but we need to get the coroner's report. He was an old man. Seems odd to me that he'd be out there at night on a hike."

"Uh-huh."

"We need to rule out any connection between your brother's injuries and Mr. Mueller's death."

"What kind of connection?"

"I'm not saying he did anything wrong here. But you can see that it's strange to find a dead man, his dead dog, and your injured brother so close together in time as well as location. We are just wondering if he knew or saw anything."

"You're not implying that my brother—"

"No, Mr. Maxwell, I'm not suggesting anything. However, I'd like to ask him some questions. He might know something."

"Well, we know he went to look for Toni last night. And he doesn't have a pet snake."

Sherriff Tate looked down as a slight smile crossed his face. "So I was told. Is that the last time you saw Sam?"

"Yes."

"Do you know if he knew Mr. Mueller?"

"I doubt it. But if he did, he never mentioned him to me."

The nurse walked back up and interrupted. "Neuro has looked at the CT and is ready to talk to you Mr. Maxwell."

"Okay."

The sheriff asked if he could listen in. The nurse looked at the sheriff. "Is he under arrest? You do know he hasn't awakened?"

"No, no. I just wanted to get eyes and maybe speak with him, but after talking to Mr. Maxwell here, I don't think that's necessary."

Dave said, "It's okay with me, Sheriff."

"Okay, then." The three walked into Sam's room.

Dave gasped. Sam's leg was in a splint with a large bulky wrap. His head was bandaged, and this made him look like a swami. His eyes were slightly opened, but it was clear that he was unconscious.

The sheriff took one look at Sam and turned to Dave. "I'll leave you now. Call me if my department can do anything, anything at all for you." And he exited the room.

Dave began to tear up. He walked over to Sam and took his hand. "Sam, it's me. You are going to be fine. Can you hear me?" He looked over at the nurse.

She mirrored Dave's look of concern. "He might be able to—hear you, that is."

The neurosurgeon entered the room and greeted Dave as the lawman left. "Mr. Maxwell." His eyes widened as he realized he was talking to Sam's twin. "Your brother should live. He has a blood clot that we need to drain surgically. And we will do that right away. We'll have to see how he does after. We may keep him in a medically induced coma for a few days while the swelling around and in his brain goes down. Then things will be clearer. If you have parents, you might want to speak with them. I'll be glad to speak with them too, of course. Ortho plans to put a plate in his leg, but I'll let them fill you in on that. Any questions?"

"Yes, but of course I can't think of any right now."

"I understand. I'll see you after surgery then. We need to do this promptly."

Dave went out and called his parents. He also called Logan, who volunteered to bring Dani to the hospital. Dave then went to the surgical waiting room to pray for Sam and wait on the outcome of the surgery.

Chapter 8

THE MAINSTREAM PRESS

Harold and Marion Maxwell arrived that evening and Dave brought them up to speed on the events of the past twenty-four hours. He repeated what he knew of Sam's injuries and assured them that the neurosurgeon and orthopedics would soon brief them. Dave didn't mention the fiasco surrounding the Elijah pageant. He also had mentioned Sam's heroism in his willingness to help find Dani's friend, even though no great peril had been anticipated at that time.

Sam's surgery went according to plan and Sam, was put into the medical coma to await resolution of his brain's swelling. The orthopedist told the family that he had put a plate and screws into his lower leg bones. Since Sam was in excellent physical condition, and as the ankle was not involved, a quick and full recovery was anticipated. In fact, he should be up and about on crutches as soon as he regained consciousness.

As Dave sat at the hospital, Logan sent him periodic updates on the search for Toni. No word yet that she or the mysterious Dixon had been found. Toni's parents were expected to arrive at Camp Sequoia soon. Dave was relieved that he would not have to be present for that episode and that Dani was now safe with Mom and Dad.

* * *

The following morning, Dave's mom came to the breakfast table at their motel, holding a newspaper. It was a local tabloid called the *Western Star News.* "Dave, do you read a newspaper out here?"

"Rarely, Mom. Why?"

"There's an interesting theory about the Toni's disappearance in this news article."

Dad chimed in, "It's a tabloid, Marian. Not a newspaper."

"Still, Harold. It's an interesting article."

Dad muttered something incomprehensible as Dave's mother handed the paper to her son. "Read it for yourself, Dave. Let the boy make up his own mind, Harold."

Dave took the paper and rolled his eyes as he read the headline. "Local Girl Abducted: Secret Air Force Project to Blame?" Dave read the lead paragraph.

> People are again wondering if this weekend's disappearance of a young woman from a Yosemite area church camp is related to the military's mysterious Project Zebulon. The *Western Star* first broke the Zebulon story two years ago after receiving a tip from a man claiming to be involved in the project. He stated that he helped operate a large electronic device on the Mono Lake Air Force reservation. This machine was reportedly able to open portals to parallel dimensions. The informant (whom we will call Captain X) came forward after a rash of five incidents over fifteen months in the area involving nine missing people. Of course, the air force denied the existence of such a program; however, since the time the *Western Star* broke the story, no further disappearances have occurred.

Dave smiled at his mom and said, "Zebulon, UFOs. Really, Mom? Not really much about our girl."

Dave's father looked up from his cereal, smirking.

"Forget the UFOs. Keep reading," she said.

> Early this morning, the *Western Star* called a local consultant, John H. Lipps, for his insight into this latest

occurrence. Mr. Lipps has just returned from a crystal gathering expedition in Mexico. He is the chief shaman of the People's Unity Family. Mr. Lipps was exhausted following his treacherous journey but graciously gave us the following comment: "I feel most strongly that the timing of this poor girl's disappearance is suspicious. The People's Unity Family will perform a crystal truth ceremony tonight to determine its cause after we have taken some rest and nourishment. By the way, I am now in possession of a fine assortment of magical Mexican stones which I have available for purchase."

"Ignore the last part of that paragraph," said Mom.

The air force has stonewalled our journal's repeated requests for information on Project Zebulon. The authorities continue to maintain that such a project does not exist. However, three men were overheard by a *Western Star* correspondent at Zippy's Tavern two nights ago speaking the phrases "Pike's Peak" and "weather program." We have reason to believe that these are code phrases related to the Zebulon project. It is historical fact that Pike's Peak was named for Zebulon Pike. Furthermore, control of the weather has always been a goal of the military (see official USAF document "Weather as a Force Multiplier: Owning the Weather in 2025"). The speaker was seen to be wearing a Pacific Gas and Electric T-shirt and a Lockheed Martin windbreaker. It was unstated what his two companions wore. It was also noted that the speaker's eyes "looked kinda funny."

"It doesn't say anything about this man except he wears retro band logo tees, and he had strange eyes—at least to the observer, Mom."
"Well, Dani said that this Dixon was weird and had dark eyes."
"Okay, and?"
"And what? Read on. The article is almost finished."

Dave read the final paragraph aloud.

> Our correspondent reports that upon being challenged
> as agents of the military-industrial complex involved in
> Zebulon, the men quickly ducked out, issuing threats
> to our intrepid reporter. One of the conspirators stated
> he "would punch the lights out of the next idiot who
> interrupts our fishing trip." The *Western Star* will continue
> to follow this story and bring you all developments, even
> if we have to pursue these men to their homes.

Dave's dad had finished eating and was now leaning back in his
chair, fingers interlocked behind his head. He burst out laughing as Dave
finished reading.

Marian scowled and turned toward the orange juice dispenser.
"You'll see."

"I'll keep an open mind," Dave said.

"I won't," Harold remarked. "Those men were probably just tourists,
as they said, on a fishing trip and didn't want to be hassled. The people
who run that paper are crazy. They're conspiracy nuts, Miriam."

"We ought to get back over to the hospital." Mom surrendered.

Chapter 9

DAVE AND LOGAN GO EXPLORING

Nothing had changed with Sam. He was still in his artificial sleep, except now his eyes were taped shut and his airway held a plastic pipe connected to a respirator that toned out a monotonous rhythm. The neurosurgeon told the Maxwells that Sam's morning CT scan showed an encouraging decrease in brain swelling and if this trend continued, they'd discontinue the medication and wake him in a couple days. His leg was now in a splint with a bulky wrap and was elevated on a pillow.

Sheriff Tate returned to check on Sam. "How is he doing?"

Dave shrugged his shoulders. Mr. Maxwell said, "The CT scan was better this morning according to the neurosurgeon, so we're staying optimistic. Say, Sheriff, has the girl been found?"

The sheriff looked solemn. "No, and in cases like this, no news is *not* good news. I'm starting to fear the worst."

Harold shook his head and Marian took out a tissue and wiped her eyes. "Oh Lord, help the LaRussos."

The sheriff said that calls had been made to Nevada and Utah to check on weddings, but none involved a Toni LaRusso. Dave figured that was a really long shot. Yet he had to admit that he did not know Toni well and Dixon at all.

Logan called Mr. Adamson Sunday morning after his conversation with Dave and explained the situation. The camp director returned from his trip two days early, swinging by the hospital Sunday afternoon. He stayed for over an hour talking with the Maxwells. He was sincerely sorry for these events, and it showed in his speech. He seemed to think none of this would've occurred had he not been away.

Mr. Adamson looked Dave in the eye and shook his hand as he left. "I had you pegged for my assistant next season, but now I wonder if there will even be a Camp Sequoia."

Two days passed with no change, and Dave decided he needed a break from the hospital. As he drove back onto the campus of Camp Sequoia, the scene was organized chaos. Police vehicles from all jurisdictions in the immediate vicinity were present. About a quarter mile from the camp headquarters was a roped-off area. There was a handwritten sign indicating this was the "Media Parking" lot. Three TV trucks parked within the cords had satellite dishes deployed. There were also several vans with radio station call letters and logos painted on their sides. Dave saw a number of people milling around these vehicles engaged in unfamiliar activities. Some were working at portable tables. One stood in front of cameras while reporting on the air. And the remainder seemed to Dave to be just milling about.

Dave parked his truck and stepped up onto the office porch, encountering another crudely lettered sign declaring, "Private. No Admittance." As Dave reached for the doorknob, the door burst open toward him and a woman hurried out, bumping into him. A man carrying a TV camera followed her.

The woman complained loudly, "How am I supposed to cover this story when I get no cooperation?"

The man scuttled along behind her, shaking his head and mumbling to Dave, "Excuse us."

Dave entered the office to find Logan with his feet propped up on the desk while reading a magazine. Seeing Dave, he shouted, "No comment!" He laughed and smiled broadly as he stood up. "Hi, Dave. How's Sam?"

"He's still out, but he's sedated. The neurosurgeon plans to wake him up tomorrow. Orthopedics fixed his leg while he was already in surgery.

"Good. Mr. Adamson met with two FBI agents yesterday afternoon, and he didn't look happy when they all came out of his office."

"Did he say anything to you about why the feds were here?"

"No, nothing. But I heard him calling the sheriff right after they left. Ten minutes later, Sheriff Tate showed up. They went into his office and came out some time later. Then the sheriff and Mr. A took a German shepherd out of the squad car and headed to the backwoods."

"Did they speak with you when they came back?"

"No. I missed them. Ron was having an issue with a couple of his campers fighting and I went to his cabin to help settle things down. This is weird, Dave. All week there have been confrontations, fights, and commotions."

"Wow. I haven't ever seen a fight here in—what?—ten or twelve years."

"Well, this week's day campers are making up for it. I'm sure glad this is the last week of camp. I remember the last fight." Logan chuckled. "Sam was an eighth or ninth grader. He knocked out that senior high camper who kept teasing him."

Dave lowered his head and smiled. He remembered Sam, the hothead back then. "I wouldn't have bet you a dollar that we'd ever be back here after that. Wasn't that kid's father on the camp board of directors?"

"He sure was, but to hear Mr. A put it, the man was a constant pain in everyone's backside and the boy got what he deserved. Ha ha. He never came back, you know."

"Hmm, I had forgotten all about him. Wonder how the boy turned out."

"He's a pastor in a San Diego megachurch. In any case, Mr. Adamson came back while I was gone. He left an envelope on my desk with instructions to turn it over to the FBI agents in the morning."

"Has anyone else looked at that clearing since Saturday morning?"

"I don't know specifically, but the sheriff has had search teams out every day."

"Don't you think it's strange that the old man died, Sam was injured, and Toni disappeared in the same area within hours?"

"Sure, and I think the police agencies feel the same way." Logan saw that Dave looked sad and hurried to add, "But that doesn't mean there was any connection or foul play."

"Yeah, I guess."

"Hey, you haven't been out there yet. Why don't you and I take a hike and see if fresh eyes can see anything?"

"Aren't you working the desk?"

"Naw, I'm just sitting here repeating, 'No comment,' to every knucklehead who can't read the sign and comes in—present company excluded. Madeline should be back from lunch any minute."

"Okay then. Let me check my mailbox and swing by my cabin first."

"I'll come by your cabin as soon as Madeline gets back."

Dave glanced at the magazine on Logan's desk as he walked out. On the cover, there was a picture of a large bird—no, a dragon—in flight. There was a man below who seemed to be standing in a crowd and shooting a pistol skyward. He read "Michigan Madness: Detective Brings Occult Killers to Justice." The name of the magazine was *America's Fortean Life*. Dave walked out.

Dave was going through the mail while standing alongside his bunk when Logan poked his head in. "Knock, knock. Ready, Dave?"

"Yeah, let's go." Dave dumped the few pieces of mail, all junk, into the wastebasket and headed out. "So any idea what was in the envelope Mr. Adamson left?"

"No, but it felt like it was just papers."

"Hmmm."

They walked on in silence until seeing the tree line, up the path from the swimming pond, then stopped. Logan pointed to an area below a steep drop-off by the stream. "That's where they found Sam."

Dave nodded. They stood looking down at the trampled weeds. Dave slid down the embankment to get a closer look. There were dried mud tire tracks made by the rolling stretcher. Peering down, Dave found a rock with reddish-brown stains and a few strands of hair partially buried in the mud. He picked it up and clambered back up the bank.

"Whatcha think?" He showed it to Logan, who nodded.

Logan looked away from the path, toward the tree line. "Look, Dave, at the far edge of these waist-high weeds, about seventy-five yards away. Doesn't it look like something moved through here in this direction?"

Dave nodded. "Could be a deer or bear."

They continued on the main path about a hundred yards farther. Failing to observe any other break in the weeds, they turned back to the spot where they'd encountered the trampled path.

Dave commented, "Did Sam leave the path? Did he see something in the trees? Dooley said his flashlight was on but not working when they found him. That's strange—unless he tried to turn it on as he was running and succeeded as he fell."

"I see, and his batteries burned out as he lay there through the night."

"Would he have fallen if he had his flashlight on, just walking along? I don't think so. He must've been in a hurry and misjudged exactly where he was. And he wouldn't have been running with his light off unless—I think he was running away from something, Logan, and Sam just happened to get his flashlight turned on as he fell."

They followed the trampled path through the weeds. From the direction of the broken stalks and trampled weeds, it was clear something, or someone, had indeed moved through here toward the bank.

About thirty yards farther in was the tree line so they headed in that direction. After a minute, Logan asked, "See that ahead?"

Again, the weeds had all been crushed down as if something had been there. But farther ahead just inside the trees, something caught the men's attention.

"Yeah, it looks like a clearing."

"Sheriff Tate said that the old man was found near a clearing. This might be it."

They entered the clearing and looked toward the center. The trees formed a nearly perfect circle around them.

"This looks odd. Logan, and that smell—do you get a whiff of that?"

"Yeah, what is it?"

"It smells like blood. I remember that smell from when Dad would gut his deer and bleed it, back when Sam and I went hunting with him."

"I don't see any blood, but it did rain last night."

The grass on the ground was short here and looked as if it had seen a lot of recent foot traffic, but neither Dave nor Logan could see any blood.

There were many rocks of various sizes scattered throughout the clearing.

Dave examined them. "Odd how they're all lying on top of the grass."

As Logan reached the center of the clearing, he kicked into some trampled down grass, sending up clouds of buzzing flies.

"That smell again?" Logan swatted the flies from his face then bent to study the ground. "It's nauseating!"

"You're not kidding." Dave poked around in the grass and pulled back quickly as something sharp grazed his hand. Bending closer, he pulled up a triangular piece of shiny, black stone. He noticed it appeared to have been sharpened and polished. A dull, reddish-brown stain covered the sides of the stone, and some had rubbed off onto Dave's hand when he picked it up. It stunk. He pulled out his hankie and wrapped up the stone fragment, pocketing it. Dave raked a hand though his hair.

Logan had moved across the clearing and climbed onto one of the larger stones, looking out through the trees to another area of high grass opposite their entry point. The trees were much thinner there. "Nothing obvious out there. Wait. I see another disturbed place in the weeds."

They walked about twenty-five yards out of the clearing, finding another area where the grass was matted down.

Dave scratched his chin. "Do you think that is where the old man died?"

"Don't know. It is near the clearing and opposite where the other disturbance in the weeds had been."

"Did the searchers miss these tramped-down areas?"

Sam wrinkled his forehead. "Hard to say. Could be they just attributed them to animal beds. There is a lot of wildlife around here."

"I guess. Maybe that's what they are."

"Maybe, but that's still a lot of coincidences."

They were silent as they headed back to the path where Sam had fallen. All they'd found were areas of pushed-down weeds and a sharp stone with a dusty brown coating. Were they being too suspicious?

They carefully climbed down the steep ground and looked over the area where Sam had fallen. "I don't know what else I'm looking for, other than I know that this is where my brother fell." Dave closed his eyes and inhaled deeply. He held the rock on which Sam had hit his head. He willed himself to relax and let impressions come to him. He opened his eyes and—

Nothing.

He looked at Logan. "We're wasting our time here. I did find this stinky, odd-looking stone in a weed clump while you were looking around in the clearing. I wanted to show it to you, but I got distracted." He pulled out and unwrapped the piece of black rock from his pocket and held it out to Logan, who took it and turned it over in his palm.

"This looks like the tip of an aboriginal knife. I've seen these in museums. I think you solved one aspect of this, Dave. That faint, pungent smell is from this artifact. See this brown powder on the flat side? That's dried blood. It stinks! Maybe we've stumbled onto an Indian hunting area. Who knows how old this knife fragment is?"

Dave was incredulous. "You've read a lot into a piece of stone with some dirt smudged on it. And why would old blood still stink?"

"I don't know. Let me send this to my cousin Daisy—after we show it to the sheriff. She's on the anthropology staff at the University of Nevada at Reno. Heck, it might even be worth something. I can see it now: the gleaming centerpiece in a new museum showcase called 'Obsidian Hunting Blade Fragment.' Courtesy of Professor David Maxwell."

Dave laughed. "Go ahead, but let's not get ahead of ourselves." The young men helped each other up the side of the drop-off and headed back to camp.

Chapter 10

PASTOR ADAMSON OPINES

Back at the camp office, Pastor Adamson and the sheriff stood just inside the director's office. They spoke low and earnestly with occasional glances up at two very large men leaning on the reception counter. Those men were unknown to Dave, but Logan whispered, "FBI." Dave looked at the two men and quizzically back at Logan. Sheriff Tate remained in Mr. Adamson's office and could be seen turning the stone fragment over in his hand.

Mr. Adamson looked at Logan and waved him over. "Logan, where is the envelope I left for you to give to these gentlemen?"

Logan walked across the room and bent down, unlocking and opening his side desk drawer. He pulled the envelope out and Mr. Adamson took it.

He walked over to the feds and handed it to them.

The taller of the two said, "Thank you, Mr. Adamson," in a monotone. Both agents turned and walked stiffly out of the building, leaving the entry door open.

Mr. Adamson then walked back into the office and closed the door. He turned and leaned out. "Logan, can you please close the door?"

Dave looked at Logan. "Did that seem a little strange to you?"

Logan laughed and walked over, shutting the door without looking. "No kidding. He acted like Jesse Ventura's 'Man in Black' on *The X-Files.*"

At that moment, the outside door again opened up and a man and woman entered. "Hello, Mr. and Mrs. LaRusso." Logan nudged Dave.

The man looked at Logan and Dave. "Have the FBI agents arrived yet?"

Dave looked at Logan, who answered. "They just left."

Mr. LaRusso looked confused. "They just left?"

"Yes, sir. Pastor Adamson and the sheriff were here speaking with them. We just got here ourselves, in time to see them leave. Mr. LaRusso, this is Dave Maxwell."

"I don't care who he is," LaRusso snapped. "Let me speak with the sheriff and Mr. Adamson, unless they just left as well."

Logan walked to the office door and knocked. "Just a second." He knocked a second time, and the door opened a crack. Mr. Adamson whispered something to Logan before opening the door fully. "Mr. LaRusso, how are you and your wife doing?"

"How in the Sam Hill do you think we're doing? Our daughter is missing from your camp. Your sheriff's department is incompetent, and we understood that we were going to meet with FBI agents here. Where are they?"

"I don't know. They never mentioned to us that they were meeting anyone."

"That was their SUV that was pulling out as you drove in. If you hop in your car and gun it, you could probably catch them," Logan put in.

"Catch them? I have no idea where they were going," Mr. LaRusso sputtered, oblivious to Logan's warped sense of irony.

The sheriff entered the room from behind Mr. Adamson. He held his Stetson in both hands at his waist. "Mr. LaRusso, we're doing everything we can to find Toni. The FBI is involved in the search now, but we will continue to assist in any way we can."

"Dandy. In other words, my daughter leaves with a man whom she believes is a camp employee but is actually unknown to everyone, and now I'm supposed to get in my car and chase down the FBI?" Mr. LaRusso turned to his wife, who had begun to cry softly. "Come on, Nancy. Let's go. I've seen enough of this clown act." The couple walked toward the door and stopped. Mr. LaRusso turned around and opened his mouth to speak, but only a chuffing noise came. They walked out the door.

Pastor Adamson looked at Sheriff Tate. "I don't know what more we can do, Otis."

"Neither do I." The sheriff put on his hat and handed the stone fragment back to Dave. "Just a piece of rock, Dave. I won't need it." He walked to the door. He peeked out between the curtains and watched until the LaRussos had driven off. Then he said, "Later," and left.

Dave and Logan looked at each other. Logan shrugged and described his and Dave's search of the area to Pastor Adamson. He detailed their findings on the path and around the clearing. Mr. Adamson listened, and he asked a few questions, but his mind seemed elsewhere until he looked closely at the piece of black rock in Dave's hand.

The elder man's eyes then lit up. "Is this what you showed Sheriff Tate? Where did you get this?" He snatched the rock. At this point, handling had removed virtually all of the dried blood residue.

Dave answered, "Yes, it is. I found it in the clearing under a pile of grass in the clearing."

"Do you know what it is?" the pastor smiled broadly.

"Logan thinks it's a piece of an Indian knife, but he was going to confirm this with his anthropologist cousin."

"He's partially right. It's the tip of a ceremonial dagger. See, there's dried blood residue on it." He rubbed the flat side of the piece. "My uncle was head of the anthropology department at Fresno State back in the seventies. One summer, I went to a dig site in Mexico for a month with him. It was at a place called Chinocuan or Wanachachuan or something like that. My job was to dust off samples and sort them. One of his best finds was an intact Toltec ceremonial dagger and the blade tip was just this shape. I remember that he sold that piece to a private collector for $30,000." He looked up at the boys and laughed. "Yeah, my uncle wasn't the most scrupulous academic. *But* he always had a nice car."

"What kind of ceremony was the knife used in?"

"He said human sacrifice, but I never believed him. In fact, I think he made up a lot of what he put forth as original research."

Dave and Logan looked at each other as Logan took the piece back.

"How in the world did this piece get to our camp?" Mr. Adamson wondered.

Chapter 11

SOMBER NEWS

The next day, the neurosurgeon withdrew Sam's sedation; however, Sam showed no sign of waking up. The medical staff didn't seem concerned though. His nurse assured Mr. and Mrs. Maxwell that this was fairly common. In fact, he might sleep for a day or so until all of the medicine was metabolized out of Sam's body.

The orthopedist also came by to check on Sam. He took off the dressing and closely examined the surgical wound. He then reiterated his expectation of an uncomplicated and full recovery. This all seemed to reassure Mr. and Mrs. Maxwell and they headed to Camp Sequoia to pack up Sam's and Dave's belongings. Yet Dave was worried. He was anxious to talk to his twin, hoping for some new direction. He stared out the window as they pulled back on to the wooded campus.

"I remember when this camp had a bell pole for a meeting place and a natural pond swimming hole," Dave's father reminisced as they drove in.

"We still do, Dad," Dani called out from the back seat.

Everyone laughed.

It took about forty-five minutes to pack up the young men's gear and load the car. The parents waited in the vehicle as Dave and Dani ran into the office to turn in Dave's key. "Hey, Logan, if you haven't sent the blade fragment off yet, I'd like to show it to Dani."

Logan brought out a small box from the back. He placed it on the counter and opened it. "Here it is." The knife tip was nestled between two pads of soft cotton.

"It stinks." Dani wrinkled her nose.

Expecting at least a "Wow!" Dave frowned when Dani just looked at the piece with no change in her expression. "This is a part of a genuine Toltec ceremonial knife blade, we think."

Dani picked at her chipped nail polish. "Hmmph. It looks like a chip off a shiny, black stone to me."

"That's what they made these blades out of, Dani," put in Logan. "This one that your brother found even had dried blood residue on it."

"Yuck."

"It might be worth a couple thousand dollars," Logan added.

"Or a named exhibit in a university museum." Dave beamed.

"You said there was dried blood on it. Whose blood?"

Dave and Logan both shrugged.

"We don't know," said Logan. "Probably a from a deer."

"You don't think it was Toni's, do you?"

The smiles were immediately gone from the young men's faces as they answered, "No."

"But you don't know, do you?" She hiccupped down a small sob.

Logan began to dissemble. "Dani, Toni is alive and probably went off with this Dixon guy on some adventure trip. Heck, the sheriff thinks they might have even gone to Nevada and gotten married."

"Logan, she just met the boy that morning. Why in the world would anyone think she would marry him?"

The mood again turned somber. Logan quickly changed the subject. "Well, it has been an eventful summer, Dave. I'll be around to see you and Sam in a couple weeks, work permitting," he said proudly. "Maybe we can go to a UCLA football game. You too, Dani."

"Logan, you know I hate football."

"Okay, Dave, see you then. God bless you." They shook hands, and Dave and Dani left the office.

As they walked to their car, the two FBI agents pulled up. "Sir," said the taller one through his open window, "We understand that you recovered a piece of a knife blade in the clearing. Is this correct?" He pushed his sunglasses up on his nose.

"Yes, sir. I don't know if it's a knife blade or not. It looked like a rock chip to me. Logan plans to send it off to his cousin who works in the University of Nevada anthropology program to have it examined."

The agents nodded. "We are going to need that blade fragment."

"Evidence," his partner added.

"Logan has it at the counter right now. Evidence?" Dave was clearly doubtful. "Sheriff Tate agreed with me it was just a sharp piece of rock."

The agents ignored Dave's comment. "Thank you, Mr. Maxwell." They parked in front of the door and walked in.

When they reached their car, Dave's father craned around in his seat. "Who were those two men? They were dressed like what's his name Jones and Will Smith from *Men in Black*. What did they want?"

Dani blurted out, "Dave and Logan found the murder weapon that killed Toni!" She started to cry.

"What?" cried both parents simultaneously.

Dave explained about his hike out to the scene of Sam's accident and how he found the stone fragment. He doubted that it was anything more than a rock, and it certainly was not part of a knife, regardless of where the imaginations of his coworkers led.

Nor was Toni dead.

Harold raised his eyebrows and looked at his son. "Strange."

* * *

Sam was resting comfortably. The neurosurgeon came in and asked the Maxwells to sit down. He spoke to Harold and Marian directly. "I am at a loss to explain why Sam hasn't awakened. Last evening, I consulted Dr. Eckhauser, our neurologist. He examined Sam, looked over his scans, lab results, and did an EEG. He can't see any reason why Sam remains asleep either. It's our recommendation that Sam be sent to the neurological unit at a specialty hospital for further evaluation. There are excellent centers located in Los Angeles, San Francisco, and San Diego. I understand you are from Westwood, so I assume that you would prefer LA. Maybe UCLA?"

"Is this really necessary, Doctor?" Miriam asked.

"I'm afraid so, ma'am. We've reached the limit of what we can do for him here. It's a real puzzle. His test results are all normal. We even tested him for toxins and drugs. We cannot find any structural abnormalities on the scans to explain this. He needs evaluation we can't give him in this hospital."

Harold asked, "What if they can't wake him up? What then?"

"In that case, he would need placement in a long-term care facility."

Dave shuddered. The thought of his twin in a convalescent home or worse was hitting home. *Please, God.*

"On the other hand, Sam could wake up tomorrow and be fine. We just don't know. I know you need some time to think this over. It's a lot to digest. For the present, we can watch and see how he's doing, but if he hasn't awakened in a couple days, we can make arrangements for the transfer." He stood to leave.

"Thank you, Doctor." Harold gave his wife a worried look.

"We'll have to talk to Sam's advisor at Cal Tech. I can call," she observed.

That night, Dave lay awake trying to figure out what he could do to help this situation. Both being postgrad students at Cal Tech, Dave could take over his brothers teaching responsibilities for the fall semester and put his own research project on hold. He was sure his advisor, Dr. Foley, would support this, as Dr. Foley also advised Sam. This would handle the autumn semester, but what if Sam did *not* wake up? Well, he'd have to leave that in God's hands.

Chapter 12

BACK HOME AGAIN

The next week found the Maxwells back in Los Angeles—Dani and her parents back in the family home in Westwood and Dave returned to the apartment in Pasadena he'd shared with his twin for seven years since their undergraduate sophomore year.

Sam had been moved to the UCLA Medical Center's neurologic unit, where the staff pored over him. They subjected Sam to an unending string of tests, combing through his history with every family member several times. *At least he is in good hands here.*

September arrived and with it came football season. Dave and Sam had loved the game since they were in grade school and both earned honors as regional California all-stars for their junior and senior years in high school—Sam at quarterback and Dave as a wide receiver and defensive back. However, they felt their future lay elsewhere than sports and both enrolled at Cal Tech. Sam was a mathematics whiz, earning his degree in three years, while Dave completed his degree program in physics.

Dave's mind wrestled with the fact that his brother lay in a hospital bed while he and Logan filed into the Rose Bowl to watch UCLA take on the Oregon Ducks. Throughout the game, which UCLA won, Logan tried persistently to cheer Dave up but he ceased trying as the game moved into the fourth quarter.

After the game, they drove from the Rose Bowl down to Westwood for a pizza. Dave tried to relax and enjoy the meal but was aware that he was lousy company. Logan offered, "You know I'm worried about Sam too, but remember he's in the Lord's hands. I'll be in to see Sam tomorrow," then went home.

Dave decided to walk over to the UCLA Med Center.

Dave walked into Sam's room and was startled to see a gorgeous brunette sitting in the chair beside Sam's bed, reading aloud to Sam from a beat-up paperback edition of *To Your Scattered Bodies Go*.

She continued to read for about thirty seconds, unaware of Dave's presence. She looked up as Dave cleared his throat and said, "Good evening."

"Hi, uhhhh, Sam's doppelganger. You've got to be his twin. I'm Lanie Martin."

"Hi, I'm Dave. Doppelganger." He reached out and shook her hand.

The girl stood to leave and Dave said, "No, no, don't stop. I enjoy Farmer, and I know Sam does as well."

She laughed. "He's one of my favorites too. The hospital hires students to read to the patients in the evenings. They say hearing is the last sense to go and the first to come back in head trauma."

"What's your major?"

"I'm a nursing student. I know Sam is a grad instructor at Cal Tech, but I don't know what program he's in."

"Mathematics."

"Yikes. What do you do, Dave Doppelganger?"

"Grad school also. Physics."

"Yikes again. Sounds like I'm in the big brain room."

Dave chuckled. "Not really, but it isn't every day I stumble into a room with a nurse reading classic sci-fi."

"Do you think he might prefer *Valley of the Dolls?*"

"No, I'm trying to compliment you. And failing miserably, I see."

"No, no. Not at all. Well, anyway, it's time for me to head out. I've got a test Monday morning and Sam needs his rest."

"Is that a hint for *me* to leave?"

"Not at all. I'm sure your presence will relax him. Just keep givin' those good vibrations."

"Ooooh, bop. Bop. Excitations."

"Not too much excitation, Beach Boy. Good night." Lanie's eyes crinkled with a hearty laugh as she pulled the heavy hospital door closed behind her.

"Good night." Dave sat down and looked at Sam. He swallowed hard at the tight knot that had formed in his throat. With a deep exhalation, he took Sam's hand in his and began to pray.

As he finished, he thought he heard something from Sam that sounded like a mumbled amen, but he waited several minutes and there were no other sounds. Dave decided he was just getting tired. He sat with his brother for a while longer then got up and left.

He returned to see his brother the next several evenings, but there was no sign of the reading girl. He had pushed her from his mind when she was suddenly there on Wednesday.

"Hello," Dave chirped.

"Hello, Professor."

"Just Dave, please."

"Okay."

"Different book, I see."

"All I could find was this. *Nine Princes in Amber*." She held the black book up so Dave could see it.

"Ahhh, Zelazny. His writing changed sci-fi."

"Wouldn't you say Zelazny's work is more fantasy?"

"Maybe. Six of one, half dozen of the other." Dave sat down opposite the young lady. "Please go on."

Lanie resumed reading, and Dave looked at his brother. Sam's face held a peaceful expression.

Dave leaned back in his chair. He closed his eyes, listening to the hypnotic rhythm of the narration. Dave's breathing became slow and regular.

Before long, Lanie stopped reading, looked up, and smiled at the gentle snoring from across the bed. She chuckled while watching the two sleeping brothers. "Like bookends."

*   *   *

Sunday afternoon Dave brought Dani to visit Sam. He was surprised to see Lanie reading the *LA Times* to Sam. She was in the middle of the UCLA game report and stopped to greet Dave. "Hi. Just trying to bring Sam up to date on the Bruins' football season."

"Hi, I'm Dani, Sam's sister. Sam likes football, but he prefers USC. You know he almost went there to play quarterback."

Dave smiled inwardly at the protective, proud words of his little sister. She'd been unusually quiet lately, since camp, the accident, and disappearance. There still had been no word or any leads on anything regarding the whereabouts of Toni.

"No, I didn't know that. But the *Times* covers USC games as well." Lanie looked at the strapping young man. "How about you, Dave? Did you play football?"

"This is Lanie, Dani. I played a bit in high school."

"Don't let him kid you, Ms. Lanie. He was an all-state receiver and had several football scholarship offers."

"In spite of Dani's enthusiasm, I wasn't good enough to play at any major college so I, and Sam for that matter, decided to skip college athletics."

"Dave goes to a lot of UCLA games. In fact, he always asks me to go, but I hate football so he goes with Logan or Sam—or alone."

"I like college football," volunteered Lanie. "My dad played a season and a half for UCLA."

"What is his name?"

"Raymond Martin."

"But why a year and a half?" Dave raised an eyebrow.

"Junior Smith."

"I don't understand. Junior Smith played linebacker for USC," said Dave.

"That's right. My dad was a running back and was tackled three plays in a row by Junior, although Dad says he only remembers the first.

"Oh."

"Finally, he didn't get up. He was taken to the hospital with three broken ribs, a ruptured spleen, and a concussion. Thus, ended the career of Raymond 'Blazer' Martin."

"Smith was a monster on the field, but as I recall, he was a real gentleman otherwise."

"In fact, he came to the hospital and visited my dad."

"That level of concern would be unusual, even back then. You're a born and bred Bruin then."

"I guess so. I mainly follow their basketball team. The idea of my dad being permanently injured playing football put me off a bit."

"Well, if you'd like to go to a game next Saturday, you could come with me. They're playing Arizona State and it should be a pretty good game."

"You don't have to do that. Your friend Logan might object."

"He'll be out of town for a work conference."

Dani put in, "Please go, Lanie. I don't want to turn my brother down again."

Lanie laughed. "Oh. Okay then. I'm free and haven't been to a game in several years."

Dani let out a deep breath. "Good. Now at least I won't feel bad."

Everyone laughed.

Chapter 13

THE NERVOUS BARISTA

The rest of the week went quickly for Dave, who was serving as the substitute teaching assistant for Sam. As a physicist, Dave had a strong mathematics background, but teaching at this level dictated that he be fully prepared to handle the extreme demands of Cal Tech students. His first two recitation sessions were nerve-wracking. He'd fretted that his preparation was inadequate, but he was getting into a groove. The sessions were well attended. Dave tried to keep them interesting with humorous anecdotes, but these left some of the bookwormy pupils scratching their heads.

Saturday bloomed sunny and warm—a great day for football. Dave and Lanie had a good time watching the Bruins win 23–21 in the last minute on a fifty-seven-yard touchdown pass. Afterward, they ran into Dani, who was studying at the Beaniac Coffee House, a favorite hangout of her and her friends.

Dave asked the girls what they'd like and went up to the counter. The young male barista looked hard at Dave and hesitated noticeably before taking his order. He then mumbled something to a coworker and went into the back room, leaving her to make Dave's beverages. When Dave returned to his seat, Dani leaned over to Dave, motioning him forward urgently. "Dave, I think that was Dixon who waited on you."

"What? Did he see you? I thought he acted a bit strange, going into the back like that. I guess we can see if it is Dixon when he comes back out."

"Who's Dixon?" Lanie inquired.

Dave gave an abbreviated version of the happenings Camp Sequoia that led to Sam's injury and the disappearance of Toni LaRusso.

After twenty minutes, the young man hadn't reappeared so Lanie volunteered to go ask the barista if she would fetch him. Lanie had decided to pose as an old friend of his.

Lanie returned to the table. "The barista was puzzled when I asked for Dixon. She said his name was Wilbur and that he left. Apparently, he suddenly felt ill. She wasn't very happy about that either. In fact, she was downright angry. I'm glad I didn't need to use the lie that I had worked with him at another coffee shop, or she might have begged me to work his shift.

"Dave, did you notice a tattoo?" asked Dani.

"No. He had on a long-sleeve shirt and the vest that the workers all wear here."

"Doesn't matter. I'm sure it was him."

"Why did he run? Are you sure he didn't see you?"

"I think he may have seen either you or Sam around the camp at some point. I don't think he even looked over at our table. It's funny, but I remember distinctly him saying he was from El Cajon."

"Why is he here then?"

"Don't know."

Lanie crumpled her napkin into a ball. "If this Dixon is involved in the girl's disappearance, and from what I've heard, that is still a supposition, he may be prospecting. This kind of job would give him the opportunity to chat up young women and girls all day long."

"Hmmm. You're right. I agree that's suspicious, and from his actions, I think he's certainly a person of interest. But I won't call him a criminal suspect yet since we don't know what happened to Toni. I need to speak with Sheriff Tate *ASAP*—or maybe those FBI agents who came to the camp."

The ladies agreed as the group left the coffee shop. They headed to the hospital to check on Sam.

On the short walk across campus, Dave called the sheriff's department and left a request that Sheriff Tate return his call at his earliest convenience. When they arrived in Sam's room, Dave's eyes widened. "Logan, I thought you would be in Las Vegas until Monday."

Logan sat in the chair beside the bed and grinned back at them. "Nope, I gave my presentation and fulfilled the demands of courtesy. Then I left. You'd have thought that my presentation of a visual computer model of geological progression in the Sonoran Desert from 1500 to the present would have enthralled my listeners. These archeologists seemed more interested in rolling the bones on the dice table than discussing soil samples and rock formations. Besides, we were at the Buckaroo Casino. I'd never heard of it. Have you? It certainly wasn't Caesar's Palace."

Lanie, Dani, and Dave all laughed. Dave introduced Lanie as a friend and fellow science fiction devotee.

Logan screwed up his face. "You can have that malarkey. I mean science fiction, not you, Lanie."

"No offense taken."

Logan stood up from his chair and stretched, motioning for the girls to take the seats. "No change in Sam that I can see. What else has been going on?"

Dani plopped into an empty chair and blurted out, "We just saw Dixon, and Dave called the sheriff."

"Where?"

"At Beaniac's. He was working the counter there and took off when he saw Dave."

"Probably recognized your face from camp. Did you show him any sign of recognition?"

"Nope. I'd never seen him before."

"That doesn't mean he hasn't seen you—or Sam."

"That's what we figured."

"What did the sheriff say?"

"Left him a voice mail to call me."

"Sounds reasonable. Well, I'm gonna take off now. Just wanted to see how Sam was doing." Logan walked around to the other side of the hospital bed. "Hey, Dave, will you be home later this evening?"

"I should be. Why?"

"I have a little something for you I picked up in Vegas."

"Not towels from the Buckaroo, I hope."

"Nope. I think you'll find this interesting."

"Now I'm intrigued."

Dani grinned at his brothers' old friend. "What did you bring me, Logan?"

Logan reached in his pocket and pulled out a silver Buckaroo poker chip. He leaned over Sam while handing it to Dani. He bowed low with great solemnity. "For you, my princess. Sorry, Lanie, I'm out of presents this trip."

"That's okay. None expected."

"See you later, Dave."

All exchanged goodbyes and Dave looked down at his brother. Sam's eyelids flickered when Logan said goodbye.

Lanie watched as Dave and Dani studied their brother. "Those are movements indicating a person is dreaming. They're called rapid eye movements or REMs."

"Like the band?" asked Dani.

"Just like. Although you have to wonder if *that's* what *they* meant."

Sam's nurse walked in to take vitals. "This has been a really nice day, Dave—and Dani. Thank you. I'm going to head back to the dorm. Monday is our test day and I need to study."

"Dani, I'm going to walk Lanie out. I'll be right back." Dave walked Lanie to the hospital doors, then looked out across the street to Lanie's dorm. "Let me walk you across."

There was little traffic, but as they stepped across the centerline, a car suddenly came racing toward them. Dave grabbed Lanie and pushed her to safety on the grass. Dave then felt a push himself and he tumbled down next to Lanie. The car whizzed by so close that Dave wondered how he'd been missed.

A large man in a jogging suit stood over the two. "That was a close one. Thank God we were paying attention, eh?"

"Thank you." Dave was wondering where this man had come from as the jogger turned and trotted quickly away.

"Yes, thank you so much, Dave. Who were you talking to?"

"That jogger who pushed me out of the way." Lanie scratched her head at this.

"Was that driver trying to hit us?"

"I don't know. He had his radio on really loud. He was probably just distracted—or maybe drunk."

Lanie looked at Dave still somewhat confused when she saw him looking around and up the road as if searching for someone. "Enough coincidences for one day. You know that you lead a pretty strange life, Professor Doppelganger? Good night, Dave."

"No one has ever said *that* to me before."

She smiled and went into the building.

Dave went back to Sam's room. He decided not to tell Dani about the near miss.

Dani sat there looking glumly at her injured brother.

"All we can do is pray for him, Dani." He helped her on with her jacket, and they bid Sam good night.

Chapter 14

HOG HEAVEN

Dave had just arrived home and put on a pot of coffee when he heard the unmistakable rumbling and felt the vibrations of a Harley pulling into the parking space directly in front of his apartment. He looked out the window and saw Logan hop off a custom-chopped motorcycle. He was dressed in Bermuda shorts and a Hawaiian shirt with a canvas bag over his shoulder, not looking anything like a hog rider. Dave shook his head.

Dave went and opened the door for his friend. "What's with your wheels?"

"Have you ever met Bonser, my next-door neighbor? No? I remarked to him that I was going to Vegas, and he asked if a couple of his biker buddies from out of town could leave their bikes in my driveway while I was gone. Being a good neighbor and thinking that seeing some Harley-Davidsons in my driveway might discourage any potential burglars, I said okay. Well, when I got home this afternoon, there were thirteen bikes in my driveway and my car was in the garage. I explained to Bonser that I needed to come here pronto. One of his friends, who called himself 'Sea Dog,' offered me his bike. Looking at thirty-odd bikers through a living room filled with smoke, all playing cards, and hundreds of beer bottles, I figured it prudent to thank him and not annoy his guests. That's why you see me with 'Matilda,' as he calls her—or it. Actually, I sort of enjoyed the ride over."

Dave just shook his head, then turned and went to the kitchen. "Coffee? I just brewed a fresh pot."

"Sure, cream and sugar if you please. Thanks."

Dave returned and they sat down.

Logan opened the bag. "Pretty good coffee. What brand do you use? Mine always tastes weak and bitter."

"I use Kona from Trader Wong's. I think the secret is having a coffeemaker that gets the water hot enough. I actually spent a lot of time looking for just the right machine and settled on this higher-end Mr. Coffee brewer. It's been a good choice, I think." Dave took a long sip from his steaming cup and sighed.

"Hmmm. And here's what I brought you." Logan changed the subject as he pulled a small dagger out of his bag. "Recognize it?"

"Not really. Looks like a knife."

"It is a high priest's ceremonial dagger used by a pre-Anasazi civilization here in the Southwest."

"Well, I can certainly see why you and Mr. Adamson thought the fragment I found looked like the tip of this blade. Where did you get this? You didn't steal it, did you?"

"What? Of course not. I found this in the Buckaroo Casino gift shop of all places. This is a replica, but a well-made one. The originals are either in museums or private collections and cost thousands of dollars. Forgive me, but you are not *that* close of a friend. It's funny, but I went in to buy a bag of potato chips and saw this in a display case right next to the register."

"Well, thank you, I guess." Dave was a bit uneasy about having this artifact in his home. He didn't like its association with pagan rites and blood sacrifice. "Logan, thanks, but—"

Logan read his expression and interrupted. "Dave, I know how you feel about these things, so I can hold on to it."

"Yeah, that's fine. I appreciate the offer and you showing it to me."

"Education, my boy. I also stopped by the camp on my way back. I asked Mr. A what the latest on Toni was. He said that there has been no trace of either of our missing persons, at least until today. They've cut back the scale of the search drastically. In fact, they've basically ended it. With the summer camp season over and the media gone, Mr. Adamson struck me as a bit lonely."

"That doesn't sound good, but it doesn't much surprise me."

"Did the sheriff call you back yet?"

"No."

"Mr. A remarked that Sheriff Tate had been acting a bit strange lately."

"In what way?"

"He said that every time he asked the sheriff how things were going with the case, the sheriff would fly off the handle and say things like 'Don't rush me' or 'We are a six-man department. Why don't you just you keep your shirt on?'"

"Geez, this is the biggest case in that part of the state in years. What are the police doing? Doubling up on traffic patrol? Plus they have a second death at the same time and place."

Logan shrugged. "Yeah, but you realize it was only in the news for three or four days. Doesn't that seem odd?"

"Sure does. It seems like there'd be daily follow-ups—at least for a while."

"Pastor Adamson also said he went to the US Forest Service and asked for help. A ranger told him they had no jurisdiction in cases not on US government property. He said the ranger never met his gaze once he asked for help on this. Camp Sequoia's western boundary borders Yosemite National Park for almost six miles. Isn't that enough to warrant a little assistance?"

"I'd certainly think so."

"I'll tell you what, Dave. I have a feeling Sheriff Tate may not return your call."

"I'll try again in the morning, and if I can't reach him, I'll call the FBI and speak with the two agents who were at the camp. What were their names? Do you recall?"

"The big one was Hogan and the other one was Page, I think."

Chapter 15

A CONVERSATION WITH PASTOR ADAMSON

Monday morning came and went. Still unable to get ahold of Sheriff Tate, Dave decided to call Mr. Adamson before talking to the FBI.

"Pastor Adamson, how are you, sir? This is Dave Maxwell. Do you have a minute to talk?"

"Hi, Dave. Sure. What's on your mind?"

"We saw Dixon. He was here in Westwood. Working at a café."

"Are you sure it was him?"

"I didn't recognize him, but Dani saw him and is 100 percent sure it was him. The way he acted supports that. When he saw me, I think he panicked. He immediately left the store through the back door. I stopped in this morning and spoke with the cafe owner, and she said, Wilbur—that's the name he is now using—quit yesterday. I'd wanted to let Sheriff Tate know about this directly, but I haven't been able to reach him. I let the police here know and figured they'd coordinate with him. I've been calling the sheriff since Saturday but haven't been able to reach him."

"No one has, Dave. The sheriff hasn't checked in at work or been home for three days. I spoke with his wife and she said he stormed out of the house Friday in a foul mood. She hasn't seen him since. Apparently, he has been acting moody at home lately. Since the disappearance, she says he's been on edge, but he's never stayed away overnight. The deputies have been looking for him since Saturday, but they've had no luck finding him."

"That's odd. I guess I need to go to the FBI with my information then. Do you remember the names of the two agents who came to the camp?"

"The lead agent was named Hogan. I can't recall hearing the other one's name."

"Was it Page?"

"Maybe. You know, as I recall, I don't think they ever told me his name. I can tell you one thing though. They sure weren't what I'd have pictured as FBI agents."

"My dad said the same thing but didn't elaborate."

"Well, first their demeanor was wooden and overbearing from the start. And their way of speaking—they sounded as if they were reading from a TV cop show script and using a lot of slang. One time, the second agent referred to me as 'the suspect.' When Sheriff Tate corrected them, Agent Hogan looked at Tate as if he were going to kill him. Since that time, Tate seemed almost afraid. It's as if the agents read Tate the riot act sometime after they all left."

Dave remembered their approach to him regarding the stone fragment. Mr. Adamson's observation gave credence to Mr. Maxwell's comment. "Did they ever say to which FBI office they were attached?"

"Yeah, and that's another thing. I remember Agent Hogan saying they worked at the Los Angeles office. I thought, *Why did the FBI send out two agents from LA when Reno is only a stone's throw from here?* Then I asked who had contacted them in the first place, and Hogan just gave me the stink eye and mumbled something about keeping my nose out of FBI business. Logan hadn't. Tate said his office hadn't. I guess it could have been Toni's parents, but they were so angry I hesitated to ask them.

"You're right. It is strange that the response time of the FBI was so *timely*."

"Right."

"Thank you, Mr. Adamson. You've been a big help."

"Dave, maybe I'm just starved for drama out here in the woods, but there seems to be something strange going on in all of this. I feel I should warn you to be careful when you contact these FBI agents."

"I will."

"Tell your parents that we haven't forgotten Sam. Our camp maintenance staff prays for him every day at devotions. He was really a favorite here."

"Thank you. Goodbye, Pastor."

Chapter 16

WILL THE REAL AGENT HOGAN PLEASE RISE?

Dave hung up and leaned back in his chair. He laced his fingers together behind his head and considered Mr. Adamson's warning. He decided to call the FBI's Los Angeles branch office to get an update from someone other than Agent Hogan. He spoke to the switchboard operator and was put through to the agent in charge. "Federal Bureau of Investigation. This is Agent Rhodes. How can I help you?"

Now that Dave was on the line actually talking to a federal agent, he was having second thoughts. "My name is David Maxwell, sir, and I'm trying to get an update on a case involving a missing person."

"How are you involved, Mr. Maxwell?"

"She was a camper under my care at Camp Sequoia, and my brother was injured while searching for the missing girl. He's in the UCLA neurology unit.

"What was the missing girl's name, please?"

"Toni LaRusso."

Another minute passed. "I've searched our regional database and have no information on any FBI case involving the surname LaRusso."

"Can you check the name Sam Maxwell, please?" Dave hoped this might trigger a hit on Toni by using another search term.

"Certainly. Please hold for a moment." The line went silent as Agent Rhodes did another computer search. "Mr. Maxwell, I ran a computer search and there is nothing on a Sam Maxwell in connection with any ongoing FBI investigation. I'm sorry. Did someone at the Bureau tell you that we'd been involved in this?"

"Well, not exactly." Dave dissembled. He stared at the phone receiver. Nausea was rising. "I must have misunderstood. One last thing, sir." Dave was going for broke with this. "May I speak with Agent Hogan."

"I can leave him a message. Most of our agents are downtown at the National Law Enforcement and Medical Examiners Death Conference for the next few days, so unless it is urgent, I can't guarantee he'll respond until he's back in the office."

"That's okay. No message. Thank you. Goodbye."

"Goodbye."

Dave looked up at the ceiling. *What now? It sounds like the FBI was never even involved in this case. Then why did someone claiming to be Agent Hogan show up at the camp?*

Dave flipped open his laptop and opened his browser. He typed in FBI and the conference name in the search window. There it was. A three-day conference at the Los Angeles Conference and Convention Center. Dave read the program syllabus online. The description of lectures seemed a bit morbid for his taste, but he understood the topics catered to the needs of law enforcement personnel. They just made him feel a bit queasy. However, he knew he needed to speak with Agent Hogan, and since he was free this afternoon, he headed out to his car for the trip downtown.

* * *

Traffic was light—for LA—and in forty-five minutes, Dave was walking into the convention center. He looked up at the signage for the event and whistled. This appeared to be a big deal. Nominally, it was a major national conference devoted to county medical examiners and police personnel. There was a long list of speakers; some of the names even Dave recognized from the network news shows. A gigantic poster hung above the main auditorium entry door showing a picture of two distinguished-looking men gazing down at the entrants. Today's lecturers were Dr. Harry Leigh and Dr. Wilhelm Spencer. *Impressive.*

Dave walked to the registration table where a young man and woman sat. The young man turned away from Dave, hunched over his cell phone while agitatedly speaking. "Mr. Eddie will get his money when I get paid. No, I don't have it now. Just tell him to leave Maggie out of all this. Threatening my dog isn't going to make money appear."

The woman looked up from the table with a bored expression. She appeared to be a bit put off by Dave's interruption of her current task—rearranging the remaining name tags on the table. "Can I help you?" she asked with an edge in her voice.

"Yes, I'm looking for Agent Hogan of the LA FBI office."

"Well, you can't just go interrupting Dr. Leigh's talk now, can you?"

Dave stood there. He began to grow annoyed at these two who were working the reception desk. "I don't intend to—"

"Well, in that case, you'll just have to wait till he's finished, won't you?" The man had now finished his phone conversation. He turned to see what was going on. He looked up at Dave, his mouth gaping and his expression vacant.

Barely holding his anger in, Dave said, "And how long will that be?"

"Well, it *is* written on the program. Are you even registered for this event?"

Dave was now at the end of his patience. Thinking quickly, he looked down at the table and saw the name tag "Dave Barclay." He leaned over the table into the face of the sneering woman and announced in a loud voice, "I'm Special Agent David Barclay of the governor's special 5-0 task force. Now you'd better give me my name tag before I call the governor's office and have you two cuffed and marched out of here to jail." He reached into his sport coat and pulled out his cell phone.

The woman shrank back at this outburst, but the man responded quickly in a frightened voice. "No need for anger, Agent *Barclay.* She was just playing with you. You know, she's trying to have a little fun. Here, I can help you." He punched a few keys on the laptop and asked, "Who were you looking for?"

Dave glanced over to see the woman sobbing into her handkerchief. "FBI Agent Hogan."

She had gotten up from her seat and, sniffling, walked slowly around the table. She picked up Special Agent Barclay's name tag and offered it to Dave. "I'm sorry. I was just funning with you." Her hands were trembling to the point that she almost dropped the tag.

The man said, "Here he is. Seat B37. That's in the middle of the front section in the VIP area, so you really might do better to wait till the presentation is complete."

"When will that be?"

"About forty-five minutes, but the speaker is Dr. Leigh. We hear he's a wonderful lecturer."

Dave had seen his share of lecturers, "wonderful" and otherwise. He started toward the large door but stopped when the man said, "Your seat is in row E, number 64, on the right-hand side." The man pointed right. "If you use that door, you can go directly down to your seat. It's on the end of the row, right on the aisle.

Dave nodded and walked to the right. As he approached the door, he turned at the sound of whining. He saw the man take the woman under the chin and look at her sternly. "No, Candy, I don't think he can arrest us. Remember we are state employees. We can do *anything* we want. If the public doesn't like it, that's just tough!"

Dave shook his head as he entered the auditorium. *Now I know why I stand in line for two hours to get my driver's license.*

On stage, a sharply dressed middle-aged man addressed his audience with professional polish. "That brings me to my primary subject, Joe Warren Gatsby, or as many of you know him the 'killer circus man.'"

For the next forty minutes, Dave found himself alternately enthralled and repulsed by Dr. Leigh's presentation. However, the nincompoop at the desk was correct. Dr. Leigh was a terrific speaker. He described the interplay of the serial killer's childhood in a mentally disturbed family, his troubled school years, and his military experience, all peppered with episodes of sadism. He then detailed how these factors combined to create this maniac. Dr. Leigh then detailed the criminal activities of Gatsby through the years and how he was finally nabbed. The talk was concluded with a number of points that Dave assumed would be useful to those in the audience tasked with chasing these monsters.

When the lecture ended, the house lights came on and Dr. Leigh received a standing ovation. Dave walked around to the front and counted over the number of seats to identify Agent Hogan from his seat assignment. Dave waited until the crowd was leaving before approaching the agent but could already see something was amiss. Rather than the behemoth agent he'd met at camp, this Hogan was about six feet tall with cropped sandy hair in a receding line and wore wire-rimmed spectacles.

Dave approached the agent and said, "Agent Hogan?"

The man turned from another conversation. "See you in the lounge, Wilhelm. I'm looking forward to your lecture on Garza. Yes, young man?"

"Agent Hogan, my name is Dave Maxwell and I'm looking into a missing persons case that occurred some weeks back at Camp Sequoia, near Yosemite."

Dave was startled when the fed replied, "I've read about the case in the paper. The FBI isn't involved at this time. Are you a reporter?"

"No, sir. I am a counselor from the camp, and my brother was seriously injured searching for the girl. I have some information that might be useful to investigators. Previously, I'd understood the Bureau to be involved. A man presenting himself as Agent Hogan from the LA office showed up at camp. I had come here expecting to find that man."

"I hope you aren't disappointed."

"No, sir, just *surprised*. He showed what appeared to be genuine credentials."

"Have you ever seen genuine FBI credentials?" Hogan laughed as he withdrew his wallet and flipped it open.

"No. I guess not."

"Most people haven't, so they assume any piece of card stock with a seal, dull-looking gray picture, and 'FBI' printed in a bold blue is real."

"I see."

"That's the magic of TV. In any case, how can I help you?"

"Well, I don't guess you can—thank you."

"If you email the information to me, I will see it gets to the proper people. Impersonating a federal agent is a felony and the Bureau takes it seriously. I have a question for you, Mr. Maxwell."

"Yes?"

"Why are you wearing Agent Barclay's nametag?"

Dave muttered, "It's a long story. I'll put it back, and I'll send you that email."

Hogan grinned and handed Dave his business card as he left. Dave thought about the email for a bit and decided it could wait. He really needed to talk to Sheriff Tate.

He walked to his car considering all that he had learned today. His cell phone rang as he entered the parking garage. "Hello?"

"Hello, Dave, it's Winston Adamson. I've got some bad news."

Immediately Dave thought of Toni, "Is she dead?"

"No, it's about Otis Tate. He was found dead in his cruiser about an hour ago."

"How? Where?"

"All I was told by Deputy Hennessey was that it was a gunshot wound to the head. They are assuming it's suicide at this point."

"Thanks for letting me know." Dave was stunned. He dropped his keys as he went to open the car door. Getting in, he put his head on the steering wheel and prayed for Sheriff Tate's family.

Chapter 17

THE INTERVIEW

August 2020.

Lou Decker bent over and plucked up a long stem of beach grass. He stood at the edge of the bluff. He put one end into his mouth and gritted his teeth. Below him the Lake Michigan surf rolled gently in. The sand beneath his feet slowly slipped off the verge of the bluff. He took a step backward. The sun was continuing its downward drift toward the horizon, but the rays softly warmed Lou's face. The deep blue of the sky and lack of clouds seconded the weatherman's prediction of continued fair weather.

From his elevation above the water, he could see quite a distance. At the horizon, a freighter headed south. Knowing he was about forty-five feet above the surface of the lake, Lou tried to recall enough trigonometry from high school to calculate the distance to the ship, but he always confused the formulas in his head and, laughing, gave up.

From behind, he heard the sound of a vehicle crunching up the gravel driveway. He turned to look and through the big wall window saw Lenore walking to the entry door. She let a man in.

Seconds later the patio door slid open and she called, "Lou, Martin's here!"

Decker smiled and waved. With long strides, he trotted toward the house: up the steps, across the deck, and through the open door.

Lou shook his friend's hand heartily. "Martin, great to see you. Have a seat."

Martin settled himself on the sofa. Several months back, Martin Hammer had performed the wedding ceremony in Minnesota between Lenore and Lou as a newly ordained minister. However, contact had been nonexistent since.

"Great to see you too, Detective."

Lou laughed. "How's the church going?"

"The church is small but it's growing—*slowly.* People seem wired to want entertainment nowadays, even in church."

Decker nodded. He leaned back in the big easy chair. Lou reached for his glass of iced tea from the side table and took in the view. Out the window wall, he watched the sun disappearing behind a distant lone cloud. Golden rays reached down to the water.

In from the kitchen walked Lou's bride, Lenore, carrying a tray of crackers and smoked whitefish spread that she put down on the coffee table. She handed Martin a tumbler of iced tea as well, then she walked over and plopped down on the overstuffed couch.

"Thank you, Lenore. Wow, Lou, what was it that your uncle did?" Martin asked, looking about the great room.

"He was a cement contractor. Did pretty well for himself. A lot of the roads in these parts were his projects."

"He certainly had a wonderful home." Martin looked around at the furnishings in the great room where they sat and shook his head. "And this view is spectacular."

"Yes. He did." Lou thought back on his uncle Bart, recalling fishing trips taken out on the big lake and the annual family Christmas parties his uncle would host. He certainly loved to entertain. So long ago. Now that entire generation was gone.

Lenny sensed Lou's sadness. "When did your journalist friend say he'd be coming?"

Lou stood up and walked to the window wall. "His plane landed at five o'clock, so I expect him anytime now." Lou's attention had drifted away.

He looked across the lake to the horizon. Nothing but calm. The water was perfectly flat. Not a ripple in sight.

Martin turned to Lenore. "It's nice to get to see you again, Lenore."

"Call me Lenny."

"Well, Lenny, it's obvious to me that you're a good influence on the detective here."

Everyone laughed.

Lou turned around and smiled at Lenny. "I don't know, Martin. She's a lot tougher than she looks."

"Why do you *always* say that, Lou?" She smiled and tossed a throw pillow in his direction.

Lou grabbed the neck of his T-shirt and pulled it down over his shoulder to expose the big surgical scar. "See, I've got the marks to prove it."

"Hey, buddy boy. Don't blame me for that one. Your Acapulco high dive act wasn't my idea."

Lou looked away. Unexpectedly, Decker felt an icy pang as he recalled his frantic jump from the high bluff above Lake Superior to escape the monster.

The doorbell rang. "That must be Nash."

Lenny walked over to let the visitor in. Her eyes bugged as she opened the door and saw the entryway filled with the giant frame of the journalist. "Hello," she said.

"Hello, ma'am. I'm Scott Nash. I have an appointment to see Lou Decker. Is he—?" Nash looked over Lenny's head and waved to Lou, who gestured him to come on in.

Lenny moved aside and Nash strode past into the room. Behind Nash's back, Lenny grinned hugely. She lifted and spread her hands and mouthed the words "He's so big!"

Scott walked over to Lou and Martin, who had now stood.

Nash thrust out his massive hand and enveloped Lou's in a warm handshake. "Hi, Lou. I hope this isn't a bad time. I really appreciate you seeing me on such short notice. I thought I might stop in here and speak with you on my way to Los Angeles. I'm speaking Wednesday evening at the national Fortean week conference. I was hoping to get some material." He grinned as he said this.

"No, Scott. No problem at all. This is Lenore, my wife, and this is Martin Hammer." Lou glanced over at Martin, who was also staring up at the big man. "Martin was with me when it all went down last fall. He's one of my oldest friends." Decker laughed at this running gag between himself and Martin, whom Decker had "met" once when Martin was a baby and their families were visiting.

"Lenny, Martin, meet Scott Nash, editor and reporter for *America's Fortean Life*"

They exchanged greetings and Lenny offered Nash a drink. He opted for an ice water. "The plane was really warm and I feel dehydrated. But maybe that's because I've been chasing around Florida on an investigative tour for the last two weeks." They sat and Scott spoke. "I guess I ought to congratulate you on winning such a beautiful bride. I'm sure you'll both be very happy."

"Thanks." He smiled across the room at Lenore.

Lou spoke. "I suppose you're here to ask about the events of last fall?"

"Yes. As with most of these 'events,' as you called it, I suspect the reality of what actually happened eluded my mainstream journalist colleagues. In fact, had *we* not met on our flight over to Minnesota, I probably would've tossed out the letters I received from our readers, without a thought. But the letters kept coming. So I dug a bit into the news archives and when I saw your name mentioned, and recalled our meeting, I was intrigued." He glanced between the occupants of the room. "Based on what we discussed on the phone, I sense there may be more to your experience than came out in the media. So here I am."

Martin's face had taken on a look of concern as he glanced at Decker. Lenore brought in Nash's water and she sat on a corner of the couch, her legs curled under her.

Decker looked at Nash intently. "There *is* more. Much more. At first, I assumed it was just lost in the issues surrounding my apprehension of the child killer Garza and the FBI investigation of the cult that abducted my sister, which by the way, has gone nowhere. You might not like where this takes us, but here goes."

Nash grinned but leaned in.

"I'm not sure where to start. You may recall I was on my way out to find my sister, Shelley, when we met on that flight."

Nash nodded at this, recalling their conversation on the plane.

For the next hour, Decker laid out the facts of the story, from his eerie initial encounter with Brother Love and his assistant to his time in Minnesota and how it had fundamentally changed his perspective on life and the supernatural. Lou described growing to love Lenore, this beautiful, brave woman who'd rescued him after his leap from the bluff.

"But it wasn't really a fall, as was reported, was it Lou?" Lenny commented.

"No, it wasn't." As he explained, Lou wondered whether Nash would think him a fool, delusional, or—worse—a liar.

Scott Nash listened quietly, never once interrupting Decker as he spoke. He looked thoughtfully at the detective. "What finally happened with the Garza thing?"

Lou studied the wall behind Nash. "He was killed. In jail. Out of the blue, he recanted his charge that I had illegally arrested him. A week later, he was shanked. No connection between those events, at least as far as I'm concerned."

"I see. Then whether the bulk of your adventure was ignored or suppressed, it's quite a story. Mind control, dragons, angels, a national criminal cabal involved in human trafficking, and a lunatic preacher heading it all. The whole thing sounds like the script of a bad TV movie." He laughed softly, but his face remained serious.

"I told you on the phone you wouldn't believe me and would probably be wasting your time coming here."

Martin interjected, "Detective Decker is telling the truth, Mr. Nash. He's the most honest man I know."

Nash put his hands up. "Don't misunderstand me. I believe it. Every word. Lou, do you remember on the plane when I said that perhaps our meeting was a 'divine appointment'?"

"I do."

"Well, now I'm convinced of that."

Lenore looked quizzically at the big man. "Why would anyone not privy to everything that happened behind the scenes believe Lou's story? You must receive letters and stories from cranks every day."

"Lenore, I think you know I'm a journalist, or at least I attempt to be one. I've investigated these kinds of reports my whole career, some credible, others not. And I like to think I'm a pretty good judge of character." Nash has a serious expression as looked around again at the three. "To paraphrase Jesus, 'This is a man in whom there is no guile.' I believe that Detective Decker is being totally honest and everything he described is totally real." Nash then broke into a grin. "Besides, you know I make my living printing crazy stories."

Everyone laughed except Lou, who wore a weak smile, still troubled by his recollections.

Nash continued. He looked hard at Lou. "You know, I had thought this might make an interesting article. But that's not really why I wanted to come here. I needed to know if my suspicions about what might have actually happened were correct. There are a lot of very weird things happening in our world right now, and many seem to have a spiritual dimension. I'm not talking about sea serpents in the Great Lakes or Elvis at Burger King in Kalamazoo." Nash stood to leave and shook his head. "Sometime, you'll have to let me tell you about my Florida trip. Right now, I'll say good night and get out of your hair. My flight to Los Angeles in the morning is an early one. The conference out there is always a zany affair." He chuckled. "You know California is the land of fruits and nuts."

Chapter 18

FORTEAN LIFE

The next evening, Logan stopped in at Dave's apartment. Logan wasn't riding the Harley this time but was in his own vehicle. Logan's knock on the door roused Dave from a light slumber. Dave got off the couch, shook his head, opened the door, and groggily greeted his friend.

Logan was carrying a rolled-up newspaper as he entered. He had a big smile on his face. "Looks like you need some coffee, buddy. Let me start a pot." Logan walked directly to the kitchen without waiting for a reply. He got out the coffee grinder and began preparations.

Dave walked into the kitchen and sat while Logan brewed the coffee.

The young men sat at the table for nearly an hour drinking coffee and chatting about the peculiarities of the LaRusso situation. Dave laid out his experience hunting down Agent Hogan and what he found at the death investigator's convention. Logan had also received a call from Mr. Adamson concerning the death of Sheriff Tate. "They think, or at least they said, the sheriff shot himself. He had a gunshot wound in his left temple. The driver's window was open, and Tate's arm was hanging out with his gun lying on the ground."

Dave thought back to the recent death investigator lecture he had attended. "Who found the sheriff?"

"I think Mr. A said one of the deputies."

"Yeah, but why would he kill himself? This is another thing about this whole affair that doesn't make a lot of sense."

"I don't know. Granted I didn't know him very well, but he never struck me as the suicidal type."

"I guess I'd better call the department and let them know that Dixon is—or was in LA."

"Good idea."

Dave picked up the paper that Logan had tossed on the table. It was open to the entertainment section of the *LA Times*. "What's going on in this town that you need a newspaper?"

"Scott Nash."

"Who?"

"Scott Nash. He's a contributor to, and some readers say secret owner/editor of, *America's Fortean Life* journal."

"Journal? Don't you mean tabloid? And—"

"He's coming to town."

"Don't make me slap you, Logan." Dave broke into a smile. "So is Santa Claus—in about three months. Why should you care about some humbug conspiracy nut?"

"David." Logan now put on a deadly serious expression. "Scott Nash is coming to speak Wednesday evening at the Bovard Auditorium. His topics will be, of course, UFOs, then the Black Rock Men's Desert Retreat, North American Cryptozoology, and get this: the Michigan-Minnesota Cult Shootout. I'm going and—I think *you* need to come with me. There are hints of the paranormal in Toni's disappearance. We might get some insight into something we're not considering."

"Logan, I'm not conceding there is anything mystical here."

"You can bring Lanie if you'd like."

"Lanie? We're not married, Logan. I took her to one football game."

Logan mumbled under his breath, "Not yet." Then he said, "I'm not blind. I see how you look at each other. Ask her if she'd like to come. Heck, she likes science fiction anyway."

Dave chuckled. "If, and only if, I see her at the hospital. I'm not going to cut into her study time." He laughed. "Would you want to be the chest pain patient whose nurse had not studied the material on heart attacks because she went to 'the Crazy Show' instead?"

Logan sighed. "It's not like that, Dave."

Dave realized that he had hurt his friend's feelings and tried to apologize. "Okay, I'll go with you. It should be entertaining and a break from thinking about all of this. Hey, we might even see someone in an Iron Man or Wonder Woman get-up. But you buy pizza afterward."

"Deal." Logan brightened. "And Lanie?"

"If I see her. Nonnegotiable."

"Wednesday night then. We can meet there at 7:30."

*   *   *

The next morning, Dave stopped by the hospital early to see Sam since his teaching responsibilities did not start till after lunch. He was surprised to see the back of a uniformed nurse looking up at Sam's monitor and writing on the clipboard. Dave walked around. He was startled to recognize Lanie.

"Hi," she chirped.

"Hi. You're here early today. And where's your book?" He laughed.

"I'm on the job. Sam's my assigned patient for medical management class. I had to ask for him, but there it is."

"Great. I think." Dave looked very serious then broke into a big smile. "It'll be nice knowing you are with him. So what's the story, Nurse?"

"No change. He's still asleep, as you can see. His vitals remain stable, and his latest labs are all normal. But Dave, I did see him move his arm and mumble something when I came in. I'm certain that he was dreaming. It seemed he might be afraid of something."

"Just a dream, Lanie."

"I know. But—"

"Change of subject, then I'll let you get back to your nursing duties."

"He gets a shampoo and trim today. How do you think he'd look with a Mohawk?"

"Like one of those boys from the skate park, I guess." Dave needed to get this out before he lost his nerve. "Hey, Lanie. Are you free tomorrow night?"

"Yes."

"Logan asked me to go with him to a lecture tomorrow, and he suggested you might come with us."

81

"So is Logan asking me out?"

"No, I'm asking you out. I guess I just assumed you'd be busy."

"So this isn't really a date? What's the lecture about?"

Dave blushed and repeated the topics Logan had mentioned to him.

Lanie laughed. "I'd love to go. Sounds like fun."

"Good. I'll pick you up about 6:30. I've gotta run now. Maybe I'll see you later?"

"Fine. Dave, do you think there'll be any—" She stopped. "Never mind."

"Be any what?"

"Nothing. I was just thinking."

"Okay, see you later."

Dave walked over to his brother and looked down. Sam appeared to be in a peaceful, dreamless sleep. "I'll see you later too." Dave squeezed his shoulder and walked out.

Chapter 19

THE LECTURE

Wednesday evening Dave, Lanie, and Logan walked into a nearly full auditorium, about twenty minutes before the beginning of Nash's talk. Dave was truly surprised to see droves of people streaming in.

Logan read Dave's expression and commented, "See Dave, I'm not a lone nut. And as you can see, almost all the people here look normal. Well, almost."

Lanie was looking beyond the other two and trying not to laugh at a patron down the row who was wearing white coveralls, a white Kabuki mask, and a big, black fright wig.

"I said almost."

The lights dimmed. The emcee came out and introduced Scott Nash, who received a standing ovation from the packed auditorium.

Nash began. "Yo. It's just too sweet being here tonight in my favorite American city. Thank you all for coming." He then talked for five minutes about *America's Fortean Life* magazine. Nash outlined its purposes, its history, and its intended future. While he talked, the crowd began a low, rhythmic clapping that increased in volume and intensity. This puzzled Dave, who looked over at Logan.

Logan turned and whispered, "Tradition. This crowd isn't interested in all that stuff. They don't need a commercial since most of them subscribe already. They want him to get to the meat of the presentation."

Lanie and Dave glanced at each other with Lanie giggling. "They're certainly not a very patient or polite lot."

The room went totally dark, and a large map of the United States came up. The room erupted in raucous cheers. The map zoomed in on Lake Michigan.

For the next twenty minutes, Nash told of his failed expedition to find Mitch, one of the several Loch Ness-type legends of the Great Lakes. The tale was amusing to Dave, but he thought parts of the anecdotes were borderline silly. He looked to Lanie, who watched the presentation with rapt attention. Logan had a matching expression. Dave muttered, "Brother," to himself and, smiling, slouched down in his seat.

For the next hour and a half, Mr. Nash spun yarns of his travels around the world investigating the odd and mysterious and meeting with varying levels of success. He spoke about the latest Ohio River Mothman Cluster, the Giant Snake of Tulum, and the Bigfoot, Yeti, and Sasquatch connection to space aliens.

Dave had just about dozed off when he heard Nash begin to discuss the Michigan-Minnesota Cult Shootout. "I was fortunate to make the acquaintance of one of the principals in this case by sheer coincidence. Detective Lou Decker was on a flight to Minnesota to join his brother-in-law in searching for the detective's sister. She had disappeared while attending what ultimately proved to be a cult-sponsored retreat. As you might guess, the detective had little time for the issues important to those of us interested in *Fortean Life*. He was a thoroughly mato man."

Dave whispered to Logan, "Mato man?"

"Materialistic. Uninterested in Fortean issues. It's a code word."

"Oh."

Lanie shushed them.

"On a mundane level, the missing woman was recovered; however, Decker's brother-in-law was murdered during the search. You might have even read about this part of the case in the news. I did. There were several angles touched on by the news plus obvious omissions that just did not sit right with me. After a time, I decided to fly to Grand Rapids, Michigan, and get the real story, firsthand, from the detective himself. When I did this, I discovered the high degree of strangeness involved."

Nash went on to detail Decker's involvement in quashing the dangerous cult involved in drugs and human trafficking. He highlighted the detective's interaction with demonic and angelic creatures, mystical personages, and his nearly fatal encounter and shootout with the dragon on the shore of Lake Michigan. Nash's tale was both lurid and entertaining. One thought occurred to Dave and stuck in his mind. *How does a modern American detective turn into a person involved in this? There must be a lot more to this story than Nash is saying.*

The presentation ended, and Lanie and Dave hung around the lobby while Logan waited in line to purchase an autographed copy of Nash's latest book, *Pursuit: Chasing the Demon.* They discussed the lecture and opined about Nash's more outlandish claims. Dave remarked, "I wonder what changed the detective so—so—"

"Fundamentally?" asked Lanie.

"Yeah. That's the word, I guess."

"The things that Nash described, if they are real, would change me. You can't tell me you'd be unaffected, can you?"

"No. That is, if they were real."

Lanie shrugged. "My grandfather was a healer. I remember him helping people from the time I was a little girl. I saw him stop bleeding, take fevers away, and make burns stop paining the victim. I thought this was magic. In fact, this is why I went into nursing. I wanted to help people like he did. But I've learned in nursing school that those "miraculous" things I saw my grandpa do weren't miracles at all. They were the result of the strong belief in my grandpa's power by the people he was helping. However, this failed to address the role of prayer in his healings."

"Hmmm. Is he still alive?"

"Yes, he is. He's almost one hundred years old and lives alone on a farm in Oklahoma."

"Hope you have his genes."

"I guess so. But I lost something when I realized that there is no magic and he wasn't really healing anybody. I began to question whether prayer itself meant anything at all in healing or was a waste of time. All my life I had looked up to him and—"

"Well, he certainly was helping people heal."

"I know, but suddenly it was like he was a fraud."

"Did he claim that he was responsible for the healings?"

"No, he always maintained it was prayer, the faith of the people, and the power of God."

Logan walked up at that moment while waving his book and smiling. "Got it. Thanks for waiting for me. Let's go get some pizza."

Lanie looked down and shook her head. "I'm not hungry. I think I'll go home. It's been a long week and I'm really tired."

Logan shrugged. "You sure? I'm buying."

Lanie nodded. Dave looked at his friend. "Logan, I'm going to take a rain check as well. I'll take Lanie home. Then I'm going by the hospital and see Sam."

"Suit yourself. I guess I'll go back to the meet and greet for a while and then go home and read some Nash."

They separated and Dave walked Lanie to his car. "Gee, I didn't mean to bum you out."

Lanie looked surprised. "It wasn't you, Dave. I really am pooped, and Nash's talk was what got me thinking. Not you."

Dave opened the door for her and helped her into the car. "Okay. Let's get you home."

He took Lanie back to her nursing dorm and then walked across to the hospital. Dave entered Sam's room and went over to the bed. He looked down at Sam and took his hand.

Sam's eyes fluttered.

"Sam? Can you hear me?" Sam's eyelids fluttered again then settled down.

Dave sat down and leaned back in the chair. He stared at the ceiling and became lost in his thoughts of the lecture this evening. The noises from the monitor provided a monotonous backdrop to his ruminations, and before long, Dave was lost in dreams of giant fish, demons, and dragons.

Chapter 20

SAM WAKES UP

The next day Dave was discussing a complex mathematical equation describing the interaction between two fluids of differing viscosity with his class when he felt his phone vibrate in his pocket. He ignored it and went on speaking. The vibration stopped. In a few minutes, the vibration started up once more. Again, Dave ignored it and plowed on with his talk. Two minutes later, Dave finished discussing the topic and excused himself. He pulled out his phone and looked at the screen. He saw the missed calls. Lanie had written twice. A third call noted Lanie 911. He dismissed the class with the admonition to be here Monday "with questions. We'll be reviewing for the midterm exam."

As the class shuffled out, Dave called Lanie. "Hello, Lanie. Sorry I didn't—"

"Dave, get over here. Sam woke up," Lanie interrupted.

"I'm on my way. When did he wake up?"

"About fifteen minutes ago. He's groggy and the neurology fellow is in there with him now. But Sam is asking to see you."

Dave rang off. He gathered his materials from the desk and sprinted to the parking garage. Dave took the 101 to the 405 and headed south. Traffic was moderate, and by the time Dave parked, the trip took about fifty minutes. During this time, Dave's mind raced with questions occurring in rapid succession.

He hustled into Sam's room to find Lanie fluffing Sam's pillow as he sat up in the bed. Sam looked at Dave and a drowsy grin came over his face. "Good to see you, brother."

"Welcome back." Dave moved to the bed and hugged his brother fiercely. "Did anyone call Mom and Dad?"

"I did," said Lanie, a huge smile on her face. "They'll be here in a couple hours."

"And Dani?"

"Your parents said they'd let her know."

"How do you feel?" Dave backed off and looked earnestly at his brother.

"A little groggy, and my hearing seems off a bit. But all in all okay. I guess I feel like I took a really long nap." He laughed.

"No headache?"

"No, none at all."

Lanie tapped some key at the bedside computer, looking back to her patient. "We've been trying to reorient Mr. Maxwell. But you should probably carry the ball, Dave."

"What's this? I'm Mr. Maxwell and you're Dave?" Sam eyed the pretty nurse at his side, then his twin.

"Well, you *were* asleep. Lanie's been your nurse, and before that, she read to you almost every night." Dave kept the fact that they were dating to himself.

"Is that why I keep thinking about the Amber series stories?" He smiled at Lanie. "Thank you. I must have seemed an indifferent audience, but at some level, you were apparently getting through. In fact, maybe I just walked back into this dimension." He laughed.

"Sam, lots happened while you were out. I don't know how much of this you want me to tell you now, but I need to know what happened to you. How were you injured?"

"I went out—" Sam hesitated as if trying to collect his thoughts. "I remember going to look for Toni and someone else, but I can't remember who."

"Dixon."

"I guess. In any case, I was walking through the field, swinging my flashlight around, and calling out to her when I heard human voices. They seemed to be chanting, and I saw lights. I moved through the weeds in that direction, and I saw a clearing. On the other side of the clearing, a man suddenly stood up and fell down. I remember that clearly."

"Was it the old German man who lived over that way?"

"I'm not sure. Dave, you said lived."

"Yes, he died the same night and was found with his dead dog about where you describe the man falling."

"How'd he die?" Sam gnawed at his lower lip.

"They said he had multiple snakebites. So did his dog."

"That fits. I remember hearing a hissing noise and a man who seemed to be watching the clearing grabbed me and told me to run."

"What did you do then?"

"I ran."

"Back toward the path?"

"I guess so."

"Tell me about the man, Sam."

"Not much to tell. Must've been a local. He just kind of appeared. It sounds weird now that I'm saying it aloud." He shrugged, struggling to recollect events, and continued. "I must've misjudged where the path was because I remember falling and a sharp pain in my leg just before the lights went out." Sam was rubbing his forehead and remarked, "Dave, I'm getting a bit of a headache now."

"We can stop. Just rest. Everything should be fine now that you are awake."

Sam pulled aside the bedsheet to look at his leg. It was in a posterior splint with a bulky wrap. "My leg is sore. I must have bruised it pretty good."

"You broke it, Sam. The orthopedist put several screws and a plate in there."

Lanie piped up, "We changed the surgical dressing every day and your wound is almost healed. You should be up and about with crutches tomorrow."

Dave considered telling Sam about Sheriff Tate's death but figured it could wait while his brother rested. Just then Dani entered the room. She ran to Sam and jumped on the bed.

"Careful with his leg, Dani," Ms. Maxwell called from the hall.

Dani gave her brother a big hug, smiled, and looked into his eyes. Disengaging, she teared up. "Sam, we were so worried about you."

Dave hugged both Dani and Sam and held them tightly.

A short time later, Logan stuck his head into the room. "Pssst, Dave." He nodded for Dave to come out into the hall. Dave had called Logan on his way to the hospital to tell him about Sam awakening and Logan had rushed over. He asked, "Is he, you know, all there?"

Dave laughed. "As far as I can tell. He hasn't begun to recite the multiplication table yet, but his speech is coherent and his memory seems pretty good, if that's what you mean."

"Yeah. Guess that sounded rather insensitive."

"No. Actually, I think we were all wondering the same thing."

Chapter 21

THE MAGIC BUSHMAN

The evening was spent talking about family issues. Sam was concerned that Dave had put his doctoral thesis on hold to teach Sam's recitation class, but Dave pooh-poohed the idea as something any brother would do. The Maxwell parents were thankful that their son had come through this and chatted happily. Mrs. Maxwell had gone on about her hopes for rejuvenating the Westwood garden club after being elected president and described in detail the plan for replacing palm trees on Westwood Boulevard. Mr. Maxwell spoke briefly about work and then sat back and listened to his wife, a big smile on his face.

The nine o'clock hour arrived, and Sam yawned. He was visibly tired, and everyone got up to leave, promising to return tomorrow. Logan gave Sam a rough hug before walking out.

"Dave, hang on a minute. There is something I want to talk to you about, okay?" Sam called.

Dave came to the bedside. "What's up?"

"You never told me. Did they find Toni?" Sam searched his brother's face intently.

Dave glanced downward and shook his head. "No. She hasn't been found, and the searches have pretty much ended. I think the general consensus is that if she didn't run away, she's probably dead."

Sam stared out the window into the blackness. "Dave, I know how this sounds. I think Toni was murdered. I'm remembering more now, and I think I stumbled on some kind of ritual or sacrifice." His voice trailed off.

"Sam, don't start. You can't blame yourself. Toni made a bad choice. It's sad, but this isn't on us. Besides, you probably dreamed it. You were out a long time." In spite of his protestations, Dave now was being forced to consider that this was sounding less and less like a straightforward abduction.

"I don't know."

"Well, I do, and I need to tell you that Sheriff Tate is dead."

"I didn't know him, but how did he die?"

Dave sat down in Sam's wheelchair and related the facts surrounding Sheriff Tate's suicide as he understood them. He also told of Dixon's appearance as a barista at Beaniac's.

"Did this Dixon know you from camp?" asked Sam.

"I don't know, but we think he saw us around the camp. It was clear he wasn't expecting to see anyone from Camp Sequoia around here." He gave a short laugh.

Lanie came back into the room. She had changed out of her nursing uniform into civvies and cleaned up. "How do you feel, Sam?"

"Okay. I was getting pretty tired, but now I'm wide-awake again."

Dave remarked, "We were just talking about developments in the LaRusso affair."

"I've been thinking about that, Dave—and Sam. Maybe we should talk to Scott Nash about this."

"You mean Scott Nash the reporter?" asked Sam.

Dave answered, "I don't know if I'd call him a reporter. Hey, how do you know about Scott Nash?"

"Logan and I have shared a subscription to *Fortean Life* four or five years now. He reads it first and then I read it when he's finished."

Dave shook his head. "Why am I just learning this?"

"Anyway, this case reminds me of the disappearances of people in national parks that have been reported on the *Sea to Sea FM* radio show." Lanie continued. "Don't look at me like that, Dave. Nursing is a twenty-four/seven job. Sometimes on the night shift I need a little help staying awake."

"Do *you* know Scott Nash?" Sam asked Lanie.

"No, but Logan met him last night at the lecture we went to."

"Wait. Do you mean that Dave went to see Scott Nash?" Sam laughed. "Dave, you'd better be careful. You'll get bounced out of Cal Tech if the administration finds out."

"Don't worry. He slept through most of it."

"True." Dave gave a solemn nod.

"Okay. Good. Dave, you had me worried there. But I don't see how Scott Nash could help us with this. Even if he will talk to us."

"Logan and I can approach him," Lanie volunteered. "I'm sure Logan would be thrilled to get a sit-down with Nash."

"Now wait a minute, you two. Again, even if he will talk to us, how can he help?" Dave had the look of a man who was losing an argument he had not realized he was in.

"Perhaps there's an angle here we aren't considering." Sam glanced between the two of them.

"What is that?" asked Dave.

"Maybe he can shed some light on the man who helped me—you know, the mystery man."

"Well," said Lanie, looking at Dave.

"When I was looking for Toni, remember I said I was stopped by a man hiding in the bushes. Well, that isn't exactly correct. As I was going to enter the clearing, he did say I was in danger and helped me escape."

"What was a man doing out in the bushes that time of night?" Lanie asked.

"Beats me, but it seemed like he was spying on whatever was going on in the clearing. In any case, when I think about him, it—"

"It what?" Dave asked.

"He wasn't like a normal man."

"How so?" asked Dave.

"He was very handsome—like movie star handsome. I could see him plainly and it was pitch-dark. He gave off some kind of light, and he was muscular. Not like a bodybuilder but solid—and perfectly proportioned."

Dave commented dryly, "And he wore a big S on his chest, right? Sam, you hit your head really, really hard. You probably dreamed this."

Lanie looked at Dave with a combination of irritation and disappointment. "Dave, it isn't getting us anywhere to make fun of your brother."

"I'm not making fun of him, but humoring his delusion isn't helping matters either."

"Remember the other night. The man you said pushed you out of the way of the car. You were talking to him."

"Yeah. The jogger."

"Dave, there was no one there. I looked around to see who you were talking to. There was no one there but you and me. I didn't call you a liar, did I?"

"No." Dave initially started to respond but turned and looked out the window.

"Why can't you accept that there are things happening that may not fit in with either your particular Christian worldview or with a Cal Tech scientist view."

Dave considered Lanie's words. Things definitely weren't fitting nicely into the boxes he'd like them to. "You're right, Lanie. I'm sorry, Sam."

"You two sounded just like Mom and Dad." He laughed. "No problem. I don't know if I'm sure about this magic bushman myself."

Dave flushed a bit at Lanie's mild scolding. "Lanie, why don't you and Logan set up a meeting with Nash?" He twisted around to look quizzically at her. "You mean you really never saw the jogger?"

Chapter 22

DINNER WITH NASH

Dave wasn't surprised that Logan knew at which hotel Scott Nash was staying. However, he was surprised at how quickly Nash agreed to meet with them. That is until Dave learned that Logan had promised Nash a meal at Musso & Franks. Dave watched in awe as the six-foot, nine-inch Nash squeezed into the booth. The dinner meeting went well. Nash entertained the group with anecdotes about aborigines, voodoo, and flying saucers. He proved to be a very amiable and educated man who treated his subjects with a charming blend of skepticism and sensitivity. Dave found himself liking Nash.

They were on dessert and coffee when Nash asked, "I understand that you all have had some *unusual* experiences lately. How can I help you?"

Dave took the lead in explaining the events at camp and subsequent developments. He barely mentioned the two encounters with the unusual men. At the end of Dave's summary, Nash remarked, "I am not sure how I can help you with this. It sounds like a job for the police."

"That's what I told my friends, but they thought you might have some mystical insights. I'm sorry that we bothered you."

Nash was clearly surprised by Dave's attitude. "I understand that you are on the faculty at Cal Tech, Dave."

"Technically I'm still a postgrad student with a temporary teaching position."

"Still, I appreciate that. Tell me: have you ever been to Egypt?"

"No."

"How about Maccha Pichu or the Australian Outback?"

"No."

"Do you have any experience with voodoo? Or druidic witchcraft?"

"I think you know the answer to that. Of course not." Dave shifted in his seat.

"Well, I'm wondering if maybe you as a scientist ought to be keeping a more open mind about things that you are not familiar with. After all, science is all about observation and inquiry, right? I've seen a lot of unexplained phenomena and while I won't say there isn't a rational explanation behind them, I haven't heard it yet. I'm also wondering if there isn't a bit more to this story than you've been telling me."

Sam piped in. "Actually, there is." He proceeded to tell Nash about his encounter with the "glowing man."

Nash listened intently, giving no hint of disbelief or impatience, surprising Dave.

Lanie then related the story of the jogger. Dave interrupted her with the objection that he was the one who'd seen the jogger and they exchanged comments.

Lanie persisted. "I never saw him. I heard you talking to someone and looking for him a moment later, but I never saw anyone. You expected me to believe you, didn't you?"

"I guess I did," answered Dave.

Nash turned to Sam. "Sam, think back to when you were approaching the clearing. Specifically, what were your impressions?"

"I don't know. My recollection of that night is hazy, but I guess I wanted to know what was going on."

"Sam, I didn't ask what you were thinking. I'm more interested in whether or not you can remember if you felt something."

"I think I felt that this was where Toni was."

"Did you get any sense of what was going on?"

"No, not until I met the glowing man in the weeds. At that point, I remember feeling like I had stumbled into something that was somehow *wrong.* I remember becoming very scared. I think I took off running at that point."

Logan described Dave's finding a piece of what Logan thought was the ceremonial stone blade used at the scene later in the clearing when he and Dave were searching. He explained his plan to send it to Reno for analysis at the college and how the strange FBI agent had confiscated it.

Nash listened closely and steepled his fingers. He looked at each of the four young people and said, "I don't think I can help you with this, but there is someone I think you should talk with."

Logan asked, "Who?"

"Detective Lou Decker. You might remember from my talk that he was the detective involved in the Michigan-Minnesota cult shootout." He looked directly at Dave and smiled. "You know, you remind me a lot of Detective Decker when I first met him."

Logan arched an eyebrow "Did he change from that first time you met him?"

Nash laughed. "Big time." He pulled out a business card and wrote Decker's name and phone number on it. "Give this a try," he handed the card to Dave. "Feel free to mention my name."

Nash pushed back from the table and glanced at the faces of the three seated with him. "Well, I've enjoyed meeting you all and I wish you well in your efforts. Perhaps you might contact me if anything comes out smelling like a *Fortean Life* article. Thanks for the great dinner and the good conversation. Now back to the hotel for a phone consultation before packing. Good night."

Nash roused his giant frame from the seat and walked out.

Chapter 23

BEACH BLANKET BINGO

That weekend Sam asked to go to the beach. They all decided on Santa Monica, but there was a professional beach volleyball tournament going on when they got there. They didn't feel like fighting the crowd so they drove up the PCH to Malibu. They turned in at Zuma and found the parking lot nearly empty.

As they helped get Sam out of the car, he remarked that the saltwater should help his healing. Sam was on crutches but did not need to keep his leg wrapped. There was only a thin pink line marking the incision. Dave shook his head, and the nurse in Lanie came out. She commented, "Your surgical wound looks great. It's well healed, but there is a plate in your leg now and your bones are still knitting. Just be careful."

"Oh, I intend to."

Lanie smiled, and Logan nodded his head seriously.

Dave set up the beach umbrella and they all laid out their blankets.

Logan opened up the cooler. "Anyone want a drink?"

Dave and Sam simultaneously answered, "Water." Logan tossed them each a cold bottle. Sam rubbed his across his forehead.

Dave saw Lanie coming back from the changing room with a frown on her face. "What's up, Lanie? Was the changing room a mess?"

"No. I want to show you something. Come with me." She motioned for Dave to follow her.

Dave shrugged and the other two guys grinned. He followed Lanie back to the building. She stopped at the corner and pointed down the beach. About 250 feet away, a young man was standing over two bikini-clad girls who were lying in the sun trying to ignore him. He was talking with increasing agitation, but the distance and noise of the waves hitting the shore prevented Lanie and Dave from hearing what he was saying. Dave recognized the Camp Sequoia T-shirt.

Lanie asked, "Is that who I think it is?"

"Dixon? Sure is. Good spotting, Lanie. Go get Logan, okay?"

At just that instant, Dixon kicked sand on the girls, and they screamed. Dixon turned away and fast-walked toward the parking lot. Dave picked up his phone and snapped several photos of the sand-kicker. Then Dave took off at a run after the escaping Dixon, but Dixon easily reached his car and drove away. Dixon was driving a bright-red, late-model Mustang with California plate "Majk Man."

Dave walked over to the girls, and his other friends were already helping them shake the sand off their belongings. Logan asked the girls if they knew the guy who was hassling them. They said no.

"What was he saying?"

The two girls looked at each other, and one made a disgusted face. They said he was trying to persuade them to come to a party. "He said it's in the canyon tonight. He went on and on about all the celebrities who come to these parties. He said he would have something special for us if we came. But we said we weren't interested, and he got angry. He started saying some pretty mean stuff and then kicked sand on us and he left."

"Canyon? Did he say which canyon?"

"Laurel Canyon."

They walked back over to their towels and Dave pulled up the photos he had snapped.

"Not very good," opined Lanie.

"Yeah, but on this one, we can at least see his face."

"Yeah, I see it now. It's kinda blurred against the sand cliff in the background."

"Well, it's all I could get."

They reached the towels and Logan yelled, "Last one in buys the pizza!" He and Dave sprinted toward the water.

Sam countered, "Not fair!" as he crutched it down the beach to the water.

Lanie stopped to help Sam hobble along, but when they neared the water's edge, he put a crutch between her legs and tripped her. Putting his feet into the water, Sam yelled, "Lanie buys!"

*   *   *

They sat on their blankets as the sun lowered over the ocean. Dave told the others of his encounter with the real Agent Hogan at the forensic conference. Logan and Lanie both expressed concerns that the faux agents were in on that night's events.

"Dave, remember the activity in the clearing?" Logan added. "That is something that we need to consider closely. We don't know what went on there, but I think it's important, and it may be the key to this whole thing."

Sam opined, "Logan is on to something. My memory is still hazy about that night, but I do remember going toward the clearing with the sense that something evil was going on. What did the muscular man I met in the weeds mean when he told me that their 'guardian' knew I was there and it was not safe for me to stay? Who or what the heck is their 'guardian'?"

"Or the man in the weeds?" asked Lanie.

"What does this have to do with Toni—or Dixon, for that matter?"

Dave added, "Why did those phony agents show up? And so soon? How did they know about Toni's disappearance? The whole investigation, such as it is, seems screwy when I look back on it."

"Dave, remember Hogan showed up again as you and Dani left camp. He came in and confiscated the knife tip you found? He said to me that it was evidence. Evidence of what? Has anyone else tried to contact this fake Agent Hogan? When you talked to Mr. Adamson, did he say anything about Hogan or the FBI?" Logan asked.

"Nothing of use that I can recall. I told you about my contact with the real Agent Hogan at the conference."

Logan nodded, but Lanie shook her head no. Sam said, "I was asleep, remember?"

"Mr. A told me about Sheriff Tate's odd behavior. Then he called back to tell me about the sheriff's death because I had told him that I had been trying to reach the sheriff. Logan, did our first Agent Hogan leave contact information?"

"Yes, in fact he did. I remember handing Hogan's card to Mr. Adamson, but I didn't even think to look at it. I never figured things would go this way. I can call him and get Hogan's number."

"Good. But don't let Pastor know about any of this. He's got enough on his plate."

"Okay, but—"

"Excuse me," Lanie interrupted. "Those girls that Dixon tried to hustle are packing up to go. Do you think maybe we should talk to them again and see if they know anything more about tonight's party?"

Logan quipped, "Are you looking for something to do tonight?"

"Yep. If the bigwigs are there as Dixon said, maybe I'll be discovered."

The boys laughed. "We don't want to lose you too," Dave said, causing Lanie to blush. "Maybe Logan could be your date. Dixon doesn't know either of you."

"Now wait a minute," Logan objected.

Sam said, "Sounds good. Logan, Dave and I can drop you off and wait in the car in case you need us."

"Need you? For what? First, I didn't say I was going. Second, I'm not looking to start a brawl."

"Dave, Lanie, let's go talk to those young ladies. Come on. Let's see if we can get an address? Logan, why not call Mr. A right now?"

Logan shook his head as the other three walked off. He called Mr. Adamson. He got the number; however, Mr. Adamson noted that he had been unable to reach the agent through this number and that Dave had recently also called to inquire about the investigation. "Right now, I'm thinking that this guy is not really an FBI agent. Heck, I doubt if the Bureau is involved at all." Logan thanked the director and looked up to see the others headed back. "Any luck?"

Dave answered, "No. Nothing more than before. Except that Dixon has changed his name again. He's now calling himself Willis."

Lanie said, "Not true, Dave. Sam had some luck. He got two phone numbers and Charlotte's offer to go with Sam to help him find the party, if he decides to go."

Sam laughed. Dave and Lanie smiled. Logan asked which one was Charlotte. Lanie answered, "She is the tall, pretty blonde with the perfect teeth and nice figure." Logan craned around to look.

Logan related his conversation with Mr. Adamson. No one was surprised that Agent Hogan was incommunicado. Dave took Hogan's number and they decided to pick up Lanie at 9 p.m. and head out to Laurel Canyon to do a little prospecting themselves.

Chapter 24

WE'RE GOING TO A PARTY—PARTY!

Dave drove around Laurel Canyon for nearly an hour before finally pulling into the Laurel Country Store parking lot. Logan got out from the back and stretched his arms above his head. He looked uphill above the store and pointed to an old house on the road. He said, "I think that is the house where Jim Morrison lived, and he wrote 'Love Street' about that place."

"What a dump. Seems like he could have afforded something a bit nicer," commented Sam.

"It probably was nicer at the time, but that wasn't the main thing. Living in the canyon itself was the attraction. Just think how many important musicians and actors lived here in the late sixties and early seventies."

"I've heard my dad talk about that," Dave said. "He has some opinions on what was happening as he looked back."

"Like what?" Lanie asked.

"Well, it seems odd how all of these musicians just kind of showed up at roughly the same time. There was no big, popular music scene in LA at that time except for the folk bands who played in clubs and dives along

Sunset Strip. Dad also pointed out that many if not most of those folks had serious military intelligence connections in their family backgrounds."

"That *is* strange," said Lanie. "I remember reading or hearing that Frank Zappa's dad was some kind of bigwig in military research. However, I can't remember what it was he supposedly did."

"Frank Zappa was some kind of genius. Ever hear of 'Wild Man Fischer'?" Dave continued.

"No," the other three answered as one.

"Was he a genius too?" Logan asked.

"No, he wasn't a genius. He was a psychotic street performer Zappa took a shine to. Why? Who knows? Zappa promoted Fischer's career, such as it was, until an incident where Fischer did something to threaten Zappa or Zappa's kids or—in any case, that's how I heard it. He wasn't much of a singer anyway. He just rambled, squeaking out goofy phrases in a loud, quavering voice."

"Oh, like Tiny Tim."

"No. He just screeched out words and was borderline incoherent. How did we wind up talking about Wild Man Fischer anyway?"

"You brought him up."

"Oh yeah."

"At any rate," Sam observed, "Dad listed a whole bunch of bands and singers who fell into this category: Crosby, Stills, and Nash; the Mamas and the Papas; the Byrds; and the Doors were some of them. Jim Morrison's father was a career navy officer. He was involved in some way with the Gulf of Tonkin incident that led us into the Vietnam War."

They were sitting on a picnic table outside the store. Dave decided to go inside to buy drinks for everyone. As he returned, he heard music and laughter coming down from the mountainside. He asked the others if they could hear it. The music was getting louder now with shouts and cheering also audible.

"I think we've found the party."

They hopped back into the car and headed up the mountain on Laurel Canyon Boulevard. Reaching Mulholland Drive, they turned right and then a quick right onto Woodrow Wilson Drive. The music was definitely louder now, and cars were parked everywhere. Four houses down, they saw the site of the party. Women were walking up the driveway. Boisterous music and voices indicated that a party was underway. Dave stopped the car for Lanie and Logan to hop out.

"Remember Willis invited you. Don't get too nosy. Just look around for him and try to talk to some people. Logan, just try to fit in." Dave laughed, leaning across his brother to speak out the window.

Lanie was dressed to fit in. She looked splendid, but Logan looked like junior faculty from the seventies in his tweed sports coat with arm patches. Lanie looked at him and shook her head. "Come here." She took off his coat and threw it into the back seat of the car. She told him to roll up his sleeves. She took off his glasses, unbuttoned his top two shirt buttons, and mussed up his hair.

Logan grinned. Lanie said, "Not bad."

Sam laughed. "You sort of look like Al Jardine. You know, from the Beach Boys."

"We'll drive around the block and come back by here. Assuming you get in and we don't see you, we'll head down to the store and wait there for your call."

Dave, being unfamiliar with the layout in this area, continued for about a mile on the street. Then he turned around and headed back by the party house in the other direction. No sign of Lanie and Logan, so Dave and Sam drove back down Laurel Canyon Boulevard toward the store. As they entered the lot, the clerk who had sold Dave the drinks was locking the place up as it was closing time.

"Hmmm. I don't think we want to hang around in their lot with no one here. The days of 'peace and love' are long gone, and I don't want to be mistaken for a burglar."

Sam was already on his phone map app and quickly located a nearby park. Dave pulled out of the store lot and they headed back up the mountain.

This time he turned left on Mulholland Drive. On the right was a sign for a gated compound: West LA Treatment Center. Sam remarked, "Otherwise known as the Hollywood Hall of Fame. I saw some of the directional arrows pointing to wings on the building with some pretty famous names on them. Wonder if they are donors or patients—or both?"

They continued a bit farther and saw the park on the left. Dave pulled into the gravel lot and looked at the sign for Laurel Canyon Dog Park.

"No times listed. That's good." He opened the car door and was assaulted by the odor of dog poop. He closed the door and looked at Sam. "I guess I missed the *dog* part…"

"You'll get used to the smell in a minute. Look. There's a picnic table by the bushes on that hilltop. Let's go sit over there." Sam was already out of the car and crutching it in that direction. Dave shook his head and followed.

As they approached the table, they saw a man sitting nearly invisible against the large hedge. He was dressed all in black with a hoodie. He held the end of a long, extension leash, the other end of which held a small, white dog. The dog began to yap furiously as the pair approached.

"Do you mind if we sit down?" Sam asked.

"How many of you are there?" the man replied.

Dave wondered if the man were intoxicated. Sam laughed. "Just the two. We're twins. We get that a lot."

The man slowly shook his head. "Whew. I was worried for a moment. Sure, take a load off."

The dog had quit barking and was sniffing at Dave's shoe. "What breed of dog is it?"

"She's a mix. Chihuahua and Maltese. A rescue. She's as smart as a whip. When I got her, she was in pretty bad shape, but she's fine now. She's adjusted to the Hills' lifestyle and thinks she owns the place."

"Do you live here?"

"Across the street and up the road a piece. We come here most nights, Lizzie and me. It's usually empty at this time of night. How 'bout you boys?" The man pushed his hood back off his head and smiled. It was now obvious that he was older than he initially appeared.

"Pasadena," Sam replied.

"Oh. Like those goofball actors on the tube."

Sam looked at Dave who shrugged. Both were puzzled.

"You know. Those nincompoops who design our spacecraft and weapons systems but can't figure out the cafeteria menu. I think it's supposed to be a comedy."

"We don't watch much TV."

"Okay. By the way, I'm Jack Holmes."

"I'm Sam, and he's Dave Maxwell. Nice to meet you."

"Same here. What brings you gentlemen out here tonight? Can't help but notice you don't have a dog with you."

"Killing time. We're supposed to pick up our sister from a party in about an hour."

"Oh, the release party."

"Release party?" Sam asked.

"Oh, you don't know. It's a celebration of sorts, for the release of Rock Rollins's latest CD: *Freak Out in the Darkness.*"

"Never heard of him."

"Hmmm. No TV. No music. What do you boys do for fun?"

"School keeps us pretty busy."

"Ahhh. Pasadena Community College, eh? I hear that's a good school."

Both laughed and let it go "Yeah, I guess so. What do you do?" asked Sam.

"Well, I used to be in movies. But now I work as a guard part time over at Universal."

"Oh? What movies? I've seen a lot of movies."

"Not these. My only legitimate film part was back when I was a kid. I was a space monster in an old Ed Wood film. That was before I was 'discovered.'"

"Oh."

"Well, I've enjoyed talking to you boys, but it's time for Lizzie and me to head back to the ranch."

"Nice meeting you, Mr. Holmes. Good night."

The man turned back after taking a few steps. "And I hope your sister doesn't get the part."

"What?" Dave asked.

"I assume that she's there to audition. Those are not nice people, boys. I'd keep her clear of them."

Sam and Dave looked at each other as the man walked off. "What is he talking about, Dave?"

Dave was also suddenly registering alarm. "Not sure, but did we send Lanie and Logan into the lion's den?" He pulled out his phone and dialed Logan. No answer. Same thing with Lanie. They hustled back to the car.

Chapter 25

PARTY POOPERS

From the street, the party house itself appeared to be a rather long but unimposing ranch-style. There was an odd-looking sculpture of a large man with a pitchfork in the front, but this *was* LA so neither paid it much notice. Moving up the driveway, they could see that the home was built onto the side of the mountain, with lights and sound coming up from below in the back.

Opening the door, Logan and Lanie were met by a tall, white-haired, muscular doorman. Opposite the door was a full wall window looking down on a large room filled with revelers, and beyond that, a second large window wall overlooked the mountainside. The doorman greeted them in a German accent. "Good evening. How may I be of service?" His body completely filled the doorway into a short hall leading to a stairway downward.

Logan looked up at him, thinking he had seen this man before. "Agent Hogan?"

The man looked down at Logan and grimaced in confusion. He did not answer.

"Hi," said Lanie. "We were invited by Willis. You know, today at Zuma—"

"And your name, miss?"

"Becca. Becca Tramell. It probably won't be on your list because I told Willis that we couldn't make it tonight. But I canceled my plans. I decided that I did not want to miss this."

Logan persisted. "You are Agent Hogan, correct?"

A brief exasperated look flashed over the doorman's face. "No, you must have met my twin brother." But then he again looked "Becca" over, nodded, and smiled. "I see. Go right in, ma'am." He moved aside and let her in but then stepped back in front of Logan, blocking his entry. "And you, sir, do you have an invitation also?" The man now looked menacingly down at Logan.

Logan was about to respond when Lanie interrupted. "He's my security man. Ari was Mossad. The only weapon he carries is his pen. Go ahead. Frisk him if you wish. He won't mind." Lanie smiled and Logan looked at her with a grimace.

The big man looked incredulous. A wry smile passed over his face but disappeared when Lanie continued. "Sir, Willis promised that your host has something special for me. He said I would meet the big boss himself. I think he might be disappointed if we were to leave. You don't want to disappoint the boss now, do you?" Lanie put on a pouting smile.

Logan had begun to sweat. He was wondering just what kind of party this was. He stood there with his arms extended out from his sides, like a cormorant drying its wings.

The doorman looked back to him and his smile returned. "Of course not, Ms. Tramell." He stepped aside for Logan.

"And your name is?" Lanie asked.

"Dolph, ma'am."

"Thank you, Dolph."

"Shalom," Logan added, struggling to maintain character. He didn't see the icy stare the doorman gave them as they descended the stairs.

They entered the great room where they were greeted by a man holding a tray of drinks. Logan took one and nudged Lanie. He whispered, "Take one, Lanie. You don't have to drink it."

Across the room, the far wall was glass from floor to ceiling, revealing a twinkling panorama of the city below. It was magnificent, with cars moving along the freeways like blood cells through their vessels, red and white lights aglow. Below was a large deck with a swimming pool, hot tub, and a DJ set up over the pool at one end. He stood on a transparent platform that made it look like he was floating above the water. Lanie could feel the bass thumping the plate glass of the window more than she could hear the music. In the room were fifteen or twenty beautiful LA-type women in small groups drinking, laughing, and talking. On the patio deck, they could see another twenty or so. Some were walking, others sitting on loungers. There were a few in the hot tub and pool. Lanie was already having second thoughts about this party when she noted that several of these women in the spa were topless.

Logan looked around and counted five men, not including the help. He stepped closer to Lanie and leaned in. "I don't see Willis, and from what I do see, I think we should skedaddle."

At that moment, Willis, wearing a brown, corduroy sport coat over his old Camp Sequoia T-shirt, came bounding down the steps into the great room. He stopped on the fifth step from the bottom. Willis waved his hands above his head and gave a loud, sharp whistle. The music stopped, and all eyes were on him. "Those of you who received a white rose on entry will be taken back for auditions shortly. Those receiving other flowers, enjoy the party and leave a contact number with Sally on the veranda. Live it up!"

A cheer and several squeals met this announcement out on the deck as well as inside the house. Willis then turned and trotted back upstairs as the music now resumed and intensified. Apparently, the party was now in full swing.

Dolph entered the room and walked directly across to a tall man with a thin moustache. The man stood sideways while looking out the window. He had a drink in his hand and was engaged in earnest conversation with a six-foot, five-inch version of Daddy Warbucks and a fit thirty-year-old who looked like a movie star. Dolph said something to the mustachioed man. Then the man scanned the room. His eyes settled on Lanie and Logan. As he looked at Lanie, a smile played across his face. *It's her twin.*

Logan elbowed her. "Hey, let's get moving."

Lanie answered, "Don't act scared. He is just eyeing me. They aren't moving in this direction."

"Yet."

The tall, mustachioed man turned and spoke into Dolph's ear, then the doorman nodded his head and walked briskly to the stairs. He resumed his conversation with Daddy Warbucks.

"Lanie, it's time to go," Logan urged. "Dolph is probably on his way to get Willis right now. We'll be busted for sure."

"Logan, you worry too much. I can handle this. Besides, if I can't, you'll get to show some of your Israeli Defense Force skills."

"This isn't funny. I'm not even Jewish."

Logan felt a tap on his shoulder and nearly jumped out of his skin. He quickly turned around to see a fiftysomething man stumble backward and knock a ceramic jug from its stand as he fell onto his back. The only sound in the room was the thumping of the music as all conversation stopped. Logan could feel every eye on him. The tall, mustachioed man had walked over and reached down to help the fallen man up. Getting to his feet, the fallen man said, "Sorry, Benjamin. It was an accident. I'll pay for it." He looked frightened and then looked at Logan. "Sorry, man. I was just coming over to say hi. You *are* Al Jardine from the Beach Boys, aren't you?"

Logan was bewildered by this. He thought Sam had been joking. Logan remembered his mom's old collection of Beach Boys hit records while growing up. Each tune dealt with the California teen concerns of the day: cars, girls, and surfing.

The mustachioed man was clearly the host. He gave a lighthearted chuckle. "No problem, Rock. I think you've mistaken our guest. His name is Ari Cluckman. He's Ms. Tramell's private security. I can see how you thought he might be one of the Beach Boys though. Ha ha." He turned to Logan and stuck out his hand. "Happy that you could make it, Mr. Cluckman. Allow me to introduce myself. I'm Benjamin Buckley. Please enjoy the party. If there is anything you need or desire, just ask Dolph, okay?" He turned to Lanie and said, "So you are the lovely Becca Tramell. You're even more beautiful than I had been told. I'm pleased that you came here tonight, and I hope you are having a good time."

Lanie was surprised by this warm personal greeting. "Oh, I am. You have a spectacular home, Mr. Buckley, and you throw a wonderful party."

"Thank you. Cashwell will be around in a bit and we can all talk then." Buckley looked at Lanie and smiled. Then he turned and moved off through the room.

Rock Rollins then rejoined the conversation. He stuck out a paw toward Logan. "I'm Rock Rollins, Ari. Sorry, I didn't mean to startle you, but I guess that security types always need to be on guard, eh? Thanks for not killing me." He laughed loudly at his witticism. "How do *you* know Mr. Buckley?"

Lanie answered for him. "He doesn't really know him, Mr. Rollins. But I'm sure you know that Mr. Buckley is the type of man who knows everyone who comes into his home."

"Agreed. And you, my young lovely, must be the leading lady for our new project. I've seen your picture in Mr. Buckley's office."

Logan looked at Lanie over Rock's shoulder and raised his eyebrows. Lanie was confused by Rollins's comment and answered coolly, "I don't know if anything is finalized yet, but thank you."

Rock suddenly reached out and grabbed Lanie's hand. He bent over at the waist and kissed it. Rock pulled Lanie toward the stairs, eyeing a small dance floor. "Hey, let's dance. DJ Maestro Mousehead is kickin' it out. We don't wanna waste the night now, do we?" Rock reached into his pocket and took out a tiny, pink, dissolving tablet he put into his mouth. "Want one?"

Lanie shook her head and followed Rock down to the deck reluctantly, leaving Logan standing alone in the great room.

As they danced, Rock held Lanie close, even though the music was fast-paced. Lanie could smell the liquor on Rock's breath. He whispered in her ear, "I'll be singing the main theme and most of the soundtrack for *Nero's Heat*. We're in the middle of shooting the videos right now. You know Mr. Buckley threw this coming out party for my new album, *Freak Out in the Darkness*. He's a big fan." Rock beamed. "Do you own any of the Rock's work?" He saw her confusion and said, "No matter. I'll have an autographed set of my greatest hits sent to you."

Lanie looked confused. She gathered that Rock Rollins must be a musical artist, but she had no idea what kind or who he was. "Mr. Rock? My parents were missionaries and I've just returned to the United States this past summer so I'm afraid I am unfamiliar with most American music."

"Missionaries, eh?" Rollins totally missed the holes in Lanie's ad hoc backstory. "Well, I'm surprised that *they* don't know my work. I am what they call a Christian rock artist. However, I've been on a creative hiatus for most of the past year. I was injured in a concert when the venue caught on fire. It was back in Michigan about a year ago. I'll never go back to that dump. The crowd panicked. I was helping two little, old ladies escape and stumbled and hit my forehead on the fence. Man, did that hurt."

"Sorry. Were you hospitalized or injured anywhere else?"

Rock stared at her for a moment, confused, then he continued. "Naw. In fact, I wrote a song about it, 'Jump Out of the Fire.' I had a big gash here." He pointed to a miniscule reddish spot on his forehead. "But I decided not to have stitches. My manager said a new scar would add character to my face. She suggested I lie low for a while to focus my creative energies."

"I see."

"Then about three months ago, I got a call from Buckley offering me this gig. They're paying me a ton of money and my manager says it should be the start of another comeback." Rollins suddenly moved in close to Lanie and began to sing in her ear. "Ne-ro. Ne-ro. A Roman colossus and he-ro. He burns with Greek fire." He waved his arms mechanically and did a little stomping dance with legs spread out as if struggling to lay a giant egg.

Lanie took this opportunity to pull away from Rock. She looked up toward the window and scanned for Logan. "Sorry, Rock, I gotta run. Mr. Buckley is indicating he wants me upstairs. Thanks for the dance." Rock stumbled again as Lanie disengaged and trotted back up the stairs.

She looked around for Logan as she emerged into the great room and spied him through a glass door talking on his cell phone on a small side deck. Lanie moved directly toward him.

Suddenly Dolph stood in front of her. "Can I help you, ma'am?"

"No thank you, Dolph. I am feeling a bit queasy and think I'll be heading home. I'm going to collect Ari. Then we'll be off."

"I'm sure Mr. Buckley will be in touch with you. You know you made a good impression on him, ma'am. Good night then."

Lanie was puzzled by Dolph's comment, but she was too eager to leave to think much about it. She continued to the door and opened it. Logan turned and saw her. He hung up the phone and grabbed Lanie's arm, turning to walk her down the deck stairs into the side yard.

They quickly reached the street and walked east. About six houses down, they saw their ride parked. Dave saw them, flashed the lights, and they trotted to the car. The ride home was filled with discussion of this weird night.

Chapter 26

"BY THE SHINING BIG SEA WATER"

Lou Decker stood on a high bluff overlooking Lake Superior. He had his usual long, grass plume in his teeth and felt the sun and a warm breeze on his face. He loved the big water, and standing out here above the lake brought him peace. He was thinking about the changes in his life over the past year. He smiled. Lenore, his wife, walked quietly up behind him. As she reached out to tickle his ribs, Lou spun around, taking her in his arms and swinging her around.

She laughed. "Careful, Detective. No flying today." He set her down and hugged her tightly. She smiled up at him. "What are you thinking about? Are you worried about being asked to be the rodeo clown again tomorrow? I have it on good authority that Mrs. Eagle is keeping a tight rein on Buster nowadays. She's had him in AA for six months now. Seems that Mrs. Eagle has had it with his drinking. I also suspect that last year they missed the money Uncle would pay him to be the clown."

"What? You mean Uncle paid Buster? And you had me perform for free? You people are pirates!"

Lenore squealed as he began to chase her across the bluff toward their bungalow. She laughed as she easily outran him.

They slowed as they approached the wooden porch, seeing a paint-splattered Hank standing there and smiling. He leaned against one of the porch posts.

"Hey, Lou, you had a call in the office. I offered to take a message, but the man said he needed to speak directly with you. From the area code, it looks like the call might be from Los Angeles." Hank, who was Lou's closest friend, Lenore's cousin, adoptive brother and Uncle's son, turned to walk back to the barn to resume his task of painting the walls. "Hi, Lenny."

"Hi, Hank."

The man everyone had called Uncle had purchased this rundown campground years ago, using funds he made in Hollywood playing Indian roles in the movies. He was married to Lenore's aunt, and they took her in to raise as their daughter when her parents were killed in a car accident. Uncle had died this past spring after a long battle with leukemia, but he had lived to see Decker's spiritual awakening and to see Decker and Hank overcome a murderous cult in Michigan. His death was sad for those remaining, but Uncle's triumphant life eased the loss. Decker often walked to this edge of the bluff where Uncle was buried. It was a "good place to think about things," Uncle had often said.

"Thanks, Hank. I can give you a hand with the painting in a few minutes. Just let me finish spanking your sister and I'll be right along."

Lenny laughed and bolted into the house, slamming the door closed. Hank just shook his head as he walked away.

Lou changed into work clothes and headed up to the lodge to get the caller's phone number. On his way to the horse barn, he took out his mobile phone and dialed.

"Hello."

"Hello. This is Lou Decker. I'm returning a call from this number—"

"Hello, Detective Decker. Thank you for calling me back. You don't know me. My name is Dave Maxwell. Scott Nash gave me your number. He said you might offer some insight into a situation that has developed out here."

Decker laughed. "Scott Nash, eh? Mr. Mysterio himself. Well, how can I help you?"

Dave then outlined the events from the time of Toni's disappearance to the intervention of the faux FBI agents and the party at the movie producer's home in Laurel Canyon.

As was his habit, Decker listened without interrupting. When Dave had finished, he said, "This is an interesting situation, but I don't see how I can help."

"Detective, there is—"

"Call me Lou. I'm not a detective anymore. I'm retired."

"Okay. Lou, there seems to be more involved here than just a missing person and some shady movie production company. We have experienced several *odd occurrences* in connection with these goings-on. My friends think there is a supernatural element in play. I'm not so sure, but we'd really value any insights you might have."

Lou felt the hair on the back of his neck begin to stand up as he remembered the actions of Miguel and Brother Love. "If Nash told you about me, he probably told you about our experience with the Congregation of Light cult. I agree—no, I *know*—that supernatural forces are at work in our world and some of these are profoundly evil. They're also very dangerous. I would advise you not to get involved with them in any way."

"Mr. Decker, we're already involved. Thank you for your advice." Dave hung up.

Lou was a bit put off by this sudden ending of the call. But as he thought about it, he realized that he had sounded dismissive of this young man's problem and understood the man's pique. Lou did not know how he could help; however, he decided he ought to at least give the problem some thought and prayer. And that meant running it by Hank and Lenny. He dialed the number again. "Hello? This is Lou Decker. Mr. Maxwell?"

"Yes."

"I apologize for acting so dismissive of your situation. This whole issue of the supernatural at play in our world is still somewhat painful for me. But I promise to give it some thought and prayer. You don't mind if I run things by my brother-in-law, do you?"

"No, of course not."

"Good. It seems like there's more going on than you've told me so far. Is this the case?"

"Yes, there have been several occurrences I thought were just coincidence or oddities, but now I'm not so sure." Dave went on to explain about the glowing man, the sighting of a giant snake, the jogger, and most importantly, the strange activity in the clearing.

"Mr. Decker, I'm twenty-seven years old and a doctoral candidate in particle physics at Cal Tech, not a carny worker. I deal with things that are unimaginable to the public every day. I'm also a Christian. I accept that the supernatural does occur in this world, but to intrude like this on our normal, daily life? Do you think I'm overspiritualizing things here, or maybe I'm just going nuts?"

"No to both, Dave. Your story sounds very credible. At least to me."

"I'm not sure if that's really reassuring." Dave gave a quiet chuckle.

Lou had to laugh. "Tell you what. Let me run this by my colleagues here at camp. We'll talk and pray about this, and I'll get back to you within a couple of days."

"That sounds great. Thank you."

Decker had not considered that Dave Maxwell might be a scientist. That gave him another point to ponder.

Hank looked up as Decker approached. "You look like you just got a call from Miguel's brother."

"Maybe about his brother. We should talk about this at dinner. I need you all to hear it." Lou picked up a brush and went to work on the barn wall.

Dinner that night was prepared by Lou's sister, Shelley. While recovering at the camp from her ordeal with the cult and the death of her husband, Shelley bonded with Lenore and Hank and accepted the position as camp cook.

They were sitting back while drinking coffee and munching on homemade chokecherry pie when Lou began the story. "The call today was from a young man in Los Angeles. He described a series of events that has no rational, mundane explanation and has him considering a supernatural element." Lou went on to detail Dave Maxwell's story insofar as he understood the details.

After about a minute of silence, he asked for comments.

"Looks like your interview with Scott Nash is paying off," his sister observed.

"How is that?"

"Well, you've got another case."

"Hold your horses. There is no case. He just asked for an impression of what was going on."

Lenny put in, "She's got a point, Lou. You can't just tell him he's facing a demon and turn him loose."

Lou looked plaintively to Hank. "Help me, Hank. I'm outnumbered."

Hank looked at the women then up to the ceiling. His gaze came back down to Decker and he smiled. "Sorry, Lou. I'm with them on this one. Let me run a remote viewing session on it and see what I find." Hank asked Lou a series of specific questions to set up his parameters. Hank had served as a trained remote viewer in the US government's secret military RV group and his skill had played a big role in their ability to overcome the cult. However, this activity was not without risk because in running sessions, Hank potentially opened himself to powerful malignant forces.

Lou looked around the table. Seeing there was no way to win this one, he capitulated. "Okay. Let's talk again at breakfast."

The girls went off inspect the barn-painting job while Hank and Lou poured a second cup of coffee and went into the living room.

Hank swished his cooling coffee around in an old mug. "I really miss Dad at times like this. He would always offer encouragement seasoned with sound advice."

"He was very special, Hank."

"You know, Lou, it sounds like these kids are dealing with the real McCoy here."

"Yeah. Sounded that way to me as well."

"Have you ever been to California?"

"Only stopped in San Diego a couple times when I was in the navy. My basic training was at Great Lakes in Chicago, not on the West Coast."

"California is a different world, Lou."

"How so?"

"There are all kind of legends about spirits being territorial, unable to cross water and the like. Most of it is just rubbish. But there were times when I was in California when I sensed a very real malevolent spiritual presence—different from anything I've experienced elsewhere. Some of those desert canyons around LA have seen some pretty gruesome and dark happenings. I don't just mean Charles Manson either. Everything from the Valley Stalker to Pablo Machado to Nix's coven. Even the local Indians spoke of the presence of demons from the time of the 'old people.' Stories of witches and shape-shifters are as common as avocados." Hank paused and looked out the window. "Lou, I'm not trying to spook you. It's just that I'm worried about these young people."

"Me too, Hank. I think you've covered it. But how can *I* help them?"

"*We.*"

"Okay, *we.*"

"You know I'm in with you on this stuff. I'm going to go run an RV session now. Then I think I'll turn in. See you in the morning."

"Good night, Hank. Thanks."

Lou wandered over to the desk and picked up the day's newspaper. He walked back to his and Lenny's cabin. He lay on the bed and read until he felt Lenore shaking him and lifting the paper off his face. "Lou, you were asleep."

Lou got up and wandered to the bathroom where he readied for bed. "By the way, the barn looks great, honey."

Chapter 27

RODEO REDUX

In the morning, the counselors were setting up for the rodeo as Lou and Lenny entered the lodge for breakfast. Buster Eagle was twirling a lasso out in the parking lot, prompting Lenore to observe, "He's a bit rusty, but it looks like he's serious about reclaiming his comedic crown. See, Lou, you *were* the star last year."

"Hmmph."

Hank came in and sat down with a smile on his face.

Lenny asked, "Why the big smile, brother?"

"Why not? It's a beautiful day."

"Was the RV session that good?" asked Lou.

"Nope. In fact, what I could determine was problematic. But it's a beautiful day and I'm really up for a plate of Shelley's blueberry flapjacks."

At that moment, Shelley came through the kitchen door with a platterful of golden pancakes, and everyone's attention instantly focused on the food.

As they ate, Hank went over what he learned in his session. "It's real. These young people have stumbled onto an evil outfit. However, at this juncture, the evil group seems to consist mainly of humans. The 'glowing man' and 'jogger' were definitely nonhuman entities, but since their actions preserved the well-being of the young people, we can assume they are beneficent. The one entity that I couldn't penetrate was the 'guardian.' However, I would attribute that to poor targeting information. Once I talk to the Californians myself, perhaps I can refine the search coordinates and take another look."

"What do you mean 'talk to the Californians'?" asked Shelley.

"Well, we are going to need to help these young people since the authorities will probably tell them they are crazy, and we know what they are facing. Besides, this is the last week of camp here, and I feel like doing a little traveling. How about you, Lou?"

"I don't know, Hank. I can make some calls and maybe get some professional cooperation. Besides, you said the enemy they face is human."

"Yes, I did say that—with the possible exception of this 'guardian,' but that doesn't mean they are not connected to a supernatural force. I'm not saying we go out to LA with the idea of cleaning up the streets. In any case, I can't offer anything other than what I've said here, unless I have more information."

Lenore looked at her brother and knew his mind was made up. He was going to LA with or without Lou. "Hank, at least let Lou call out there and see if he can get the authorities moving."

Hank smiled at Lenny and Lou. "Fair enough."

The rodeo went off without a hitch, except Buster seemed to garner an inordinate number of catcalls from the crowd. The chant of "We want the cop!" was heard several times. Buster Eagle's ropework was inept and his singing was off-key, but he took his paycheck and left without staying for the awards ceremony.

Lenore opined, "Buster's feelings were hurt. I suspect he'll stop at the American Legion hall to kill the pain."

Shelley, who reprised her role as Chuck Wagon Cora, was more succinct. "Buster stunk, and I don't just mean his act. He smelled like booze when he walked by. He wasn't funny, and his ropework was awful. Lou makes a much better rodeo clown."

With everyone assembled in the chow hall for closing ceremonies and awards, Shelley decided to take matters to the people. She called out, "Quiet. Quiet. How many of you were here last year?" About 75 percent raised their hands. "Who was the better clown? Buster or last year's clown?"

Lou tried to cover his sister's mouth, but he was too late. "Shelley, knock it off!" Shelly and Lenny were now laughing loudly, and Hank waved his arms over his head and grinned broadly as he encouraged the crowd's unanimous roar, "Last year's clown." That eventually morphed into a chant of "Bring back the cop! Bring back the cop!" Lou turned a deep shade of crimson. He tried to get into the spirit by performing a deep theatrical bow. In doing so, he ripped out the back of his pants, which delighted the crowd even more.

It took Hank a full five minutes to restore order. Hank began the customary final devotion with prayer and then turned to his subject. "In our lives, we are constantly called on to make choices. Some big, some small. Being a Christian in today's world puts a big target on your back. People will always be watching you. Friends, families, and onlookers. You will find yourself in the crosshairs of people who just can't wait for you to slip up so they can call your faith into question. Many of us ask the wrong question when considering our options as we face life's choices. We ask, 'What would Jesus do?' Maybe what we should be asking is 'What would Jesus have us do?' This may sound like a small point, but think about it. Jesus is and was perfect. Are you? No, none of us are. That's why we need Him in our lives every day. No one knows us and loves us more than Him. Scripture says God will help anyone who asks according to His will. Remember those last four words. They are important. I hope that all of you will live your faith through your decisions and actions at home, at school, and in the community. May God bless each and every one of you. We'll see you all next year!"

After a few moments of silence, Lenore asked, "Were you talking about your decision, Hank?"

"Maybe a bit. Yeah, I guess."

"Well, you're right. Making decisions is tough. I think Shelley and I can handle closing down the camp if you and Lou go to Los Angeles."

Lou had heard only parts of this exchange as the campers surrounded him. One youngster near tears asked why Lou had not performed for them. This saddened Decker to think that this is how they saw things—that he let them down. He thought about what Lenny and Hank were saying. It made him sadder yet to think that the young adults out west would feel the same way and face this danger alone, should he decide to stay home. He looked to Lenny, who was nodding. "Lenny is right, Hank. I'm in. But I'm still going to call the authorities."

125

Chapter 28

WESTWARD HO!

Lou went online that afternoon and booked two round-trip tickets to LA with an open return date. He figured two weeks should be more than enough time to sort things out but also secretly hoped it wouldn't take that long. He and Hank might then do some sightseeing before returning to Minnesota. After booking the reservations, he called Dave Maxwell. "Hello, Dave. Lou Decker here."

"Hi, Detective. Did you come up with anything?"

Lou was about to correct Dave again but figured he might as well let it go. If Dave was comfortable calling him Detective, it wouldn't hurt anything. "Yes and no. My colleague is sort of a *psychic* spy."

Dave thought, *Oh no. No wonder Nash recommended him.* "Oh?"

"No, that's not quite right. He was a military-trained remote viewer in the marines, and he has some *opinions*. However, he would like to come out there and clarify certain aspects of this situation. I think I'll just let him explain what he does when we get out there; otherwise, I'll probably make it sound like mumbo jumbo. In short, we'll be flying out Saturday. I'm hoping you might have the evening free to go over things with us in detail and maybe set up a tactical plan."

Decker was correct. It sounded like "mumbo jumbo." Dave wondered what remote viewing was. However, Dave would wait and see. *Now is this where he hits us up for money for the tickets and hotel?* But Decker never asked for money. Dave remained silent.

Instead, Lou offered a word of caution. "Dave, my colleague Hank and I strongly suggest that all of you refrain from any involvement with or attempting to look any deeper at these people for the present. Just go about your daily affairs until we get there. We feel these people are very evil and dangerous. Hank thinks they are connected to an even darker power, although he has not confirmed that yet in his viewing. Are you okay with this?"

"Yes, we all have regular jobs except Sam, my twin, who is still recuperating from his head injury. I'll let them all know. When do you get in? I can pick you up. LAX?"

"We get in at 4 p.m., but we've booked a vehicle already so thanks anyway. How about if we meet at the Pasadena Marriott at, say, 7 p.m.? That's where we are staying."

"Sounds great, and thanks, Detective."

"See you then." Being called detective evoked a warm sense of nostalgia in Decker. He looked back with pride at his work and accomplishments while wearing the badge for over twenty years. Decker was now warming to the chase. He realized what Hank seemed to know instinctively. They had made the right choice in deciding to go. Decker could feel his excitement rising in spite of himself.

The rest of the day was spent packing and getting ready to leave early the next morning. Lou cleaned and packed the nine-millimeter semiautomatic that Hank had given him in its lockbox and slipped it into his suitcase. Lou was out of the special ammunition Hank had also given him, but he figured that he could pick up ammo in LA. He packed an old badge and ID. Lou and Hank planned to take a connector flight from Duluth to the Twin Cities and then fly nonstop to LAX. There was a layover in Minneapolis, so air travel time would total about nine and a half hours. Lou and Hank both had experienced much worse flight schedules, but it still figured to be a long day. The two-hour time differential would add to this at the end of the day. Both men turned in early that night.

*   *   *

Lou slept soundly and awoke at his customary time of 6:00 a.m. to find that Lenore had already gotten up and left him a note on the bathroom counter. "Breakfast at 6:20." Lou hopped into the shower. It was 6:18 when Lou walked into the dining room. The table was set with a hearty breakfast. The three others all sat waiting for him. Lenny looked at her watch. "6:19, Detective. Cutting it a bit close, are we?"

Lou pulled out his iPhone to show it to the others. "6:17. Plenty of time."

Lenny coughed, and everyone laughed. "We should get on the road in about half an hour."

Hank said a blessing and they dug in.

On their way to Duluth, everyone was quiet, lost in their own thoughts, until Lenny asked, "What do you two really expect to find out there?"

Lou replied, "I don't know. It could be that all these events are being unintentionally conflated. Maybe they are not related at all and they've just run across some urban lowlifes, but that can still be pretty bad. Gangs and organized crime are all over LA."

Hank added, "I'm not sure either. The idea that I cannot get a read on the character that they called 'the guardian' bothers me. That they had two other encounters with specific 'unusual' types strongly suggests that there is a supernatural element involved."

Lou said, "True enough. I'm trying to apply Occam's razor here, I guess."

Lenny asked, "Whose razor?"

"Occam's. Basically, if there are multiple explanations for an event, it's usually the simplest one that's true."

"Gee, Lou, remember I just went to Indian boarding school." Lenore laughed. "That's pretty deep for me."

Hank winked at Lenore. "This is from the man who killed a dragon, sis."

Chapter 29

I LOVE LA

The flights went smoothly with no delays. Hank sat by the window and looked down on the ever-changing landforms. Greens, blues, grays, and browns all mixed in varying degrees of light and shade to paint a distinctive landscape somehow unified in form and texture. "I think that's the Devil's Tower down there."

Lou leaned to see over him, but the giant granite monolith was now obscured by clouds and the aircraft's wing. Lou shrugged. "I missed it," he said as he went back to his Robert Crais novel.

Later in the flight, Hank observed the course of the Colorado River as it wound through the great crevasse that formed the Grand Canyon. He was just about to open his mouth to show Lou but looked over to see his friend gently snoring with the book in his lap. "The view must be spectacular from the edge of the canyon."

The pilot came on to notify the passengers that they were now on their final approach to LAX. As they descended over the final mountain chain, Hank could see the strip of sand forming the beach and the endless stretch of the ocean's blue-gray ahead. He smiled, considering God's unmatched artistic genius.

While the men waited with their bags in line for the car rental area, Hank did a few stretches. Two young marines in travel gear walked by with their duffels shouldered. One turned to Hank and, seeing Hank's USMC sweatshirt, saluted Hank with a big grin on his face. Hank called out after him, "Don't salute me. I work for a living."

The young marines laughed.

Hank showed his military discount ID card to the clerk at the rental desk.

The lady looked down at her computer for several seconds and spun the screen around to Hank. "All we have left is a Humvee. You can have it at your discount price." A small smile played at the corner of her mouth.

"We'll take it," Hank nearly yelled. Lou shook his head and looked down, hiding his grin at Hank's obvious joy.

"I thought you might." The clerk laughed.

"Thank you."

Hank signed the papers and took the key fob. "Let's get on the road before she changes her mind."

Hank headed out California 110 toward Pasadena. After several miles, Hank remarked, "This must have been the first freeway in LA. The entry and exit ramps each look about twenty feet long. It feels like I'm on a Disneyland racecar ride. It's so narrow and twisty."

Lou laughed nervously. He also was tense on this road. He gripped his handhold tightly as they entered the tunnel near Chavez Ravine. After another few miles, the freeway ended. They found themselves on a main north-south business artery in Pasadena.

"The hotel is up on your left about a mile," Decker said.

"Roger that."

Upon entering the hotel, they walked past a group sitting in the common area on sofas around a fireplace. They were joking and laughing familiarly. Hank and Lou approached the check-in desk. Things again went smoothly, and five minutes later, they were up in their room. It was a nice suite with two bedrooms, a kitchenette, and a sitting area. The large window framed a view onto a park area, and beyond that, Lou could see mountains. There was a vague familiarity to the outline of the mountains. He thought of those seen around the Rose Bowl on TV.

They had been in the room less than five minutes when the phone rang.

"Detective?"

"No, this is Hank. Hold on a minute please." Hank handed the phone to Lou. "Dave Maxwell I'd guess."

Lou took the phone. "Hello."

"Hi, it's Dave Maxwell." Lou nodded his head to Hank. "We're here. We'll be in the lounge area when you come down, okay?"

"Sure, see you in ten minutes." Lou hung up the phone. "Yeah, that was him. Wonder if that was the group by the fireplace?"

"Right age. Good chance."

It turned out this surmise was correct. Dave got up to meet Lou and Hank as they exited the elevator. Introductions were made all around and the group proceeded into the hotel restaurant.

"How was your flight?" Sam inquired.

"Long," replied Hank, "but I did get to see Las Vegas from the air." Hank noticed Logan staring at him. Hank looked back at the young man. "That was an attempt at humor."

Logan looked at Hank wide-eyed. "Mr. Cloud, when Scott Nash told me about your and Detective Decker's exploits, he mentioned that you were Indian." Logan began to laugh. "LA colleges are full of Asians, so I assumed he meant Asian Indian, not—"

There was a slightly awkward silence at the table while everyone stared at Logan.

Hank screwed up his face as if in anger and stood up, towering over Logan. Gripping the edge of the table, Hank leaned down, said, "Ugh, Dakota," and burst into a hearty laugh. "I guess introductions are now complete."

There was general laughter at the table, except from Logan, and all tension dissolved. The conversation turned to Decker and Hank retelling the story of their involvement and ultimate confrontation with the Congregation of Light.

When Decker touched on the role of Hank's remote viewing in their adventure, Dave interrupted. "You mentioned remote viewing in our earlier conversation. Just what is it?"

Decker turned to Hank. "You field this one, okay?"

"Sure," replied Hank. "In the military, there are projects pretty much unknown to the general public. I think you all realize this. Most of these are connected with weapons development, but not all. Remote viewing is a means to gather information or reconnoiter. In military terms, that means it yields bona fide tactical benefits for operations. It's like spying in a way."

"Like Jason Bourne?" Logan asked. "Or James Bond?"

"No, not really." Hank went on to briefly describe RV. "But not like a clairvoyant either. Remote viewing is a discipline where the viewer connects with the collective unconscious. He is given a target generally unknown to him. He then allows impressions to come to him which yield information on the target. There is a rigid multistep protocol of writing down these impressions and refining them."

"Sounds like a séance." Logan again.

"No, not at all."

Lanie twisted a long lock of her dark hair around her finger. "It does seem pretty far out."

"Well, that was the opinion of the brass back in the day. Despite our results, many of which were impressive, the program was eventually scrapped, at least in regular military channels. With our record though, I find it hard to believe that no agency in the government is still using RV."

Dave Maxwell piped in, "Fascinating. When Detective Decker first mentioned it, well, I thought of the Hollywood Psychic Hot Line." Everyone laughed. "So you think that RV will give us useful information on our situation, Hank?"

"Yes, I do, but first I need to get up to speed on the particulars of what's happened so far. You see, forming the appropriate query is key for a successful search. It *must* be precise. I think a good starting point might be to search for Toni's current location."

"Yes. That's the reason we are involved in this in the first place." Logan opened a folder in front of him and pulled out a small map of California. He pointed out the location of Camp Sequoia and commented on the geography of the place.

Lou Decker suggested that he would start on another leg of the investigation—law enforcement and the bogus FBI agents. He then tasked the young people with gathering information on Benjamin Buckley and his production company. They agreed to meet again in the hotel lounge the next afternoon at 3 p.m.

After the group enjoyed their meals, Hank spoke with Logan and Sam for a time, discussing the events of that evening of Toni's disappearance as the boys understood them. They discussed Toni's physical appearance, her personality, and her habits.

Logan leaned back in his chair. He looked thoughtfully at Hank and Sam. "I reckon her shoe size is about an eleven." This drew stares from the others. Logan continued. "Toni came into the office the previous afternoon. I gave her a rag to wipe off her shoes because she was tracking mud all over." Sam and Hank continued to stare at Logan who blurted, "What? She has big feet."

Hank raised his eyebrows and Sam shook his head. "TMI."

At that point, Hank laughed and headed back to his room to run an RV session on Toni's current location.

Lanie, Dave and Decker had moved to a quiet corner of the lounge near the large fireplace as there was little foot traffic and their conversation would not be overheard.

Dave went right to the point. "What do you make of the phony FBI agents and the manner in which the investigation proceeded out at camp? The death of Sheriff Tate strikes me as strange too."

"That so much 'strangeness,' as you put it, is going on here raises a big red flag. In my experience, most simple crimes have simple explanations. Robbers commit their crimes because they want something, recognize an opportunity, and go for it. Means, motive, and opportunity. Understand the process and solve the crime."

Lanie and Dave listened raptly to the detective.

Lou continued. "However, here the situation is clearly different. As you have described it, there are so many odd, complicated facts that we can't consider this a simple crime. Looking at the people involved, you have the alleged perpetrator, Nixon—"

Lanie laughed as Dave corrected Decker. "Dixon." Dave handed Lou the photo he had snapped of Dixon at Zuma.

"Yes, Dixon. Face is a bit blurry, but this should help. Thanks. Well, first Dixon finagles his way into the good graces of the victim, Toni. Then he turns up here in Los Angeles, and then at the beach. Next there are the phony FBI agents and the party people. This might suggest something more than a simple abduction or killing. But as the great detective once said, 'It is a capital mistake to theorize in advance of the facts.' That being said, it's been a long day and we have a heap of fact gathering to do *starting tomorrow*. I think I'm going to head up to bed."

They exchanged good nights and Lou walked toward the elevator. He heard Logan ask what the chuckling had been about. He turned to see Logan drop his head forward and swing his hands up into peace signs while growling out, "I am not a crook."

Decker laughed. *They seem to be a pretty tight group, but they* are *young and we don't know with whom we are dealing yet.* Lou let himself into the suite and saw Hank's door was closed. Lou decided not to bother his brother-in-law and turned in.

Chapter 30

411

Lou woke early the next morning and went out to the living room. Hank sat on the sofa, drinking a cup of coffee. "Good morning."

"Good morning, Lou. How did you sleep?"

"Pretty good. I think the mountain air must agree with me."

"There is coffee in the pot. I made eight cups."

"Why so much?"

"I didn't sleep very well."

"Bed bad?"

"No, I was having nightmares."

"Hmmm. Do you want to talk about it?"

"Get a cup of coffee first."

Lou nodded and walked over to the kitchenette area. He took a mug and poured himself a large cup. The coffee was still steaming, so that meant Hank hadn't been up too long. He went over to a seat near the couch, sat down, and looked at Hank.

Hank shook his head, his lips pursed in a grim expression. "The girl is dead. I wound up needing to run two sessions. She was killed in the clearing that the Maxwells described. In any case, her remains aren't there. I can't get a firm reading on the exactly where they are, although I did see a building on a mountain, looking down at a city. Here in Los Angeles, I think, but definitely in a coastal area."

"Could you see any detail that might help us identify the location?"

"It was dark. I can tell you that there was a lot of traffic on streets and freeways. Beyond the cityscape extended more lights going right up to a pitch-blackness that seemed to extend indefinitely. It was as if I were standing on a platform or patio on a mountainside looking out across the distance to the ocean."

"Hmmm. It could be LA if you were standing, say somewhere in Hollywood Hills, looking south." Lou was fiddling with his phone's browser. He was trying to find the view of LA commonly seen in the movies, from Mulholland Drive. After a few moments, he handed Hank the phone. "Is this it?'

"Yeah, looks a lot like it. The perspective is slightly off, but yeah, that's basically it."

"I wish I knew more about the geography out here. The girl, Lanie, said that she went to a party in a place called Laurel Canyon. But then she described being in a large home that was built on a mountain. She may be able to help to clarify this."

"Agreed. Let's call her this morning." Hank took another sip of coffee and gazed out the window. "Toni's death, Lou."

"Hank, you don't need to."

"It was horrific. It was an occult sacrifice. Dixon led her to a private place where he overpowered her. He and several confederates then took her to the clearing where others were waiting. She was placed on a stone altar of sorts and was killed. I saw several spiritual entities there. One appeared to be overseeing the ritual. There was also another evil presence in the form of a very large—no, actually a giant—rattlesnake. It, whatever it was, dealt with another intruder and a dog that had stumbled on the proceedings. For some reason, the boss demon was laughing at this man. The man appeared to be wearing a World War II Nazi SS uniform. I also detected the presence of an angelic spirit who intervened to protect Sam from this snake. Lou, this is exactly what I feared."

Lou studied his coffee cup and then looked at Hank. "I guess I shouldn't be surprised. From the beginning, this is what I wondered about.

More of this craziness." Lou gazed out at the mountain view. "I'm starting to feel like the Scott Bakula character in that old movie."

"*Quantum Leap?*"

"No, not the TV show. *Lord of Illusions,* the movie where he was a detective investigating supernatural events. I'm getting off track."

"I think we should keep this to ourselves for the present—not that anyone in law enforcement would believe us anyway."

"Agreed. We can bring this out when the time is right. I'm going to make my calls to speak with the sheriff's office in Mariposa County where the camp is. I'll also contact the FBI and speak with Agent Hogan if I can. Meanwhile, are you going to talk to Lanie and find out more about the party location?"

"Yes, I will. Let's get some breakfast."

As they headed down to the hotel restaurant, Lou's mind was a jumble. He kept thinking about the young girl. How her sunshine days at a church camp had turned into a nightmare. He thought of her parents. Reluctant to let her go to the camp in the first place, they now had to live with this horror for the rest of their lives. And the odd behavior of the authorities in the investigation—was that incompetence or complicity? The mysterious movie producer—did he have a role in this or was he just an incidental creep? By the time the waitress came to take Lou's order, his appetite had vanished. "Just coffee please."

Hank looked across the table. His face was set and his eyes were hard. "I know how you feel. It's hard to think of food. But you know that an army marches on its stomach and we need to be in top shape to function efficiently. I'd suggest you eat something, even if it's only some soft-boiled eggs."

Lou took Hank's advice to heart. He called the waitress back and ordered an omelet and toast.

When she returned with their food, Lou smiled at Hank. "You're right, of course. I'll have to take you to Leon's when we are in Michigan. His breakfasts are really something."

"A good cook, eh?"

Decker winced. "I didn't say that, but his portions are generous."

Both men laughed and went to work on their food.

Chapter 31

HOORAY FOR HOLLYWOOD

Lanie was bundling up her study materials for a trip to the Medical Library when her phone rang.

"Hello. Is this Ms. Tramell?"

She nearly hung up until she recalled her pseudonym from the other night. She cleared her throat and answered, "Yes, speaking."

"Ms. Tramell, this is Bryan Cashwell. I work for Benjamin Buckley. I'm his private assistant. I'm sorry that I didn't get to meet you the other night, but Mr. Buckley has informed me that he is *very* eager for you to play Statilia Messalina, in Rock Rollins's upcoming music video *Nero's Heat.* In Mr. Buckley's opinion, this will be a stepping-stone to a successful Hollywood career. Would it be possible for you to come back up to the house this evening so we might discuss terms? That is, if you're agreeable."

Lanie's face crinkled in confusion. *Who in the world is Statilia Messalina? And what in the world is* this *all about?*

There was silence on the line as Lanie wrestled for an answer.

"Hello? Ms. Tramell, are you still there?"

Lanie's curiosity won out. "Yes, I'm, uh, just checking my calendar. I'm free about seven o'clock if that works." She decided she could always cancel later.

"Seven o'clock it is. By the way, you won't need your bodyguard, Ari."

"Okay. However, I will bring my agent."

"I think you will find Mr. Buckley's offer sufficiently gener—"

"Either my agent comes with me or I don't come, Mr. Cashwell." Lanie was not going back to Buckley's mansion alone.

"In that case, we'll see you both at seven. Have a nice day, Ms. Tramell."

Lanie ended the call without saying goodbye. *When have I ever interrupted anybody like I just did? Well, maybe a bit of attitude is what they expect. Who do they think I am anyway?*

She walked into her bedroom and the phone rang again. "Hello?"

"Hi, Lanie. It's Hank Cloud. I hope I'm not catching you at a bad time."

"No, not at all. Just headed to the library. How are you?"

"Fine, thanks. Hey, Lanie, I wanted to ask you where exactly was the party that you went to the other night?"

"It was in Hollywood Hills on Woodrow Wilson Drive, just off of Mulholland."

"Is this on a mountainside? Lou thought you said it was in a canyon."

"Yes, the area is called Laurel Canyon, but it really is mountainous." She gave a brief laugh. "I know it sounds silly, but—"

"I get it. Just curious geography names. Kind of like the Florida 'lakes' that are about the size of a small pond anywhere else in the country. Lou and I were thinking of taking a drive up there later so I needed to clarify this. You don't have the address, do you?"

"No. But you can't miss it. I remember it as the fourth house from Mulholland Drive on the right. It has a very large statue of a green man pointing a pitchfork—or trident—at the driveway. He looks like a Martian version of Poseidon."

Hank cringed. He realized that this statue reflected exactly what it sounded like—a marker for pagan activity.

"The house looks smallish from the road, but it's actually a very large house with a patio in back that goes partway down the mountainside. It's odd, but I just got off the phone with Mr. Buckley's assistant. He asked me to come by tonight at seven o'clock to negotiate for a role in a music video that Buckley is offering me. Do you think I should go?"

"Not by yourself anyway. Let's hold off on that decision. We know these people can be dangerous, and your friends are supposed to be looking at their operation. We can talk it over at our three o'clock meeting. We'll know more then, okay?"

"That sounds good. See you then."

Hank set the phone down on the bedside table and sighed. It sounded as though his RV session had actually taken him to Buckley's house. He suspected Buckley wanted Lanie for something beyond a role in some kind of video, and he figured it wasn't good. As beautiful as the girl was, beautiful girls were a dime a dozen in Los Angeles. Hank needed a break from thinking about these issues. He decided to take a walk to the bookstore he had seen across the street to look for some LA history books, particularly those with pictures of old Hollywood scenery. This should help him clear his mind.

Lou was gone when Hank came out into the living area of the suite. The clock said it was just after nine o'clock. Hank found a note on the counter. "Going downtown to the FBI office. Back by 2 p.m. Will tell you about my talk with sheriff's office then." Hank saw the Hummer keys were gone from the shelf, so he headed across the street.

Chapter 32

ON THE HUNT

Lou decided to head downtown to the FBI headquarters first. Agent Hogan was in the field and unavailable, but Lou was given Hogan's business card with the agent's contact information. Decker sat in the parking lot and dialed up Agent Hogan. They had a brief conversation in which Decker learned nothing of substance. However, he was used to dealing with the feds and expected this.

Decker then contacted the sheriff's department for the Yosemite area. "Good morning. Mariposa County Sheriff's Department. Deputy Hennessey speaking. How may I help you?" The man cleared his throat on the other end of the line.

Lou decided to play the "official" card. "Morning, Deputy. My name is Lou Decker. I'm a detective with the Grand Rapids, Michigan Police Department. My badge number is 658. I am looking into the disappearance of a family friend as a courtesy. I was wondering if there is someone in your office I might chat with informally about the Toni LaRusso case."

"I'll try to help you, Detective."

"First off, has she been located yet?"

"No, we're working on the assumption that she and the boy ran off together."

"She's not dead? *That's good then—if it's true.* Decker waited a long second. "Why are you looking at it from that specific angle?"

"We have a series of credit card receipts from gas stations and restaurants leading to an Indian casino resort. We spoke with the desk clerk there and he said a man named Dixon Mason checked in the evening following Ms. LaRusso's disappearance. We determined that he was not alone as multiple key cards were issued. He stayed for two nights."

"Which casino was this?"

"Let me check." Lou could hear papers being ruffled. "Cactus Charlie's Wild West Casino and Hotel near El Cajon.

"Do you have Mr. Mason's home address?"

"Uh, we do. Let me look. He lives at 4107 Dry Lake Drive, in El Cajon."

"Did you find anything there?"

"He was not at his residence, but according to the FBI's interview with a neighbor, this Dixon is a traveling salesman who is often out of town for long periods. So he's in the wind. That's where we are at present, Detective."

"Are Toni's parents aware of this?"

"Uh, Sheriff Tate said he'd tell them. That was before his accident."

"Accident? Oh, might I have a word with him?"

"Well, suicide."

"Oh, I see. Sorry to hear it." Lou was interested in this deputy's wild story. This supported Dave Maxwell's perception of incompetence on the part of these investigators—or maybe dishonesty.

"I know that an FBI friend of mine, Agent Hogan, was investigating the case."

"Yeah, I know him. He did most of the legwork and traveled to El Cajon. Hogan suggested we close our end of the investigation as the disappearance had been solved. She was eighteen and out on her own. That reminds me it was Hogan who told me he'd talk to her parents, not Sheriff Tate.

"Well, I guess that about wraps things up." Decker knew for a fact that Toni was barely seventeen and decided to pose a particular question to Hennessey to establish the extent of his dissembling. "I'll touch base with Hogan when he gets back from New Zealand in a couple weeks. Did he mention the trip to you or leave you a contact number where he might be reached? You know how the Bureau is about these things."

"Uh, yes, he did mention the trip, but no address or phone. He said he wanted to wrap this case up before he left for New Zealand. I'm sure he'll have more details when he gets back, if you need them. Have a nice day, Detective."

"You too, Deputy."

Decker now knew for certain the deputy was lying. But why?

He decided to call Mr. LaRusso. This might be a touchy situation, but there were some things he needed to know.

"Hello."

"Mr. LaRusso? This is Detective Lou Decker. We're running a performance evaluation on our personnel. I'd like to ask you a few questions about your interaction with one of our agents. Do you have a few minutes, sir?"

"I guess so. But I don't know how much help I can be."

"Thank you. Why is that?"

"Sheriff Tate was only here for about five minutes."

"Pardon me, sir. Did you say Sheriff Tate?"

"Yes, I did."

Lou was surprised. "I'm sorry. Our phone connection is breaking up a bit. Can you describe him?"

"Describe? You mean the sheriff? Well, he was really big. I'd guess about six feet, six inches. Pale, thinning hair. He had a deep voice. He was very brusque speaking to my wife and me. He sounded like he was reading from a cop show script."

"Was his uniform clean and pressed?"

"Uniform? He wasn't wearing a uniform. He said he was coming by on his day off as a courtesy. He had on what looked like patchwork weightlifter pants and a neon orange tank top. At first, when he walked up our driveway, I thought he was lost or maybe a hot tub salesman, but then he showed me credentials and a badge."

"Why was he there?"

"He came by with information on our daughter. I'm sure you know about her, er, problem."

"Yes, sir, I'm sorry for your troubles."

"We had just about reconciled ourselves to the idea that Toni was dead, but Sheriff Tate now said they'd traced her to El Cajon and then to San Diego. He told us the Bureau suspects that our daughter had been abducted by a man named Ahmad Shelnikov. This Shelnikov is supposedly an international criminal—a white slaver. I guess that's what they called a human trafficker back in the day. He had no further information on Toni and said he possibly never would, but the FBI was involved and would keep looking. This wasn't much comfort. In some ways, I'd rather she be dead." Mr. LaRusso's voice began to crack, and Lou heard him sniffle.

"I'm sorry for all of this, Mr. LaRusso. I won't attempt to excuse the sheriff's insensitivity." Lou's stomach soured with his pretense, especially when Hank had determined Toni's actual fate. "Thank you for your help, and God bless you."

Lou then dialed the Cactus Charlie's in El Cajon. He introduced himself and said he had a few follow-up questions for the evening clerk Agent Hogan interviewed the other night. The manager took Decker's name and phone number and promised to pass the message on. Lou then made his final stop of the morning the public library, where gathered some basic information on El Cajon and looked up the names and phone numbers of Dixon Mason's neighbors in the city directory.

With this slew of new data, Lou decided to call Hank. "Hank, I'll be on my way back soon. How about some lunch?"

"Sounds good. At the hotel?"

"No, Let's go to the Cheesecake Factory. I saw it about three blocks south on our way in."

"Okay. Half an hour?"

"Sounds good.

When Lou arrived, Hank sat at a window table looking out at passers-by. He waved to Lou as he entered. "No need to run out to Buckley's house this afternoon." Hank then described his plan to accompany Lanie to this evening's meeting. "How were things at the FBI?"

"I didn't get to meet Agent Hogan. He was out of the office. But things are evolving just as Dave Maxwell indicated. After my stop at the FBI office, I had a phone conversation with the bona fide Agent Hogan. He had dismissed Dave as a crank, but when I explained everything to him, he said he would look into the situation. He is not happy that there's someone out there posing as an FBI agent, especially him." Lou chuckled. "I don't know whether he was pissed off or amused by my description of the phony Agent Hogan. His comment was 'Geez, we're in Hollywood. They didn't need to cast me as a giant, did they?' Otherwise, Hogan had no information."

Lou went on to relate the essence of his other phone calls with Deputy Hennessey and Toni's father. He finally spoke of locating two of Dixon Mason's neighbors and speaking to them. "There was a middle-aged lady who spoke well of Mr. Mason. She described Mason as a sixtysomething male who works as a professor at the local community college. Hardly fits the description of our Dixon. He has been widowed about twenty years. His wife died of cancer. No foul play apparently involved. The second neighbor was a male who confirmed the lady's description, but he laughed when I asked about Mason going off with a young woman. Hence, it now appears that we have a local deputy giving us a full line of BS. I'm waiting on a return call from the desk clerk at the Cactus Charlie's Casino.

"You know this is looking more and more like a coordinated disinformation campaign."

Hank then described his brief conversation with Lanie.

Lou observed, "Logan shouldn't go with her, even if he is Mossad trained." Both men smiled.

"Lou, I *do* have some Hollywood roots." Hank was referring to his father who had acted in many Indian roles under the stage name Wild-Boar Cloud. "It might be time for me to embark on a new career as a Hollywood agent."

"That sounds reasonable." Lou laughed.

As Hank and Lou returned to the hotel, they planned a trip to Camp Sequoia the next morning. "You know how I feel about recon, Lou. It's rare that you get too much. Besides, I've always wanted to see the Sierra Nevada mountains and hopefully Yosemite. Heck, you might even find Lenore a bearskin robe."

"Great. She could wear it when she conducts bed checks next summer at camp."

Chapter 33

AFTERNOON WAR COUNCIL

The Californians arrived en masse at the hotel promptly at 3 p.m. and were sent up to Lou's suite. Lou led off the discussion by filling the others in on his inquiries from the morning.

Dave in particular was interested in the deputy's story. "Lou, I remember one of the deputies getting out of the patrol car and walking up to the main cabin like he didn't have a care in the world. He spoke to the sheriff and Sheriff Tate raced out the parking lot like a maniac. That struck me as odd."

"I remember you telling us this, Dave. Could the deputy have been in on Toni's disappearance?" Logan asked.

"I'm not saying that, but I wonder what he told the sheriff."

"Yeah, hold your horses, Logan. There is a big difference between incompetence and involvement in a crime," said Sam.

Lou then outlined his plan to drive to Camp Sequoia the next day and eyeball the scene. Logan and Sam volunteered to go along, and Logan said he would call and alert Mr. Adamson. Sam said it would take about five hours of driving to get there.

Lou then asked, "Sam, do you know how long it takes to go from the camp to El Cajon?"

"About seven or eight hours, but that's just a guess. I've never driven it."

The group decided to leave at 6 a.m., and the conversation moved on to a discussion of the young men's findings about Benjamin Buckley's company.

Sam led off. "It turns out that Buckley's film production company is only about two years old, but Buckley has been active as a backer for several major motion pictures since 2012. His films have uniformly been blockbusters, making him tons of money. He was a major financier on *Between the Stars, Steel Woman,* and *Hungover in Cambodia.* This last film reportedly earned him a cool $150 million. Looking at his list of projects, I didn't find one that made less than 50 million. It's as if he is wired into the wallets of moviegoers worldwide. But I've been unable to find anything about Buckley before he appeared on the Hollywood scene with a fat wallet. No personal history, no family records, nothing."

"Impressive. Sounds like he bought the Hollywood Hills property with pocket change," Hank said. "I can't wait to get a look at that place."

"Exactly. He is listed as CEO and majority shareholder of Buckley Import-Export or BIE Ltd., incorporated in Delaware in 2013. Seems a strange name for a production company. From there I found a maze of interconnected companies all related to a conglomerate called Saturn Communications."

Looking at Hank, Lou interjected, "Saturn?"

"Yes. Saturn's holdings look like a comprehensive list of every business in America. They're involved in everything from frozen food to diapers to internet service to advanced military projects. If you can make money doing it, Saturn is involved."

Hank looked back at Decker and frowned. "I think things just got a lot more dangerous than we'd figured." Hank then went on to relate how Saturn Communications had been linked to the human trafficking arm of the Congregation of Light cult. "Remember the FBI raided their headquarters in Las Vegas—or what was left of it after the company burned it and bugged out."

"You think it's the same outfit?"

"It would be another major coincidence if it weren't. I think we need to look at Saturn a bit closer before we go stirring their pot."

"Okay, that's depressing. What's the plan for my meeting with Buckley tonight?" Lanie asked.

Lou looked at Hank and started. "For some reason, Benjamin Buckley is enamored with the idea of Lanie being in his video. No offense, Lanie. Maybe he thinks Lanie is someone else. Who knows? But it would be irresponsible to send her in there alone, so Hank has volunteered to represent 'Ms. Tramell' as her agent." He looked at Lanie.

"I'm ready to go back in," Logan piped up. "Besides, they already know me."

Lanie shook her head. "No, Logan, they made it pretty clear that they don't want my bodyguard there."

"Aha! They're afraid of me."

Hank grinned. "I think your 'Mossad training' has them on edge."

"I knew it!"

Hank let out a theatrical sigh. "I guess I am the logical choice. I do have a little experience with Hollywood types and I'm probably the next best trained of us." Hank had a twinkle in his eye as he said this, causing the others to smile, except Logan, who missed the irony. "Lanie, do you have a little, black dress?"

"Of course."

"I'll ask the concierge to get me a tuxedo. We should meet with them for about an hour then leave. We can say we've committed to a party in Malibu. That should give us enough time to get some useable intel. Sound okay, Lanie?"

"Sure."

"Okay, let's meet here in the lobby at six o'clock."

Chapter 34

GUESS WHO'S COMING TO DINNER

Hank was waiting in the lobby when Lanie and Dave walked in. It was just after six in the evening, and Dave had a slightly flustered look on his face.

"Sorry we're late," Dave said. "There was a big traffic tie-up near Lanie's dorm and traffic is busier than usual for a Saturday evening." Dave reached out and shook Hank's hand. "Take care of her. That bit about Saturn and human trafficking has me concerned."

Lanie blushed and gave Dave's hand a squeeze. "We'll be fine, Dave. See you later."

"Okay. Have fun." Dave spoke to Lanie, then turned and left.

Hank looked at Lanie. He smiled.

Still blushing slightly, she said, "What?"

"I can see why Buckley wants you in his movie. You look great."

Lanie blushed even deeper, but she smiled. "We'd better get a move on it. Traffic really *is* heavy. It may take an hour to get there."

*   *   *

Benjamin Buckley looked at his watch as he pulled into his driveway. It was 5 p.m. and he was hungry. He hopped out of his new yellow Lamborghini convertible and walked up to his front porch. Buckley turned, looked at the vehicle, and nodded approvingly. The sun was in middescent out over the Pacific, giving his lawn and car a golden hue. He had just returned from the dealership where he traded in his year-old model for this one. *Yes, the canary yellow is just about right.* He laughed to himself.

Stepping onto the porch, he said, "Buckley," activating the facial recognition entry system. Before he reached the door, it was swinging open. "Cashwell!" he called as he entered. He took off his wayfarers and looked around.

"Yes?" came the reply from his assistant entering the foyer.

"Is everything set for this evening? Is she coming?"

"Yes, Benjamin, it's all set. There was one small hitch though." Cashwell told his boss that Ms. Tramell would only come if she could bring her agent. "I didn't see any way around this development, so I agreed. I am sorry about that."

"Agent?" he said as he laughed. "Now she has an agent? Let's see if our 'Ms. Tramell' has a better eye for agents than she does for bodyguards."

Cashwell joined in the laughter. "Your dinner is ready. Afterward, Senorita Solis is waiting in the study for your consultation."

"Great. Why don't you join me for dinner? You can update me on progress at the Saturn Building."

Buckley ate while Cashwell detailed the completed work on the building. Very little remained to do before opening. "Saturn's computer system will be up and running this week and the administrative sections, that is, floors one through four, will open shortly thereafter. As you know, this is mostly window dressing. The wiring for the solar panels and the grow lights is complete throughout the building. The grow vats and the hydroponic plumbing have been installed. We'll open the remaining hundred and fifty levels—that's three levels per floor—in stages over the next three months. Plants and growing medium are being delivered daily in trucks marked as electrical and other service vehicles. I've seen no indication that anything unusual has been detected. All installations are right on schedule. Your gifts to building inspectors have had the desired result. I anticipate a successful grand opening on October 31 as planned."

Buckley smiled broadly. "And my suite?"

"The entire top floor is ready for you. You'll have the option of personal high-speed elevator or the helipad. We did run into a temporary glitch in our supply of dilithium crystals to power the transporter beam."

"What?"

"I'm joking, sir. Old school, you know, *Star Trek?* Blood is *our* power source. And we don't plan to run short of that."

"Of course." Buckley looked away out the window.

"Your study is finished. The altar and celestial guide stones were all aligned using stellar navigation equipment borrowed from the JPL."

Buckley had finished his salad and a juicy Pittsburgh-style steak. He pushed back the plate and wiped his lips. "It all sounds good, Cashwell. Please tell Ms. Solis that I'll be right along."

Chapter 35

THE BRUJA

Buckley went to his bedroom. He stripped off his clothes and put on a bloodred-hooded robe. He headed to his study and stopped outside the door. He removed his sandals and stood barefoot on the threshold of the room. As he entered, a spicy aroma assailed him through thick darkness. Around the room were bookshelves holding rare metaphysical and magical works—some nearly five hundred years old—and a few seemed to glow with a pale light of their own.

He inhaled the aroma, a blend of Mexican desert herbs and grasses, and waited for his eyes to adjust. At the far end of the room was a pretty, young Latina. She wore a white robe and sat cross-legged on an ivory stool. This was the solitary piece of furniture in the room. Etched into the center of the room's floor was a pentagram outlined in iridescent yellow tiles There was a red candle at each point of the design.

Buckley dropped to his knees. He crawled into the center of the pentagram where he kneeled, waiting. The *bruja*, or sorceress, stood and asked, "Are you prepared?" Buckley nodded but made no sound. She asked, "Do you wish to consult the stars?"

This time Buckley replied, "Yes." He reached out with his left hand in front of him.

She asked, "Do you accept the price?"

For the third time, Buckley replied in the affirmative, "I do."

A feminine voice sang softly. It was a plaintive tune that evoked melancholy and seemed to originate from inside his head. Buckley began to sweat and shake as the witch moved slowly toward him. From inside her robe, she withdrew a long, gleaming stiletto. Buckley looked at it and his fear became almost overwhelming. She reached out and grasped his left hand. Turning it palm upward, she drew the knife lightly over his hand. The wound burned like hellfire and he had to bite his lip to keep from screaming.

The bruja walked in a circle around the pentagram. She placed a drop of blood from the knife blade on each of the candles. This caused them to flare wildly with a greenish flame. When she had completed her circuit, she stepped back and the lines of the pentagram began to radiate a sickly green light upward into the room. From a pouch that hung around her neck, she took three polished, translucent stones. She placed them into his bloody hand. "Shake the stars, my child."

Buckley forgot his pain and began to shake the stones in his hands like a crazed craps shooter.

Ms. Solis began to join in the song. Her voice became breathier as she sang. Finally, she shouted, "Now!"

Buckley flung the stones from his hands as if they were burning him alive. The stones stopped abruptly, held in by the lines of the pentagram. Each stone began to glow with a starlike radiance. Ms. Solis bent over the stones and studied the pattern.

"*Stand.*" A loud, male voice echoed through the room.

Buckley stood. He looked up to see the bruja floating, legs crossed in lotus position, four feet off the floor. Her eyes were closed, but through her mouth came a deep, masculine voice. "Your question is considered, my son. The answer is undetermined at this time. Processes are in flux. There is no firm time line for your request as yet. Beware of the hunter. He wears protection from the adversary, and the power of death is with him. Even the prince of California takes precautions to avoid him. The girl is not who you think she is."

The lights in the room suddenly flared to life and all seemed normal again, except that Ms. Solis was lying facedown, unconscious on the floor. Buckley was angry and shook as he spat out the words "What *is this,* bruja?" Buckley looked down at her and shook his head. "I pay with blood for some crappy B-movie dialogue? This is useless." Buckley turned and stalked out.

*　*　*

Buckley stood in the shower, letting the hot water run over him. He looked down at his left hand. There was now only a fine red line where the knife had sliced him, and that was rapidly fading to pink. He always felt uncomfortable and slightly nauseous after these sessions. Usually the rewards were more tangible, but were they worth the ultimate price? Again, he considered the answer he had received, and his anger flared again. It wasn't the cutting of his flesh or the loss of blood that concerned him. However, with each new cut, he felt a terrible burning and brief flare of terror deep inside. He began to fear these were a foretaste of his future. *This wasn't part of the bargain.*

Buckley remembered his seven o'clock meeting as he stepped from the shower. It was now 6:30 and he hurried to shave and dress. As he did so, he thought of the girl, Lanie Martin, and laughed. For some reason she had called herself Becca Tramell at his soiree. She was quick on the uptake, he mused. *I'll need some of the bruja's herbs with her.*

His mind wandered. The warmth of the shower had finally relaxed him. He thought back to his youth in Jamestown, New York. Buckley's father had owned the Old Ferrie Tavern on the Chadakoin River. It was named for the historic ferries that hauled settlers across the water on their treks to the great western frontier. This business had been owned and run by the Buckley family since his great-great-great-grandfather had established the inn in 1820. That man had been something of a local hero for his exploits in the War of 1812. He was a crack shot who had single-handedly held off the pursuing English and their Indian allies during the Jamestown militia's hasty retreat after the battle of Table Rock on Lake Ontario. This ancestor enjoyed great success as proprietor of the tavern, keeping travelers entertained with tales of the war and local legends. He was said to have a thunderous laugh that would set his double row of teeth clacking. He had never been ill a day in his life until he sat down in his rocker one autumn afternoon and fell into a permanent sleep at the astounding age of 115 years.

Buckley looked back with pride at his youthful accomplishments. He'd excelled playing basketball for St. Cunigunde High School. He had then accepted a scholarship to play at Syracuse University, but a serious injury to his left knee in his first game as a sophomore ended his career. After this, he decided that he needed a change of scenery and headed for California. His understanding of life in Los Angeles had been forged by television and the movies. Buckley naively thought his natural good looks and good humor would be sufficient to land him a contract in the movies—or at least a guest shot on *Three's Company.*

Cashwell called from the hall. "Ten till seven, Benjamin."

"Okay, thanks." Buckley finished putting on his clothes and combed his hair.

Chapter 36

THE BLOOD OATH

Traffic was not as bad as they had feared. On their way to Buckley's estate, Hank and Lanie chatted casually about her goals as a nursing student and life here in LA. They settled on a name for Hank's assumed identity as her agent. Lanie then asked Hank about his life growing up Native American in Middle America.

"I'm not sure what you are asking. We had a happy family, and I was never aware that I was different from anyone else in the community. I think that it's much more difficult to be a child in today's culture."

"You were in the military, Hank. Did you ever have to kill anyone?"

Hank was a bit startled by the abruptness of this question. "Yes. I was a marine in the Middle East during the second Gulf War. It came with the territory."

"How did it make you feel, Hank?"

He thought about the question. "At the time, there was no feeling associated with it other than the relief of still being alive. We were doing what we were trained to do in order to succeed in our mission and survive. Later, I felt a deep sadness. The taking of human life is a very serious thing."

"Oh." Lanie looked sad and turned to look out the window. "What about the cult shootout?"

Hank chuckled. "It wasn't the O.K. Corral. Actually, *we* only killed a dragon. The preacher was killed by a disgruntled customer, you might say."

"But my point is this: I'm sure Detective Decker has had to kill people in his job, and you would've killed, had it become a case of kill or be killed. How do you justify that as a Christian?"

At this point, Hank became confused. He had assumed that Lanie was a Christian, but now he had to ask. "Aren't you a Christian?"

"No, not really."

"But you are Dave's girlfriend. Right?"

"Sort of, I guess."

"Then you weren't at camp?"

"No, I've never been to the camp at all."

"Okay. Now I think I've got things straight." Hank took a deep breath. He had gotten this all wrong. "Killing does not equal murder. In scripture the two are distinct. Mistranslations and misunderstandings cause confusion between the two." They were now pulling up in front of Buckley's home. "We can continue this later, if you wish."

They got out of the car. Looking at the home and Lamborghini convertible, Hank muttered, "Wow." His eyes looked over to the statue of the titan and he laughed. "That does look like a Martian version of Disney's King Triton."

The door swung open as they approached and Cashwell greeted them cheerfully. "Welcome, Becca. I am Bryan Cashwell. You may recall we spoke on the phone."

"Mr. Cashwell, this is my attorney and agent Roy Quigley. Roy, this is Mr. Cashwell. He is Mr. Buckley's personal assistant."

"How do you do?" both men said at the same time and chuckled.

Yeah, sure, Cashwell thought. "Come on in. Mr. Buckley is waiting in the lounge." He looked over the two while noting their apparel. He let his eyes linger on Becca. "It looks like you two have plans for tonight. A shame. This shouldn't take long—at least the business part."

They walked up a short stairway and along a hall toward the back of the split-level home. Reaching a door, Cashwell swung it open. A thick, oddly sweet aroma drifted out and Hank was instantly reminded of Afghanistan. Hank could see Lanie sniffing the air and then inhaling deeply out of the corner of his eye.

"What a pleasant scent," she mumbled.

They stepped into the large room. At the far end, Buckley sat at a large, oak desk in front of a giant window wall. There was grand piano along one wall and floor-to-ceiling bookshelves along the opposite. Buckley stood and walked over to meet his guests. "Good evening, Ms. Tramell. I'm so pleased you could make it here tonight." Turning to Hank, he reached out to shake hands. "Hello, I'm Benjamin Buckley."

Cashwell completed the introductions. Then Buckley turned and led them over to the floor-to-ceiling window. Hank recognized this view revealing Los Angeles coming to life at dusk, with twinkling lights visible all the way to the ocean. Headlights and taillights were coming on and crisscrossing as cars moved across the landscape. The sun was low on the horizon and cast a dim orange glow over the land. Lanie shook her head. "It's beautiful. Look. There's the Hollywood sign!"

Hank was also impressed by this magnificent spectacle. Below he saw the pool, deck, and hot tub exactly as Lanie had described. To his surprise, Hank noticed a couple dozen people walking about below, with a few in the pool and hot tub. He then saw a new bright-red Corvette Stingray poolside.

"We're having a small party this evening to celebrate Ms. Tramell signing on to our project."

Hank laughed. "A bit premature, isn't it?"

"Well, I certainly hope Ms. Tramell won't think so." Buckley followed the line of Hank's gaze. "I see you admiring the Stingray, Mr. Quigley."

"Hard not to. With all those extras walking about, it looks like you're shooting a commercial."

Buckley laughed. "Touché. No, not a commercial. It's yours, Mr. Quigley."

Hank felt his throat tighten. He began to speak, "I don't know what—"

"Hear me out, please. Ms. Tramell will receive $250,000, plus the usual perks given the star of a motion picture. She'll also get a new car of her choice. Perhaps you'd like a Bentley, Ms. Tramell?"

Lanie's laughed happily. "Indeed, I would, Mr. Buckley. Or maybe Hank's Stingray." Hank flinched slightly at her lapse and noted that Lanie's eyes now had a slightly glassy look.

165

"And Mr. Quigley, of course the Corvette is in addition to your regular fee. If you already have a ride you like. Mrs. Quigley might enjoy a new Land Rover to take the little Quigleys to their violin and polo lessons." Buckley and Cashwell burst out in a loud laugh at this. Hank wondered if they were being serious.

"Let's get business out of the way so the party can begin, shall we? Cashwell, do you have the contract?"

Cashwell walked to the desk and set down a piece of parchment covered in writing. He held a stylus with a pointed tip. "Ms. Tramell?"

Hank interrupted. "Now wait a minute, Mr. Buckley. Please send your contract to my office Monday morning and I'll look it over and—"

"I'm afraid that will be impossible, counselor. We have a long list of prominent female actors dying to get in on this deal and we're under pressure from the studio to wrap up these negotiations tonight."

"We haven't had *any* negotiations yet."

"Your client might disagree. What say you, Ms. Tramell?"

Hank looked at Lanie and was astounded. She was staring up at Buckley with a smile and nodding. "Where do I sign?"

Cashwell suddenly took Lanie's left hand and jabbed her ring finger with the nib of the pen. "Ouch."

Hank grimaced "Wait a minute. Becca—" He reached out to jerk the pen away from Cashwell, but the man was too quick and turned away.

Cashwell put the nib into the drop of blood and said, "Sign here."

Lanie signed. Cashwell then placed a drop of blood on Lanie's right thumb pad and pressed it to the document. Cashwell repeated the exercise on himself, signing as witness. Buckley's name was already present in a large, dark-red signature worthy of John Hancock. Ben Buckley took Lanie's arm and steered her toward the doorway. "Shall we join the party?"

Hank's alarm grew as he saw Lanie smiling at Buckley and turning with him. Hank reached out and grabbed Buckley's arm, causing Buckley to stumble. "Lanie, remember the party in Malibu. I said I'd have you there by—"

Hank found himself unable to finish his sentence as he was suddenly held from behind in a crushing bear hug that made breathing nearly impossible. Hank shifted his feet to a fighting stance when he saw Lanie turn to him and give her head a small shake. This confused Hank, who was on the verge of delivering an elbow to the ribs of his assailant. Hank stopped his struggle.

Lanie frowned at Hank. "Quit it, Hank. I'm just fine here with Mr. Buckley. You run along now." She gave Hank an exaggerated smile then looked at Buckley, who had recovered his footing.

"We'll see that she gets home in one piece, counselor. Show our guest some hospitality, Dolph."

Hank felt the pressure on his chest relax. He turned to see a blond giant grinning down at him. Dolph moved to the side, whispering in Hank's ear. "You are not invited, mien freund." Dolph lowered his arm, waving it with a flourish. Cashwell turned to Hank and smiled menacingly. "I think you know the way out, Mr. Quigley."

Chapter 37

HIT THE ROAD, HANK!

Hank walked toward the Humvee while pondering what had just happened. He stopped and looked back at the house, deeply confused. At first, he thought she was signaling him to back off with her head shake, but now he was unsure. Lanie certainly didn't appear to be under any compulsion when she signed the contract. Her smile was that of a child opening an unexpected Christmas present. Was it the money? The car? The offer of a career and celebrity? And there was something a bit off about her eyes. *Maybe she was just playing along. I'll wait here for a bit to see if she comes out.* Hank took out his phone and set it on the dashboard.

As he waited, he began to mull over what he would tell Dave. *Maybe her blush earlier tonight did* not *indicate a deep attachment to Dave after all. When I asked, her response was not a ringing endorsement of that relationship.* Hank gave up after nearly an hour of waiting. He could still hear the music and laughter from the pool deck below. *Well, that sure was a nice Corvette.* He laughed and drove away.

When Hank arrived back at the hotel room, Lou was sitting on the sofa and watching the Dodgers beat up on the Tigers in interleague play. "Hi, Hank. How about we take in a ball game Sunday afternoon?"

"We'll see."

"How did it go? Did you get any intel?"

169

"Well, I learned a lot about Lanie. She signed his movie contract then stayed with Buckley at his party."

Lou laughed, but he quickly recognized that Hank was not laughing. "You're serious."

"I am. I haven't told Dave yet. I wanted to get your ideas on what we should do next."

"Call Dave, I guess. You're sure she was not faking? She seems to be a strong-willed young woman. Maybe she saw an opportunity to do some deep recon on her own."

"No way. When she signed, she smiled like she'd just won the lottery."

"Okay. Let's call Dave, and then we stick to the plan."

Lou dialed Dave's number and handed his mobile phone to Hank. "Dave, do you have a minute?"

Lou listened as Hank spent the next quarter hour describing the night's activities in detail. Afterward, Hank gave a few perfunctory okays before hanging up. Lou asked how Dave took the news. Hank chuckled. "He sounded a bit disappointed but relatively unconcerned except for her safety. Maybe we misconstrued the situation between them."

"Maybe. I guess. What was he talking about at the end?"

Hank thought for a moment. "Dave said that when he was researching Buckley, a feature article mentioned that Saturn is renovating an old office building on the edge of Koreatown. Dave finds this unusual because the building is in a rundown area near downtown Los Angeles."

"Sounds like a reasonable question unless the price was extremely low."

"Exactly, but Dave said it wasn't. In fact, he said the costs mentioned in the article seemed astronomical for the project. Hank chuckled. "He said that since it did not look like he would be taking Lanie to Santa Monica tomorrow, he'd drive down there and try to see what is going on."

Lou's eyes squinted from concern. It would probably be a good idea if he didn't go alone. I doubt Saturn would appreciate anyone snooping around their building. "What was that you told him about Lanie signing the contract in her own blood? And something about her eyes?"

"It's true. I thought the signing thing was just theatrics, but now I'm not sure, and her eyes seemed a bit glazed. I *can* place the aroma now. When I was in the Middle East, there was an intoxicant that the locals used. It was similar to marijuana but many times stronger. I remember the users acting extremely passive and suggestible. My buddies called it the 'scent of suicide bombers.'"

"I see. Well, five o'clock is going to come pretty quickly, so I think I'll turn in."

Hank nodded and replied, "I'm still a bit keyed up. I think I'll watch one of those Mexican luchador superhero movies for a bit. That should put me to sleep."

Chapter 38

TRAVELING BAND

Decker walked through a deserted downtown. Los Angeles? Weeds grew waist high in clumps all around him. It was deathly silent. Lou was puzzled. He was looking for something but didn't know what it was. He wore an old safari jacket and ragged khaki shorts but thought nothing odd about this. A thick, studded gun belt holding a Desert Eagle pistol hung from his waist. Decker walked from one ruined building to the next, looking in through broken windows. Around him he saw only rubble and scrub vegetation. He saw an old, well-worn book lying on the ground. He picked it up, and it crumbled and fell apart as he handled it. Lou turned the pages quickly. He could not read the writing but recognized many detailed ink drawings of legendary creatures. Near the back, he saw a flying dragon that resembled Miguel, the sorcerer from the Congregation of Light. On the next page was a giant rattlesnake. It was nearly as thick as the man it was striking in the back. He noted with curiosity that the man appeared to be dressed in a World War II Nazi SS officer's uniform. The snake then turned its gaze in Lou's direction. He dropped the book and it disintegrated into dust.

Lou continued his meandering quest. He approached a rundown gas station. The garage door covering the service bay began to open as he neared. He heard an old, electric motor grinding as it worked the squeaking gear mechanism. When the noise stopped, Lou heard a loud rattling. He peered into the dark bay. A gigantic rattlesnake sat coiled on the weedy floor. The snake looked at Lou as if it had been waiting for him. Its head and neck began to undulate as the reptile moved slowly toward Lou and into striking position. Lou drew his revolver and took aim, but the snake was lightning quick. It struck, and Decker felt a searing pain in his gun hand as his arm went limp. He jerked backward and fell onto his side. He tried to rise and run, but the creature was too fast. It pinned Lou under its weight and lowered its open mouth toward his face. Lou let out a yell.

He came awake to find Hank shaking him. "Are you all right? You were having a nightmare, Lou. You were shouting really loudly."

Lou looked blankly upward and nodded. His right hand had twisted in the covers and Lou had to wrestle the blanket off. "Yeah. Guess so. It didn't start out that way, but when it turned bad, wow."

Decker went on to describe his dream as he remembered it.

Hank listened without comment. "It's only 1:30, so I'm going back to bed for a few hours." Hank recalled the Californians mentioning rattlesnake noises in the clearing.

Once his friend had left, Decker lay there, staring at the ceiling and arranging his covers. He prayed for insight and protection in their quest, and after a while, he drifted into a dreamless sleep.

* * *

In the morning, Lou and Hank met with Logan in the hotel lobby. Hank asked where Sam was. "He has a headache and doesn't want to travel. Never known him to have headaches before his injury. He said not to be concerned though. Dave and Lanie would keep an eye on him." Lou and Hank looked at each other and wondered.

The trip to Camp Sequoia passed quickly. Lou and Hank marveled at the changes in scenery as they moved out of the city through the desert to mountains then back down to rich farmlands. Finally, they were climbing up into the Sierra Nevada Mountains. The miles flew by and they were soon at the camp.

They drove in on the tree-lined entry road and pulled up to the main office building. Pastor Adamson stood on the porch, waving goodbye to a young man who was driving off hurriedly in a cloud of dust. "Blogan!

Grape to shee you!" Mr. A called indistinctly and too loudly as the men exited the Hummer.

"Mr. Adamson. You look great. It's Logan, Pastor."

In fact, he did not look so hot to anyone. He was leaning against the porch post and his left arm hung limply at his side. Mr. A was slurring his words and had a distracted look in his eyes. He suddenly turned in a lurch, grabbed at the doorknob, and fell forward onto his face. As he went down, the right side of his head came into view. Swelling was obvious above his right ear and a trickle of blood ran down his neck from four long parallel cuts over the swelling. Lou and Hank moved quickly to help Mr. Adamson up.

They carried him into the cabin and asked Logan, "Is there a bed or cot anywhere?" Logan pointed to the director's private quarters and moved to the desk. He picked up the phone, "I'm calling 911 and the sheriff." Logan picked up the phone, but it was dead. No dial tone. He traced the line to the wall and trotted out around to the side of the building, where he saw the wire had been cut. Reentering the building, he said to Lou, "Gimme the car keys. I'll have to drive up the mountain about a mile to get a good signal on my cell phone. Be right back."

Lou tossed Logan the key. He heard the Hummer roar as Logan pulled out. He turned to Hank and said, "Didn't realize he had it in him." They had placed Adamson on the bed and Hank checked his neck and performed a quick survey to check for other injuries and wounds. Lou grabbed a couple of washcloths and fashioned a head bandage of sorts. The pastor lay there snoring.

Logan returned in less than five minutes. As he entered the building, he called out, "Hello! Lou? Hank? Hey, Chief Thunderthud is—"

Lou yelled, "Is what?" He got up and walked into the office to see Logan staring up at a giant bear head mounted above the door.

"How is Mr. Adamson?" Logan asked.

"Still unconscious."

"Ambulance is on the way."

"Does he have family?"

"Nope. He's a bachelor. Married to his job, as he says. Never mentioned any kids."

Lou noted there were two very large bear paws mounted alongside the head. Hank had entered the room as Logan said, "There was a marauding three-legged grizzly bear that lived in the woods way back when. It was killed by the father of Camp Sequoia's founder. The man gave this mount to his son when the camp first opened. I think the story of the kill had some spiritual aspect, but I can't remember what it was. The bear's skin is a rug somewhere and this big old head and three claws have been here for fifty-some years. Everyone calls it Chief Thunderthud."

Hank saw the connection at once. There was a paw missing from the mount. He walked over to a window that was cracked open. Looking out, Hank saw the bloody bear paw lying in the flower bed.

Lou asked, "Is it there?"

"Yes."

"Armed or pawed robbery? Maybe attempted murder?"

"Why murder?" asked Logan.

"The phone line was cut so it appears that they didn't want Adamson to call for help. Maybe assault with intent to commit murder. Just speculation."

Lou had removed Mr. Adamson's wallet. He was looking for contact information. He found none.

"Hello?" came a weak call from the bedroom. "Anyone there?"

Logan went in. "Mr. Adamson, it's Logan Williams. Do you remember what happened?"

All three men watched as Pastor Adamson screwed up his face and shouted, "Why you—" He reached out and grabbed Logan's collar and began to shake him before collapsing back on the bed unconscious.

"Looks like he was expecting you." Hank grinned at Logan.

The ambulance and a deputy arrived simultaneously. As the attendants loaded Mr. Adamson into the rig, Deputy Hennessey asked the men what had occurred. Logan explained that he had called Mr. Adamson yesterday to inform him of today's visit.

"In fact, we were surprised to see Mr. A standing on the porch. We thought he was waving goodbye to the fellow who sped out as we arrived, but maybe not."

Hennessey looked questioningly at Logan. "So you say there was someone else here when you arrived?"

"Yes. I didn't get a good look at him."

Hennessey's face turned sour. "Let's forget the mystery man for now. What are you three doing here?"

Lou cut in, "I'm Detective Lou Decker, and we're looking into the disappearance of Toni LaRusso. I talked to you yesterday on the phone. You're not suggesting that we had anything to do with this assault are you, Deputy? If so, why would we call it in?"

Hennessey ignored Lou's comment. He had his hand on his sidearm. "Detective, eh? I told you yesterday the case was closed. Where from? LA?"

"No Grand Rapids, Michigan." Lou pulled out his credentials wallet to show his ID to Hennessey. He hoped the latter wouldn't notice the date of his retirement.

Apparently, he didn't. "I remember you. Looks like you're a little bit out of your jurisdiction, Detective." The deputy sneered. "Turn around and—"

Hank sensed impending disaster and took this moment to speak up. "Deputy, you might be more interested in me." He stepped between Hennessey and the others.

"And why is that?"

"My name is Bryan Cashwell, Deputy."

Color drained from Hennessey's face. Hank grabbed the deputy by the arm and shook him. He jerked Hennessey over away from Lou and Logan. Hank spoke rapidly into Hennessey's ear, the latter repeatedly nodding his head. Lou caught a few words, including 'cleaning up your mess.' When he was finished, Hank said loudly, "I think we're done here. You can leave now."

Hennessey nodded. "Yes, sir." He turned and walked to his patrol car.

"Don't forget to call me after seven. Got it?" Hank called after him.

"Yes, sir."

The deputy, clearly shaken, was visibly pale as he drove off.

Lou looked at Hank and asked him, "What did you tell him?"

"I took a chance and figured that if the deputy was involved in Toni's disappearance, then he knew Dixon and he *might* know of Buckley and Cashwell. I had no idea that he would be so intimidated by the name. I suggested that unless he were packing antivenin, it might be in his best interest to terminate this interview *now.*" Hank laughed.

Lou joined in.

Logan looked confused. "Cashwell?"

"I'll explain later. I figure that right now we have about an hour to look around before the deputy begins to put things together." They walked back into the office.

"Is anything missing?" Lou asked Logan.

Logan walked through the room looking around intently. "Yes, the camp computer is gone. Otherwise, I don't see anything out of order or missing."

Lou asked, "Is there only one computer."

"I've never seen another. I've only seen Mr. Adamson use the stolen one. We connect through a hard wire at camp. There's no Wi-Fi. I don't think Mr. A even has a mobile phone."

"I didn't find a phone in his pockets when I checked for his wallet," Lou offered.

Hank said, "Okay. The robber came for the computer. He cut the phone line, incapacitated the director, took the computer, and left. Mission accomplished. I told the deputy everything was under control here, so I doubt he'll be back to the cabin until there is some kind of pressure to investigate."

"Or when he figures out that you aren't Cashwell."

"Yeah, there is that. Let's go out to the clearing area and have a look-see."

They hopped into the Hummer and Logan directed them out between the cabins, back into the wilderness section of the camp. As they plowed through the weeds, Hank looked over at Lou and asked, "Bring back memories?"

"No mountains in Minnesota." Both men laughed.

Hank partially explained the events of the night before to Logan, leaving out the more lurid features. "Did you meet Cashwell when you went to the house, Logan?"

"Don't know. What does he look like?"

"Caucasian. Tall, big-boned, about six foot, five. Balding."

"Sounds like our Daddy Warbucks."

"What?" asked Lou.

"That's who I thought he looked like." Lou and Hank looked at each other and shook their heads. "He and another man were talking to Buckley when we arrived."

They drove along the bank of the creek. Logan said, "This looks like the place where we found Sam. Yeah, look there along the bank where all the weeds are tramped down. You can see where they brought in the gurney. What a muddy mess."

"Where is the clearing?" asked Lou.

"See those trees about a hundred and fifty yards that way?" Logan pointed toward the woods. "Dave found the knife point in the clearing over there."

Hank wheeled the Humvee right and headed toward a stand of trees a short distance off. As they approached the trees, a clearing became visible in the midst. Hank parked the vehicle and they got out. Walking to the clearing, Hank remarked, "Almost a perfect circle."

"Agreed," Lou observed. "Too perfect to be natural. What do you make of those four big, oak trees?"

Hank was already at the center of the clearing. He raised his arm and pointed at one of the oaks. He took off his watch and held it horizontally, lining up the sun with the number twelve dial. He made a quick calculation in his head. Then Hank looked at the other three trees in order. "The oaks line up with the four cardinal compass points—that one being north."

Lou asked where the blade fragment was found, and Logan pointed to a spot about five feet from Hank. "Right about there. At least that's where Dave said he found it."

"Do you still have it?"

"No, the man who called himself Agent Hogan took it."

Hank walked around the perimeter of the clearing and looked down at the grass. "There's been a lot of foot traffic in this clearing—more than just you and Dave." Hank knelt down and pointed to a circle where the vegetation was almost scrubbed away. "People were moving about here for quite a time as if they were marching in a circle. In the center, the grass is matted and scratched away as if something heavy pressed it down."

Hank saw the worry on Lou's face and said, "Well, I've seen enough. If we leave now, we can get out of the county before Hennessey puts two and two together."

"Plus we can probably make El Cajon by dinnertime. I hear Cactus Charlie's Casino has a buffet that is out of this world." Lou laughed.

Logan looked at the men. "Is there another reason we're going to El Cajon – other than for dinner?"

Lou answered, "Yes. There are some people there we need to talk to."

Logan shrugged his shoulders. "El Cajon it is!"

Chapter 39

THE SATURN BUILDING

Despite Dave Maxwell's feigned indifference to Lanie attending Buckley's party, he spent much of the night worrying about her. He called her at 11:30 and just after midnight before accepting that he had no claim on her. *Sure, we've gone out several times. I thought she enjoyed being with me, and she seemed to be interested in the situation surrounding the camp, but—*

Dave decided to go to sleep and talk to her in the morning.

He called again at 8:30 a.m., after he got up, washed, and brushed his teeth, and got the same result: no answer. He left a message this time. "Hi, Lanie. It's Dave. Just wondering how the party went and what plans you had for today. I need to go downtown on an errand this morning, but call me anytime when you get a chance. Bye." He hung up and decided it was time to get going.

Traffic was light, the temperature was pleasant, and the sun was shining—a typical, beautiful Southern California morning. He relaxed as he drove and decided to listen to the radio. Dave didn't listen to music much because the songs became internalized and interfered with his concentration. *Not that I'm OCD or anything.*

He punched the on button and found his customary station. There was a talk show on as he expected. He recognized the voice of a local personality, Jay Chachick, who reviewed TV, cinema, and musical offerings. Chachick generally interviewed writers, directors, or artists and Dave generally found him entertaining. However, Dave often questioned the judgment of the host in referring to the interviewees as artists. "Mr. Deake, your movie *Kaiju X* is violent by any standard; however, several scenes in the movie seem to raise the level of gore to new heights."

"We give the audience what it wants, Jay."

"Are you saying then that you had emails and calls from potential viewers asking to see people crushed under the foot of your giant dinosaur or incinerated by his radioactive fire breath when you were making this cinematic travesty?"

"Well, not that specifically."

"And what about the screaming elderly lady taken aloft by the giant dragonfly and dropped into the volcano?"

"That was my brother-in-law's idea. In focus group testing, this scene resonated at a 61 percent approval rate. With some groups, we left in a preceding scene in which the lady, Mrs. Bates, was shown cutting down trees in her yard. In those groups, the approval rate jumped up to a whopping 93 percent."

Dave groaned and switched the station. He heard a song playing that he did not recognize. It was a slow number in a minor key and slightly dissonant. The voice of the singer sounded vaguely familiar. "Fire and destruction … flammable construction. Nero ignites … and we all watch it burn. Yes, we all-ll-ll-ll, watch it burn-n-n-n!" and the song faded out. The DJ came on. "That was Rock Rollins with the title tune from the upcoming movie *Nero.*"

Geez. Dave switched off the radio. *I didn't know Rollins was still recording. Is every movie and song today about violence and mayhem? A movie about Nero? Really?*

The outline of the Saturn Building towered over its neighboring structures in the distance. He reached Koreatown and decided to park a block away from his destination and walk to the building. Along the way, he passed several LA-style strip malls, complete with picturesque bilingual signage advertising attorneys, exotic eateries, and various businesses from electronics, to nail salons and bail bondsmen.

Dave stood across the street from the Saturn Building. He was surprised to see an eight-foot-high wooden fence shielding the property from view. *I didn't even think of this. Did I think I might just walk in and ask a few questions? How dumb.* The building covered nearly an entire city block and went up about forty stories, and the fence extended in both directions around the corners. Dave crossed the street to a bus stop bench and sat. *Why am I even here?*

About a minute later, a pair of white stake trucks drove by. Each bore the Saturn Communications name and logo. They were followed by another pair of trucks, and then a third pair.

With piqued curiosity, he watched as they turned the corner. He rose and followed the trucks, stopping to watch them turn onto the Saturn property about half a block away. Dave looked up. On this side were large conduits running up the sides of the building. On top, he saw the edges of a large solar power array. All of the windows above the fourth floor appeared to be covered in a shiny, metallic coating with several branches of conduit going in at every level. *Looks like they are into solar energy. Nothing illegal about that.*

He walked back to the bus stop. As he sat there deciding whether or not to just go home, a door in the fence opposite him swung open and a tall, balding man walked out. He wore a business suit and carried an expensive-looking briefcase. He walked toward a black Audi parked several spaces away. The man opened the car's back door and placed the briefcase inside. He looked over the roof of the car directly at Dave. Their eyes met briefly before Dave looked away. Dave saw a glint of recognition in the man's eyes and a small frown flicker across his face. *Does he recognize me?*

Dave heard the car door slam and looked up to see the man crossing the street in his direction; however, now the man was not wearing a business suit. He was wearing a well-worn "Duke's Seafood" T-shirt and cut-off shorts with sunglasses and sandals. He carried an old-style longboard in one hand, and a six-pack swung from his other. He was walking directly toward the bus shelter. Dave began to perspire and considered running. At that moment, a bus pulled up. Dave quickly got on. He watched as the man approached the curb and stopped, as if deciding on whether to enter the bus or not. The man kept his gaze fixed on Dave through the bus window.

As the bus moved off, the man set down the beer on the bench, scratched his head, and turned away. He shrugged and walked back toward the car.

To his utter confusion, Dave realized that now the man once again appeared to be wearing his suit. *That was really strange. Why did I feel so nervous? He must be a professional quick-change artist.* Dave laughed at himself.

A block and a half later, he pulled the stop cord. The bus driver pulled over and Dave got out. He could see the Audi still parked in the same spot. Dave scanned the area, but neither the businessman nor the "surf bum" was present, so he crossed the street. He was walking back toward the Audi when a hand tapped him on the shoulder. He turned with a start to see a short, elderly Asian man grinning up at him. The Asian held a bunch of long, thin, bamboo sticks, each having a colorful paper fish or animal clipped to the end. He held out one of the sticks to Dave and made a noise, moving his mouth oddly. "Gumma, gumma, gumma."

Is this man trying to imitate an animal noise? Maybe he can't speak English, or maybe he's just crazy.

"No, thank you." Dave turned to walk away and continued toward the Audi.

The man followed him. Now he was speaking loudly. "Gooma, gooma, one doll-uh."

Dave noticed several passers-by looking at the toy salesman and him. They gave the pair a wide berth as they walked by.

"Glucka! Glucka!" The man persisted.

Dave was growing annoyed. He stopped and turned around to face the man. He pulled out his wallet, removed a dollar, and shoved it at the man. "Here. Now leave me alone, please."

The man's smile was cold now. Dave peered closely and recognized the face of the surfing businessman now turned Asian and staring at him.

The man said in perfect English, "Thank you. Now that I have your attention, I'd like to ask you a question."

Dave found the intense anxiety returning. "W-w-what?"

"Yes, w-w-what-what is your great interest in the Saturn Building?"

"I'm an architectural engineering student and heard rumors about this building's use of solar power. I wanted to see if I could get some ideas for a project."

"Oh, and who told you about this?"

"I don't know. I heard some other students talking at lunch on Friday."

The old man suddenly reached into his pocket and pulled out a cell phone. He brought it up and quickly snapped a picture of Dave. He then placed the phone back into his pocket.

"Hey, I didn't say you could take a picture of me."

"And I didn't say you could snoop around our building. I'd suggest you leave now and don't come back. Your kind is not welcome here."

Dave turned to go down the side street.

As he did so, the man said, "Wait." He handed Dave a stick with a grinning rattlesnake hanging from the end.

Dave continued slowly down the street, using all his willpower to still the deep tremble in his gut. Several paces away, he snuck a peek behind him, but the old man was gone. He turned the corner and walked half a block then tossed the toy snake into a litter can.

The gate in the fence where the trucks had entered was just ahead. A fence board was broken near the gate. *I need to at least get a look inside the fence, or this trip will be a total waste.* He pulled on the slat, breaking out a large piece.

Looking in, he saw several trucks parked in the area near a receiving door. Two trucks had their rear doors open and men were unloading plants with vibrant red blooms. *Poppies.* He watched as the workmen loaded the plants onto a flatbed cart and pushed it into the building. Dave saw ten other pallets lined up, ready for loading with poppies in containers. Dave inhaled sharply, pulled out his phone, switched on the camera app, and shot photos. *No reason for this many poppies—except to produce heroin.*

A voice from behind Dave growled. "You got away from me once in the woods, and I just warned you again. You're not very bright, are you?"

Dave turned to see a giant rattlesnake with a vaguely human face emerging from the garbage can. He took off at a full out sprint to his car.

Only after locking the door did he look back. Dave held the steering wheel with both hands. He was clammy and shaking. He looked back and saw no snake or any pursuit. People were walking by normally on the sidewalks. None appeared alarmed by the presence of a giant reptile. *What's going on? Am I going nuts? What did he mean when he said that I escaped him?*

Just then, his cell phone went off and he jumped. "Hello?"

185

Chapter 40

TALK, TALK

"Hey, Dave, It's Logan. I'm afraid I've got some bad news." Logan then described the attack on Pastor Adamson, the robbery, and the visit from Deputy Hennessey. "We went to the clearing. Lou and Hank have some concerns, but I'll let them tell you tomorrow when we get back."

"Tomorrow?"

"Yeah. We're going on to El Cajon tonight. There are some people there that the detective wants to waterboard."

"Waterboard?"

"Just kidding. He wants to check some information concerning Dixon."

"Where will you be staying?"

"At Cactus Charlie's? Maybe I'll hit the blackjack table this evening."

"Logan, I thought your card-counting days were over."

"Yeah, just kidding. Gee, Dave, lighten up a bit. Hear from Lanie?"

"No. I left her a message to call me, but nothing yet."

"How is Sam doing? He said he had a headache this morning when he called."

"He was sleeping when I left."

"Did you make it downtown to check out the Saturn Building?"

Dave went through the events of the morning with Logan. He decided to tell what he experienced without comment.

When Dave had finished, Logan groaned. "Good grief. You'd better go home. You can tell Hank and Lou all this when we get together. This sort of thing seems to be up their alley."

"Maybe I should write this up for Scott Nash. Do you think I'd get a byline?"

Logan laughed. "Yeah, you should."

"Goodbye, Logan."

Dave was feeling somewhat normal again after talking to his friend. His phone rang a second time. This call was from an unknown number. Dave waited for the caller to speak.

"Hello, Dave?"

Dave recognized her voice. "Lanie. Hi!"

"Dave, I'm sorry I didn't answer your call. I lost my phone at the party and had to replace it this morning."

"Okay." Dave noted that Lanie didn't mention that he made multiple calls. "How was the party? I understand you were the guest of honor."

There was a brief pause on Lanie's end before she responded, her tone now more formal. Somehow colder and less friendly. "It was fine, Dave. I know you don't approve of my *involvement* with these people, but this is a big opportunity for me and there's a lot of money at stake."

Dave didn't respond.

After an uncomfortable ten seconds Lanie continued. "I'm quitting school. I'm an adult and I need to do what's best for me. And right now, I've decided this is it." Lanie waited for the angry words she *knew* were coming.

Dave could not formulate any coherent objection to this. "Okay."

"I'm going to be very busy for the next few weeks, so you probably won't hear from me for a while."

"Okay. I understand." Dave didn't really understand, but he realized what he thought was blossoming between them was over. "I'll watch for your movie. Keep in touch."

Lanie said bye very quietly and clicked off.

*   *   *

She put her phone on the desk, sat down, and began to tear up. *That's that. I still don't know why Buckley doesn't want me to see anyone from my old life. I don't even know why he wants me in this movie or video or whatever it is. Or what he sees in me. But I can't pass up this chance, can I?* Lanie's thoughts rambled as she sat on the edge of her bed crying. After a time, she felt purged and her crying slowly petered out.

She looked at her clock. *The studio's men will be here in a bit to move me out of the dorm, and I haven't packed anything. Maybe I'll just leave it all here. In any case, there's not going to be much to put in their truck.*

In the end, she piled a few items on her bed. Some photos. One of Lanie herself, her brother, and her parents on the beach. Another of Lanie at her high school graduation. A third of her older brother, grinning broadly, in his flight suit while standing next to an F-16. And a few items of clothing she put into her suitcase. All in all, there was very little in her life that she clung to.

Lanie wondered what her new apartment would be like. Cashwell told her she'd have a personal assistant now and an agent. A real one of Buckley's choosing, not "Quigley." Cashwell told her that her future looked very bright in the industry. *The industry.* She was already starting to think like a Hollywood type.

When she had completed her packing, she picked up her mobile phone to call Cashwell and tell him she was ready to go, as he'd volunteered to drive her to her new digs.

She looked out the window and saw a black Audi parked below, illegally, near a fire hydrant. There was a knock on the door.

She opened it and saw Cashwell standing beaming. "Are you ready to start your new life?"

Lanie's face registered her surprise.

I certainly hope so.

Chapter 41

THE GRAY HOPPER

Lou awoke with the bright Southern California sun streaming in through his window. His room was high enough in the casino hotel tower that the desert below crept right up to the property's edge. He poured himself a cup of coffee and sat on the couch, then flipped open his Bible to the book of Job and began to read.

"God's voice thunders in marvelous ways. He does great things beyond our understanding." In the distance, he could see mountains slowly emerging from the night. *Beautiful, and so true.* As he finished his devotions, he heard a knock on the door. "Come in."

"Good morning. Sleep well in this air-conditioned desert oasis?" Hank chuckled.

"Yes, I did. Out like a light for seven solid hours."

"What time do you want to get going?"

"I'd like to get to the first interviewee's house about 9 a.m., so maybe forty-five minutes. I'll have to plug the address into my map app, but I don't think the drive will take over ten or fifteen minutes. El Cajon isn't Los Angeles, is it?'"

"Hardly." Hank walked out and knocked on Logan's door. He heard a groggy hello from inside. "Rise and Shine. We move out in forty-five minutes."

An hour later, they turned on to Avocado Avenue to pick up some breakfast. They were about to turn into a Big Bobby's Burger Stand, but Logan warned them off. "No breakfast here. Besides, you see that big C in the window. They were investigated last year for adding kangaroo meat to their burgers. No kidding."

Hank said, "Wow. A burger stand that doesn't sell good, old American beef breakfast burritos? What is this world coming to?"

They settled on a Denny's farther down the road.

After breakfast, it was only a short drive to Wanda McCoy's house. It was 9:05 a.m. when Lou knocked on the door. He was met by a middle-aged woman who had been in the middle of her yoga class on the local PBS affiliate. She showed the three men into the living area to wait while she hustled back to another room to finish her workout. "I'll finish up and be back in three minutes, boys."

Lou chuckled and Hank shook his head.

For the next fifteen minutes, Lou, Hank, and Logan repeatedly looked at each other as moans, several screams of pain, and one loud fall could be heard from the other room. "I'm okay, boys. Just slipped."

Finally, Mrs. McCoy came limping out with a towel around her neck. She had a small smear of blood on her forehead.

"Mrs. McCoy, you have blood on your forehead. Are you okay?"

"I'm fine. Just a little argument with my coffee table. Have you boys eaten breakfast? Why don't I heat up some Brussels sprouts souffle that I whipped up last week?"

"No thanks, ma'am. We stopped at Denny's and ate big breakfasts," said Lou. The others just shook their heads.

"You policemen work so hard. You can't be expected to chase down crooks all day on a load of MSG-riddled fast-food a-churnin' in your gut. Why not let me fry you up some ostrich eggs? I get 'em from my sister. She has a bird farm near San Diego."

"No, really. We only have time for a few questions, then we have to race to the next interrogation site." Lou gave Hank and Logan a sideways grin.

"Okay. Shoot!"

Logan looked confused. Hank laughed, and Lou stood up. Decker walked over to a table lamp. He removed the shade and held the lamp up to her face. Mrs. McCoy giggled. "Do I need a lawyer?" The others laughed too as Lou reassembled the lamp and set it back down.

Decker laughed. "No, ma'am. You're not under arrest. I just need to ask a few questions."

"Go ahead."

"Do you know the man who lives next door named Dixon Mason?"

"Yes. I've known him for about twenty-five years."

"Can you describe him for me?" The men looked at each other. Either Dixon looked a lot younger than his age or—

"He's a tall man—maybe five foot, eight or nine. He's about sixty years old, I think. He's black. Sometimes I used to watch his dog Chi-Chi when he would go out of town on business. That was a good dog. It was a mix of poodle and something else. Smart as a whip. Chi-Chi was about a foot tall and lived ten years. He was white with a brown patch—"

"Mrs. McCoy, could we stick to Mr. Mason, please?"

"Of course. Mr. Mason is a good neighbor. Except when he has those pool parties. They can get a little loud and he always has this big bunch of men there. They are continually yelling and screaming. You'd think they never saw a swimming pool in their lives. Mr. Mason calls them his 'crew' or something. Sometimes Mr. Colòn calls the police, but that only happens when the fighting starts."

Lou looked at Hank. He shook his head slightly. "Do you know where he works?"

"Who? Mr. Colòn?"

"No, Mrs. McCoy. We're talking about Dixon Mason, remember?"

"Yes, I remember. He works for the community college. He used to be a slot machine designer at Honshu Games." This was a new bit of knowledge for Decker—useless, but new. "Mr. Mason says anyone who plays the slots is a sucker. He says with all the new computer chips the machines have, they can tell when you are going to quit because they've taken all your change and then the machine lets you win for a while to keep you there and goad you on."

Lou took out the picture of Dixon that Dave had given him.

Mrs. McCoy asked, "Who is this? It isn't Mr. Mason. That's a young, white boy!"

"We know that. Can you recall ever seeing him?"

"It's hard to tell. His face seems to be melting into those rocks." She squinted down her thin nose. "No, I don't think so."

"Thank you, Mrs. McCoy. You've been very helpful."

"Glad to be a good citizen." She looked at Hank and Logan and said sternly, "Now you boys should respect your boss here and do what he says. Don't get trigger happy."

They could hear Mrs. McCoy humming "Bad Boys" as they left.

Logan just looked confused and asked Lou, "What was that all about?"

"That is real police work, Logan. We meet a lot more Mrs. McCoys than John Dillingers."

Logan just grinned. "Where to next?"

"The neighbor on the other side of Mason." Lou led the way out to the dusty sidewalk.

As they approached the house, they saw a rail-thin man with bleached white hair and a big "US Coast Guard" tattoo on his bare back above a canoe holding celebrants waving tomahawks. He was squatting while watering a scrawny tomato plant. He had a boombox on his porch, along with a two-liter bottle of Faygo Orange. An old Led Zeppelin tune played. When he saw the three men approaching, he stood up, took a deep drag on his cigarette, flicked it to the curb, and greeted them. "You must be the police from LA. Are you vice?"

"Vice?" Lou was a bit perplexed. "No, we're investigators, not police. I'm Lou Decker. I called the other morning. Are you the gentleman I spoke with?"

"Yes, I'm Joe Blatz."

"Nice to meet you, Mr. Blatz. These are my associates, Mr. Cloud and Mr. Williams."

They all shook hands and Lou continued. "We won't take up much of your time, Mr. Blatz. We're looking into the recent disappearance of a young lady in the Yosemite region."

"Then Mr. Mason is not your man."

Lou chuckled. "You make that sound like a sure thing."

"I think I mentioned on the phone that he runs with a crowd of men, if you get my meaning. If not, I'll state it plainly. Mr. Mason is gay. Normally, he's a very nice fellow and a good neighbor, but his pool parties can occasionally get out of hand."

The men looked into the backyard next door and saw an extensive pool setup complete with several doorless shower stalls, a small cabana, and what looked like a tiki hut.

Blatz continued. "I think Dixon is a teacher at the community college. I know he goes out of town frequently. He told me that he consults with gaming device manufacturers. He seems to get along with everyone around here except Mr. Colòn."

"Who is Mr. Colòn?"

"He's a neighbor. He lives directly behind Mason."

"Okay."

"Mr. Colòn is pretty old and a bit of a curmudgeon. I don't think he sees very well. I know that he calls the police to report gunfire at Mason's pool parties. These guys just like their firecrackers."

Lou then showed Blatz the picture of Dixon. "Do you know this man?"

Blatz took the photo and squinted at it. "Can't say that I do."

"Have you ever seen him around here?"

"Not that I could say for sure, but I don't think so."

"How about at Mason's parties?"

"Mr. Decker, I don't swim with those fish." Blatz looked offended and turned back to his tomato plant.

Logan piped in. "Mr. Blatz, do I know you *from TV?*"

"If you watched my old TV show, you might." He squinted and bent to light another cigarette.

Logan stared at the man's face. The he burst out, "I do know you. You're the Gray Hopper!" This was a character on a kid's show in LA from the late nineties. The actor wore a gray rabbit suit with a cutout for the face and would hop onto the set at various points in the program to cite a proverb or give a word of warning to the characters.

"I was." Blatz laughed. "But that was a long time ago." His eyes had a faraway look.

Logan began to sing "Hopper's Theme," which closed out every episode as the character hopped frantically about. "Listen to the Hopper, you little scamps."

Blatz joined in. "Unless you want to turn into tramps."

And they finished the tune with the final raspberry. "Blatzzzz."

They all laughed, though Hank looked incredulous. "Who was the artist behind that musical gem?"

"Some nitwit who worked for the production company. Actually, I think it was the producer's nephew."

Lou thanked Mr. Blatz for his assistance. They all shook hands and the investigators headed back to the car. Logan asked, "Any more stops? Mr. Colòn?"

Lou said, "No, I really just wanted to get an eye on these people. Things seem pretty straightforward. I think I've about worn El Cajon out from an information standpoint. Our Dixon is not here."

"I once had a girlfriend from El Cajon," Logan offered.

"Another day," Lou responded.

Chapter 42

SPEED RACER

The drive back to Los Angeles began pleasantly enough. They headed north over of the mountains, along a twisting, two-lane highway. The road was nearly deserted, until they encountered a young driver who seemed determined to race them down the mountain. He drove a candy apple red Camaro with a tuned exhaust. They heard him coming in the distance, long before he began to ride their bumper. The man would pull up beside them and rev his engine then race ahead. He would then fall back behind the Hummer, tailgate while revving his engine again, and repeat the process. This went on for about five minutes before Hank turned to Lou and laughed, "Should I bump this halfwit off the road?"

"Naw. Logan, roll down that window." Lou pointed to the left rear window. He pulled out his cred wallet, and as the young man pulled up alongside the Hummer yet again, Lou leaned over the seat and pointed to his badge. He opened his mouth to yell at the man when a bright flash sliced through the space between the cars, accompanied by the loud screech of tires as the would-be racer threw on his brakes.

The young man's car slid to a stop on the shoulder.

Hank gasped when he saw light lingering from the flash. "What did you do, Lou?"

"Nothing. You saw that flash?"

There was total quiet in the car for a moment. Then Logan asked, "What was that?"

Hank glanced at Lou, who was staring straight ahead. "Your guess is as good as mine."

"Never mind. Probably just the sun's reflection. How far is LA?" Hank changed the subject.

Forty-five minutes later on the drive back to Los Angeles, a CHP patrol car came up alongside them near the exit for I-15. The trooper stared into the Hummer and flashed his lightbar. Getting Hank's attention, he indicated that Hank should pull off into a rest area just ahead.

When Hank stopped, the trooper pulled up alongside and exited his cruiser. He walked up to Hank's open window. "Sir, do you recall seeing a red Camaro a while back?"

Hank answered, "Yes, sir."

"Did you make a threatening gesture at the driver."

Hank looked at Lou, who opened his mouth to speak.

Before Lou could answer, the trooper broke into a wry grin. "I didn't think so. We got a call from a burner phone earlier reporting this. The driver wouldn't give his name and hung up quickly, but not quickly enough. We pinged his location and sent a car already in the area to check it out." The trooper took off his sunglasses and pushed his hat back on his head. "May I see some ID, sir?"

Hank extricated his driver's license and handed it to the trooper. Meanwhile, Lou reached across Hank and handed the policeman his cred wallet. The trooper looked at Lou's card closely and handed it back. "Thank you, Detective." He took Hank's license back to his car and could be seen writing and speaking on the radio.

After a minute, he came back to the Hummer and handed Hank's license back. "Sorry about the inconvenience, gentlemen."

He went on to detail some of the events surrounding the apprehension of the racer. "Our guy spotted a red Camaro driving recklessly at a high rate of speed down the mountain. He appeared to be racing a Mercedes. The trooper lit up his lights and gave pursuit. At this point, the Camaro bumped the Mercedes, sending it spinning off the road. The Mercedes hit a guardrail that kept it from flying down the side of the mountain. No one was injured, but our trooper radioed for backup and two deputies set up a roadblock a few miles ahead. They stopped the Camaro, and it turns out the driver was a parolee from Lompoc in possession of a firearm. He also had a description of your vehicle and the plate number on a piece of paper. Looks like strike three for this fella. We suspect him of being involved in several street racing incidents, one with fatalities. He was hysterical when we took him into custody. He maintained that he was fleeing from your car and not racing anyone, although why after forty-five minutes and a phone call was unclear. He described your car as a gray Hummer. As you can see, your Hummer is green, so we think he saw your car and made up the whole story. I've canceled the BOLO on your vehicle, but I thought you might be interested just in case you get stopped. Have a nice day, gentlemen."

The trooper chuckled, threw a salute, and drove away.

Logan called Sam to see if he was back to normal again. He was surprised to hear Dave's panicked voice on the other end. "Hey, Logan."

"Dave, everything okay? Just called to see how Sam is feeling."

"I can't wake him up. I've called 911 and my parents. I can't talk, Logan. The ambulance should be here any minute."

"Wait. What? What happened? He has a pulse and he's breathing, right?"

"Yeah. He is just asleep and won't wake up. Gotta go. The ambulance is pulling up."

"Okay, I'll see you at the hospital. UCLA Med Center, right?"

"Right. See you there." Dave hung up and bent over Sam's bed to shake him again. "Sam, wake up! Can you hear me? Wake up!" There was no response from the sleeping twin.

Dave heard an ambulance in the distance. Its siren wailed as it approached. For Dave, it was a strange feeling, knowing for whom the ambulance bell tolled.

Chapter 43

ERASING PERSONAL HISTORY

Buckley lay in bed, breathing in and exhaling slowly to slow his pounding pulse. He'd been dreaming once again of the worst night in his life.

It was a fraternity party with Gwendolyn, his fiancée. In the dream, Buckley had just handed her a capsule. It was the first time that either had ever tried drugs. They'd been drinking from the party keg liberally throughout the evening and when a fraternity brother offered them the mescaline caps, Gwen laughingly said, "Sure. Why not?" Buckley had laughed too, but he was anxious. Not too sure about this. At the last moment, he palmed his capsule, only pretending to swallow it as Gwen threw her head back and downed hers. A few moments later, a strange, frightened look came over her face. "Buck, I don't feel right. My throat is closing. I can't breathe." She began to gasp and fell to the floor.

Buckley's door flew open, and Dolph was standing there. Buckley said, "It's all right, Dolph. It was just a nightmare. I'm okay."

"Yes, sir." Dolph excused himself and backed out, closing the door.

Buckley lay there, his bed sheets and pillow saturated with sweat. His terror was easing, but he still felt nauseous. At least this time he had been able to wake himself before the dream's inevitable climax. Tonight, he was not forced to stare down into the darkness of her grave before falling in and tumbling for an eternity through the icy blackness until he awoke.

Gwen was the one true love of Buckley's life. They'd planned to marry after graduation and raise a family. He knew in his mind that her death was not his fault. She had taken the capsule herself, voluntarily, eagerly even. But in his heart, he knew he should never have taken her to that party in the first place. In his eyes, this made him culpable.

Shortly after her death, the recurrent dreams began. Sometimes he'd be able to wake himself before the ending, like he did tonight. Other times he'd cradle her head in his arms, crying and fighting the satanic appearing ambulance drivers who came to steal her away and toss her body into the pit. Many nights he would yell out, "Gwen! Gwen!" waking and frightening his household.

After a month back at home in New York after graduation, his family, fearing for his safety, took him to counseling. Buckley had taken a job in a fast food restaurant and seemed to have lost all ambition. He was being eaten up with guilt over the death. His family wanted to relieve Benjamin's guilt and hopefully end the night terrors; however, in this way, they inadvertently set him on the dark path. Unknown to them, the counselor who Buckley was seeing was a closet occultist. Rather than help Buckley, she played mind games with him and encouraged him to look to the spirit world for help. Buckley found himself warming to Ms. White when her treatment seemed to prove efficacious. As the frequency of his nightmares lessened, he found himself opening up to her about other areas of his life. In this manner, she nourished a growing dependence in Buckley. Gradually she introduced him to the idea that pursuing occult power was a natural, and even admirable, pursuit for any man. She told him that he must expunge any memories of personal guilt and erase his personal history. She discouraged his use of alcohol on the grounds that it destroyed one's self-discipline, focus, and clarity of mind. After about six months, she judged him "ready for the next step" but did not explain.

At the next session, Buckley found the conversation turning to drugs and their use in shamanistic practices. Initially he was put off by this, but as she spoke, he became intrigued and asked, "How do you know about all these things, Ms. White? I thought drugs were for partying."

"I have a wide range of experiences and learning that you yet know nothing about, Benjamin, as well as certain *skills.*" She added this last under her breath. She gave him a coy smile as she said it. Leaning across the desk, the therapist looked deeply into Buckley's eyes and touched him on the forehead as if brushing away a stray strand of hair. "In fact, a few friends and I are getting together tonight at my place to discuss some of these things." Buckley felt a stirring. He had not been out with any woman since Gwen's death. "Would you like to come?"

Benjamin Buckley looked at her. *She isn't much older than me, and she really is quite pretty.* "Yeah, I'd like that."

"Great. My house about nine o'clock." She took a business card from its holder and wrote her home address on the back. "Don't eat dinner. A friend is preparing a meal. He's a gourmet chef and I'm sure that you'll appreciate it."

Chapter 44

GUEST OF HONOR

Buckley spent the next few hours shopping for new clothes to wear to the party and readying himself for the evening. He bought a small bouquet of flowers and a bottle of wine as gifts for the hostess. Ms. White had described her home was an old farmstead located on the outskirts of town. Rows of unharvested corn from the prior season stood around it. Behind the house, he saw very tall, old, oak trees towering over it. The paint on the house was peeling, and the windows were darkened. There was a large, screened-in porch attached to the front of the house. He mounted the front steps and noted three wicker rockers, a broken Adirondack chair holding a scythe across the arms, and a spear leaning against the wall. A clock chimed inside as he reached for the doorbell.

The therapist opened the door and greeted him with a big smile. "Come in, Benjamin. We're just about ready to eat."

He could hear Santana's "Soul Sacrifice" playing on a music system, and the haze and aroma of marijuana were pervasive.

He handed her the wine and flowers. "Thanks for having me here tonight, Ms. White."

She giggled, and the sound was like a ringing crystal. "Call me Willow. Ms. White lives at the office."

Benjamin smiled. "Okay. Willow." *What a beautiful name. How appropriate for such a lovely woman. I don't remember that being the name on her card.* Her long, blonde hair rolled down over the shoulders of her white gown. She plucked one of the flowers from the bouquet and put it in her hair. She examined the wine bottle. "Charles Shaw, one of my favorites. We can serve this with dinner. It'll go great with the stew!"

A giant, Germanic-looking man took Buckley's jacket. She turned and led Buckley into the large living room where several people sat laughing and engaged in conversation. One older, bearded man was doing a spastic jig not quite in time with the music.

Willow had just finished introducing Buckley to all present when a tall, pale man stuck his head into the room. "Dinner is served!"

At this, Buckley was almost run down by people rushing toward the dining area. Buckley entered, and Willow took him by the elbow and steered him over to the chef.

"Cashwell, this is Benjamin Buckley. He's the young prospect I was telling you about, and my date for the night." She giggled and pointed to the flower in her hair. "Benjamin, this is Bryan Cashwell. He'll be your facilitator. He is tonight's chef, and my dear friend."

Cashwell gave a sweeping bow then stood erect and shook Buckley's hand warmly. "You are a lucky young man to have our Willow bestow her favor on you as benefactor."

Buckley smiled and blushed slightly. *Facilitator? Benefactor?* The therapist showed Benjamin to the seat on her left. He noticed that the old man who had been "dancing" was sitting across the table while grinning and staring at him with an open mouth. Buckley thought he heard the man mumble, "Yes, oh yes, I think he'll do fine."

Willow heard this and looked hard at the old man. "Stop that now, Lloyd. Use your manners. No ogling."

The old man quickly shut his mouth and looked away downcast.

Buckley's eyes reflected his puzzlement. He leaned over to Willow. "What did you mean 'prospect'?"

She narrowed her eyes. "I said 'project,' not 'prospect.'"

Buckley's inclination was to challenge this, but he decided she probably just misspoke and he let it slide. *Anyway, I don't know if I prefer "project" to "prospect."*

Cashwell stood and raised his wine glass. "Ladies and gentlemen, in honor of our guest, neophyte Benjamin Buckley, let me propose a toast." All present stood. "May he find power wherever it lies, and gather it till the day he dies."

"Hear, hear," resounded throughout the room. They all drank.

Benjamin thought this an odd toast.

The room cheered and Willow elbowed Benjamin in the ribs. "You need to respond with a toast to acknowledge your facilitator."

"Oh." Buckley felt slightly dizzy after his drink, but he stood to his feet, drink in hand. *I don't know any toasts.*

Willow pinched him on the buttocks. He yelped, and everyone laughed. Buckley blurted out, "Live long and prosper!" Everyone cheered raucously and drank. He stumbled back down into his seat.

Benjamin's memory of the meal was that it consisted solely of a well-seasoned stew served with a large chunk of crusty bread. The stew was not bad, but it was an alarming red color and the meat had a gamey taste. It had a lot of onions, garlic, and peppers, which made it barely palatable, but he'd never consider this fine dining. Buckley noted whole medium-sized mushrooms of a variety he had never seen floating in the concoction. He contented himself with one serving, while most of the others had several helpings.

After the meal, Cashwell stood and announced, "As is customary at our initiation dinners, we will dispense with the dessert. The devil's cake shall remain in the oven."

Surprisingly to Benjamin, no one laughed at this *joke,* except him. He thought that Cashwell had left out the word "food" after "devil's" intentionally as some sort of pun.

"Gentlemen, to the parlor for cigars and brandy." Buckley swayed slightly when he stood up, and it appeared that two Cashwells took him, one by each arm to lead him out. The Cashwells sat Buckley in an overstuffed chair near the center of the room. Before sitting him down, Cashwell took a white, hooded robe from a wall rack and draped it over Buckley's shoulders. Buckley looked around the room and saw that the other men had put on similar robes, but each was colored black. They sat on stools encircling Buckley. His curiosity grew as he looked around.

The valet assisted Cashwell in putting on his red gown. As he lit two black candles, everyone pulled up their hoods. Buckley moved his arm to do likewise when a strong hand grasped him and prevented this. He looked to see the gray-bearded man holding his arm. He was dressed in a patchwork cloak with tiny bells sewn onto the fringes. Incongruously, he also wore an LA Angels baseball cap. The bearded man then moved nimbly about the room passing out cigars and tin cups with a sharp-tasting beverage. He then sprinted around the circle, lighting the cigars for the men. Buckley was given an unlit cigar and the old man pantomimed holding it up in front of his face. As he did this, Buckley was assaulted by an overpowering smoky aroma. He coughed repeatedly.

Cashwell began to read from a very old book he held. Benjamin was having trouble following the narration. From time to time, the room would respond with a drawn out "Be it so."

When he finished reading, Buckley's cigar was lit and Cashwell told him, "Smoke now and receive the peculiar knowledge." Buckley took a deep drag and immediately had the feeling that he was no longer in his body. He moved at great speed above a barren, dim, greenish plane toward a bright-yellow light. He stopped in front of the light and saw he was in the presence of an odd-shaped, glowing cactus. Its crown was shaped like an artichoke, but Buckley saw a face with large luminous eyes. Buckley heard a voice in his mind.

"Well, it took you a long time to get here! Did you come of your own volition? Do you seek knowledge and power?" The plant cackled hysterically.

Buckley was confused. He mumbled, "Yes, I think so." He saw a tendril reach out to him and wrap around his left forearm. It burned wickedly at the site, and just before he could yell, he was back in his chair, fully awake. He now wore a black robe with the hood covering his head. He was given a large mug of a cool, greenish drink. *Limeade?*

He heard Cashwell. "Brother Buckley is back." Cashwell rolled the sleeve of Buckley's robe back and yelled, "He is now one of us! He is destined for greatness in our ranks! Let us drink in celebration!"

The room cheered, and everyone drank the brew. Buckley enjoyed the taste of this drink after all the weird smells and tastes of the evening. He looked up to see Willow enter the room. She was wearing an outfit that made him think of Salome's from the Bible or of Barbara Eden's genie costume. Music filled the room. She began a gyrating and flowing dance while circling him. Buckley couldn't take his eyes off her. She leaned over him and touched his face.

As the dance continued, Buckley felt a powerful urge to kiss her. He stood up drunkenly and staggered about the room in pursuit. The beat and pace of the music intensified as Buckley chased the woman. Finally catching her, Buckley reached out and slapped her with the back of his hand, knocking Willow to the floor. For some reason, he was angry. Why had she tried to evade him? The music stopped and the room erupted in cheers. He was feeling very groggy now.

Willow stood back up and slapped Buckley hard. He was startled by this, and after a few seconds, they both began laughing. She then took his right hand. In one quick movement she drew an obsidian blade from somewhere in her clothing and ran it across the palm of his left hand. She sucked the wound and smiled. She led him through a door into a chamber that looked like an *Arabian Nights* dream. He stumbled along, unable to speak. A tingling crept upward from his hand. She caressed him and whispered something in his ear, which he could not understand. This was the last thing he remembered of the evening.

He awoke suddenly, in the dark. Buckley heard a cock crowing outside the window. Next to him, the bed was empty. Disoriented, he got up, reached around until he found his clothes, and dressed. He saw light from under the door and wandered out to the dining area. Willow and Cashwell sat at breakfast. Willow drank her tea and glanced up at Benjamin as Cashwell munched a plate of pancakes. "Good morning, Buckley," he said.

"Good morning, Mr. Cashwell. Good morning, Willow."

Willow did not look up at him.

Cashwell continued. "Welcome to the family."

Buckley then saw the bruise on the side of Willow's face.

"You *were* a bit rough with her," Cashwell said with a smile and chuckle.

In the light, Buckley now saw the cause of the stinging on his left forearm. It was a brand in the shape of a three-pronged pitchfork—a trident.

Cashwell pulled up the sleeve of his robe and Willow's to reveal identical marks. "Family emblem," Cashwell said.

Buckley looked closely at his left palm and saw only a thin line from the laceration. It was almost fully healed. He looked questioningly at the pair.

Cashwell waved him off. "All in good time. We can talk after breakfast. Now you must eat. You need to recover your strength." Cashwell saw the look of concern on Benjamin's face and laughed. "Don't worry. They're only pancakes, and the syrup is unadulterated, good old Aunt Jemima."

Buckley sat down. Willow went into the kitchen and brought back in a stack of pancakes for Benjamin. "Thank you, Willow."

Cashwell said, "Ms. White was your benefactor. You might call her your recruiter. I am your facilitator. Now you'll be in my hands as you learn the ways of the family."

Benjamin was as famished as he was confused. So he attacked the one problem he could solve. He ate the stack of pancakes eagerly and drank a large mug of black coffee.

He pushed back from the table and looked at Willow. "Ahhhh, that was really good! Thank you, Willow."

Willow looked at Buckley and hissed.

Cashwell said, "At this time, you're not allowed to speak to her."

"What? Why?"

"It is the way of the family. Eventually, you two will resume your normal friendship, but now you must wait."

"For what?"

"To see if the seed takes root."

Buckley was confused. Then he remembered last night. "Oh."

"Don't take it so seriously, son. We've all gone through this. It is the way things have always been done."

The thought of all the other men in the group having been with Willow bothered Buckley, but not as much as he thought it might. In fact, he was noticing a creeping indifference to her.

Cashwell read his thoughts. "She was your recruiter. She is very skilled at this and virtually impossible to resist. Don't beat yourself up. Soon you'll accumulate enough personal power to see your Gwendolyn again. Wouldn't you like that?"

Buckley looked up eagerly at Cashwell. That was exactly what he wanted. He'd do anything to see Gwen again.

"Let's take a walk." Cashwell pushed away from the table.

They walked out the rear door toward the woods and Cashwell indicated a path through the trees. "Buckley, you were quite slow to get moving, but you found your ally more quickly than anyone I've ever initiated. Did he give you his name?"

"I-I don't know. I'm not sure. I can't remember."

"That's okay for now. Your tattoo indicates that he has attached himself to you and will be there to assist you in your journey for the rest of your earthly life." Cashwell saw the doubt in Buckley's expression. He pointed at a young tree and indicated that Buckley should look there. "It's *all* about power." Cashwell mumbled a few words Buckley could not understand, and the tree burst into flames. Buckley gawked at Cashwell. "I doubted too, but my facilitator was more reserved. He would've never shown himself this early in my training."

Buckley looked quizzically at Cashwell. "This 'training'— will it be more than starting forest fires?"

Cashwell laughed loudly. "Wait and see."

Chapter 45

NO ONE EXPECTS THE INQUISITION

Arriving back in Los Angeles Sunday afternoon, Lou, Hank, and Logan went directly to the hospital, where they found Dave. His sister, Dani, sat on the edge of Sam's bed while wearing a sad expression. The Maxwell parents stood near the bed anxiously. Mr. Maxwell looked away and chewed his lip. Mrs. Maxwell wrung her hands.

"What did the doctors say, Dave?" Logan asked.

"They haven't found any reason for this. They didn't see any structural damage on the CT, and there is no detectable infection."

"Is this related to Sam's earlier injury?"

Dave answered, "The neurologist doesn't think so, but he doesn't have an answer either."

Mr. Maxwell said, "They are continuing to run tests and observe him. He's scheduled for an MRI in about a half hour. And so far, his toxicology screen was negative."

"Sam told me he had a headache when he said he wasn't coming to camp, but he made it sound like it was no big deal. I got the impression that he was planning on going downtown with you."

"Well, he was up for a little while yesterday morning but went back to bed. He said he wasn't feeling well and stayed in bed most of the day. He was asleep this morning when I left to run errands. When I got back to the apartment, he was still sleeping and I couldn't wake him up."

Dave introduced Lou and Hank to his sister and parents. There was a bit of uneasiness as Dave's parents were obviously very worried about Sam.

Mr. Maxwell walked over to Lou and Hank and quietly asked, "May I speak with you two out in the hall for a moment, please?"

The three men left the room. Mr. Maxwell looked Lou in the eye and asked directly, "Why are you two here in LA? I understand that you're an investigator." He turned to Hank. "And you are some kind of psychic *commando.* You aren't encouraging my sons to play junior detective, are you?"

Lou looked levelly at Mr. Maxwell. "I was a detective. Your sons *asked* us to come out here to help try to locate a missing girl."

"Toni? I told them to give that up a month ago, right after Sam was first injured. The police and FBI haven't been able to find her. What do you two hope to accomplish? Are you getting a free vacation out of this? Now the newspapers speculate she was the victim of a human trafficker. And why is Dave sneaking around the Saturn Building project anyway?"

Hank moved toward Mr. Maxwell. "Mr. Maxwell, We pay our own way. We are not encouraging *anyone* to play detective, and if you have an issue with Dave's actions, he's an adult. I suggest you take it up with him."

Hank's phone rang, and he turned his back on Lou and Mr. Maxwell to answer it.

Mr. Maxwell walked back into Sam's hospital room.

Hank put his phone on speaker and gave a wave to Lou. "It's the CHP, Lou."

"And we found that some of the information Trooper Smith gave you was incorrect. The young man taken into custody was a Felix Hernandez. He *is* a third-strike parolee with a firearm, but then the story gets interesting. Shortly after taking Hernandez into custody, CHP troopers observed a different car on the same road engaged in a race. This car was a red Corvette, not a Camaro. We learned under questioning that the driver of this vehicle was actually the man we had been after. Meanwhile, the man who accosted you remains in custody. He continues to be agitated and keeps talking about a 'white light creature' coming after him. Our psychiatrist on duty thinks Hernandez believes he's telling the truth. We also checked on his Camaro and found it to be a rental. Hernandez was then given a mild sedative, but he still stuck with his story. However, he did give us more information. He said that his boss hired him to run you off the road and if you weren't killed, well, he was given the gun to finish the job, though he denied any intention of using it."

"His boss? Who is he?" Hank clenched the phone tightly.

"Yeah, we don't get it either. We did a little background on you and understand that you live in Minnesota. We saw you and a Detective Decker had a run-in with a church in Michigan last year. I see you two flew out together. Do you know why someone might put a contract out on you? Particularly, out here in California?"

Lou and Hank looked at each other. "No idea. You mentioned his boss. Where does Hernandez work?"

"He's a line technician for Saturn Communications. We found the Camaro was rented on a Saturn credit card, so we talked to the man's boss and he denies knowing anything about this. He says that he can't see why Hernandez would even have a Saturn credit card and suggested we speak with Saturn's legal department on Monday. Do you know anyone who works for Saturn that might have a beef with you?"

"Not really," Lou cut in. He glossed over his experience of reporting this corporation to the FBI but omitted any mention of supernatural occurrences. "I know Saturn was on the Bureau's radar, but that's it."

"Hmmm. That's odd." The officer paused for a bit and sounds of a keyboard clicking came through the phone. "The FBI has Saturn on a watch list, but access to their file is restricted."

Hank looked at Lou and mouthed, "Damage control?"

"Well, you boys need to keep a weather eye out for anyone who might have a long memory. We'll let you know if we turn up any information that suggests you are still in danger. Have a nice day, gentlemen."

They hung up and Lou and Hank reentered Sam's hospital room.

Lou walked over to Mr. Maxwell. "It was nice to meet you folks. We hope this is all clears up quickly with Sam. We'll be praying for him."

Mr. Maxwell dropped his eyes. "Thank you. I apologize for coming on so strong."

"It's okay. Not an issue. I understand you're concerned about your family. We're going to go now and get some dinner. We had a long drive today. Good night."

They all said goodbye, and as Lou and Hank walked out, Dave called, "Wait up." He turned to his parents. "I haven't eaten since breakfast so I'm going too. I'll be back in about an hour." He didn't see the questioning look his dad gave him.

Logan followed Dave. "Same here, but I won't be back. Good night, Mr. and Mrs. Maxwell."

In the car, Logan said, "Dave, your dad is really upset."

"He's just worried about this whole—whatever it is. He'll calm down soon enough."

"Well, this trip has been all business for you two so far." Logan indicated Lou and Hank. "Why don't we eat at a genuine Hollywood tourist restaurant?"

Dave looked over at Logan. "You have something in mind, don't you? The Hawthorne Grill?"

"The Hawthorne Grill is now an auto parts store. No, that's out."

"I don't know if the Magic Castle is open to the public on Sunday night, but it's an interesting place. Let's try there. If it isn't open, or we can't get in, it's only minutes from Hollywood Boulevard and I'm sure we can find something touristy there."

"Sounds good."

Traffic was light, and they arrived at the Magic Castle to find that it was booked for a special members-only event.

The valet laughed as he looked into Hank's window. "When you turned in, I thought you might be Arnold driving up in that Hummer." When he saw how the occupants of the vehicle were dressed, he added, "Coat and tie only, gentlemen."

So they then drove to Hollywood Boulevard and parked in the basement of the shopping and entertainment complex at Highland. Wandering through the property, Lou and Hank were amazed at the décor. It seemed to be themed in a "Hollywood-Babylonian" motif complete with gigantic statues of winged lions and other fantastic creatures. Hank looked at Lou.

Lou was staring at a giant, gaudily painted obelisk. "I see why they call Hollywood the dream factory."

"I know. If I had a robe, I'd feel like an extra in a Cecil B. DeMille movie."

Chapter 46

SHABU-SHABU AND THE WALK OF FAME

They found an Asian restaurant on the third floor and entered. Looking around, Hank balked and then smiled. He spied a pot of boiling water in the center of each table, and having been deployed overseas, he suspected that this was some exotic form of cooking; he was correct. Each customer would order raw meat and vegetable portions from the menu and then cook them in the hot water. It proved an unusual, but not unpleasant, dining experience for the midwesterners.

Logan kept saying "shuba" and laughing. He said this was the Asian name for the type of cooking and you were supposed to say it every time you dipped a piece of meat or the meat would go bad.

"You're making that up!" Dave fumbled with a piece of cubed beef as it slipped from his amateur chopstick work.

"Only the last part."

Dave waved the waiter over to their table. "What does *shuba* mean?"

"It's *shabu-shabu*. It means 'swish-swish.' It's how we cook here." He mimicked the motion of picking up a morsel with chopsticks and swishing it in the pot.

Lou had a seat opposite Hank along the outside wall of the restaurant. He had a nice view of the street below and watched the passers-by stop and look at the metallic stars anchored in the sidewalk. "Hank, at your four o'clock, see the man staring at the Paul Muni star."

Hank waited about five seconds then turned and scanned the sidewalk. He looked back across the table. "Do you mean the bushy-bearded man bending over and polishing the star with his shirtsleeve? He must be a real fan."

Lou glanced down. "Yeah, that's him. But he's up now dancing a jig on the star."

"What about him?"

"He's been there since we sat down."

Hank looked at his watch. "About twenty-five minutes now?"

"Sounds right."

"Okay, what about him? He looks like your typical Hollywood derelict to me. Maybe he's a Muni relative."

Lou chuckled. "He's been looking up here at us every so often. Every time I look in his direction, he looks away and does something bizarre like you just saw."

"He's probably hungry," Logan observed.

"Maybe so, but think. How did Hernandez know where we'd be today?"

"Who is Hernandez?" asked Logan.

"What does this goofy guy have to do with our road trip?" asked Hank.

Lou set his chopsticks on the side of the plate. "You're probably right. I'm thinking like a detective again. He probably just has a crush on you, Hank. Ha ha."

Lou then told the boys about the conversation with the CHP officer at the hospital. They all ate quietly.

After dinner they sat sipping green tea. Hank said, "Sorry. I prefer coffee. Although the boiled meat didn't sound very appetizing, it was a surprisingly good meal. But I've drunk enough tea in my life to fill a swimming pool. No more, please.

Dave puckered at the bitter taste of his tea, setting the steaming cup down in front of him. "Tell us about your road trip. How is Mr. Adamson, and why did you guys head down to El Cajon anyway?"

Lou described yesterday's events at camp. "Mr. Adamson was in the hospital when we left. From what I understand, they expect a full recovery, but it's too early to be sure."

Lou described his earlier interview with Deputy Hennessey. "I was wondering if Hennessey might have tipped off Hernandez, but I'm still confused about how Hernandez would know where we would be."

"What we know of Saturn's capabilities makes me think their tracking someone might not be difficult at all." Hank had his cell phone in hand. He held it up to Lou. "Here, look at this." On screen was a web page listing Adventure Car Rentals as a subsidiary of Saturn Industries, Ltd.

Lou looked up. "So they could be tracking us. I can see that if they wanted to know where we are, it wouldn't be difficult. We need to think about getting a new ride ASAP."

"Let's park this one at the hotel and not turn it in yet."

"Agreed."

Dave then described his morning at the Saturn Building. He was reticent at first, skipping over the "unusual" things, but Logan called him on it.

"Dave, you said that you'd give the full story. If you don't, I will."

Dave looked down and began again. This time, he was interrupted frequently by questions from the two men. It surprised him that they didn't think he was embellishing his story and that they accepted his description of the events and characters involved as fact.

Lou asked first about the solar panels and the plants being taken into the building. "It doesn't sound like they were bringing in plants as desk decorations. With multiple electrical feeds to each floor from the roof, it seems to me that they plan on engaging in an urban farming venture. You gentlemen are scientists. Can you come up with a figure for how much power their solar array might generate, how much wattage grow lights would use, and so on?"

"It isn't that simple. The electrical output of the solar array depends on the particular panels. I don't know. Maybe they have access to an advanced high-output technology."

"Okay, but *if* we need to take this to the FBI, it would be best if we were prepared with some figures."

"Logan and I can work on it."

"Good."

Hank focused on Dave with his voice serious. "Dave, how do you think the man at the Saturn Building was able to change his appearance so completely and so quickly?"

"I don't know how he did it. The first time I thought *I* must have lost track of time and he just quickly changed clothes. But then he was instantaneously again in his business suit when he crossed the street going back to his car. I just don't know."

"And the Asian. Are you sure it was him?"

"Yes, he had the same features on a Chinese face; however, he was at least a foot shorter. And the snake appeared to have the man's voice too, but I'd thrown the toy into the garbage can on the street and I saw his car was gone so he was gone too, wasn't he?" Conflict creased his brow.

Logan asked, "What did he look like as himself—you know, the businessman?"

"Tall, pale, balding. He looked strong but wiry, not a bodybuilder type."

"That sounds like Cashwell," Hank observed.

"Yes," agreed Logan. "So Cashwell is how Buckley ties into Saturn?"

"Maybe." Lou rested his forearms on the table and looked at Dave. "We need to know more about Buckley. Dave, how are you doing with all of this?"

Dave gnawed his lower lip as he considered the question. "Okay, I guess. It's pretty strange, but it *is* interesting."

They finished and walked downstairs to Hollywood Boulevard. Lou looked about but did not see the wild-looking tramp anywhere. They walked up the street toward the Chinese Theatre, checking out the Walk of Fame stars as they went. Ernest Torrance was the first star.

"Who is he, Logan?" asked Hank.

"Beats me." Everyone shook his head. The next star was Monty Hall. *"Let's Make a Deal!"* yelled Logan.

Then Joanne Woodward. "I think she was Steve McQueen's wife," Logan said.

"No," corrected Lou, "Mrs. Paul Newman."

They continued, looking at well-known names like Burt Lancaster and Groucho Marx and the not-so-well-known such as Mabel Normand.

Then there were the just plain strange, like Vince McMahon and Kermit the Frog.

Eventually, they reached the Chinese Theatre, where they viewed the handprints and signatures. Lou and Hank walked about looking at the impression made by Morgan Freeman. They were surprised to see the same weird man squatting over an open spot while drawing with chalk on the cement. Security guards came out from the theater. As they did, the man took off running into a souvenir shop across the street. Dave and Logan had just entered the store in search of bottled water.

Lou wandered over to the drawing and called Hank over. "Hey, look at this." Lou laughed. There was a chalk drawing of a man with a guitar and the name "Rock Rollins." The drawing was remarkably sophisticated, to the point it resembled a photograph. "Our boy Rock has some talented fans."

Just then a loud yell came from the store and the wild man burst out the door with Dave and Logan in hot pursuit. "Stop! Thief!" Logan yelled. The bearded buffoon pumped his arms crazily as he rushed directly into the path of a city bus. The driver slammed on the brakes, but it was too late. The impact made a dull crunching sound as it knocked the man twenty feet onto the trunk of a parked car. Dave was the first to reach the victim and immediately saw he was dead.

Dave took a wallet out of the dead man's hand just before police officers came up and asked him what happened.

Dave looked at the policeman. "We saw him get hit by the bus and came to see if we could help."

One of the cops looked at Dave, "Weren't you yelling at him?"

Logan quickly said, "No, it was that guy." He turned and pointed. No one was there. Then Logan scratched his head and acted as if he were trying to find someone.

Hank and Lou had arrived at this point to hear the policeman say, "Okay, we'll take it from here. Thanks for your help, gentlemen."

As they headed back to the car, Hank asked, "Why were you chasing him?"

"He stole my wallet. Just walked up behind me, reached around, and grabbed it out of my hand when I was paying for my water."

Lou asked, "Did he take anything?"

Dave held the wallet and was looking through it. "No, I don't think so. Wait. This wasn't in there before." Dave pulled out a sheet of paper that was folded in with his bills. It had writing on it. He held it up to the streetlight. "'Back off! We know who you are.'"

Chapter 47

LIGHTS! CAMERA!

The next morning, in spite of the usual beautiful sunshine, Dave drove to work in a foul mood. He thought about the threatening note from last night and decided that while Toni's fate was still unknown, that was not really his concern. It now appeared that his fruitless intervention in this problem had put his life in danger, and to what end? *The road to hell is paved with good intentions. Time to get back to reality—whatever that means. I don't have time for being chased by giant rattlesnakes or other hallucinations, and now it looks like I'll be teaching Sam's classes through the end of the semester. What if he doesn't wake up?* But Dave didn't want to go there. And losing Lanie before their relationship even had time to blossom hurt him deeply. Dave had felt that real love had been possible with her.

Since Sam's recent turn, Dave felt absolutely alone. This was something he had never experienced. It wasn't like going somewhere by himself physically, more like he felt alone in the universe—in a deep spiritual void without the connection to his brother. *Maybe Sam has been right. Maybe we are connected in deeper ways than other people.* Dave heard a voice in his mind then. "I will never leave you, nor forsake you." Dave had memorized this scripture long ago. But if he was honest, lately he hadn't given any real attention to his spiritual life. It was time for that to change. He pulled to the side of the road and bowed his head. As he prayed a confession of this indifference, a peace settled over him and he thanked the Lord for His faithfulness.

*   *   *

Logan, on the other hand, was up to his neck in this whole mystery. He was finding purpose in a belief that he might make a difference in whether Toni lived or died—not really believing her dead. He was not yet willing to accept Hank's assertion that she had been murdered. *I need to see some physical proof before I give up on her.* But Hank's information had been correct so far, and Logan once again considered the stone knife tip. Logan recalled something he had heard about missing people. Was it something he'd heard online, something Scott Nash said, or something he had read somewhere? What he recalled was that Yosemite is historically an epicenter for disappearances as well as alleged UFO activity. He decided to go to the UCLA University Library to see what he could turn up in the old newspaper files.

Logan had accrued vacation and personal time so he called work to take off the entire week. His supervisor liked Logan and would normally bend over backward to accommodate him. This time though, Logan sensed resistance. "Williams, you can't just take a week off without arranging it in advance. You know we're in the middle of a make or break program."

"Mr. Bundy, I'm entitled to ten personal paid days off per year in addition to a three-week vacation by my contract. I haven't taken a personal day off in two years, and I need this time." He paused, but the man didn't respond. "There are important, personal things I have to take care of *right now.* I just can't put them on hold any longer."

"No need to get dramatic with me, son. You're aware we have a demonstration of the Sprite analytic system scheduled next Monday with several big-money clients. We need all hands-on-deck until then. Besides, Logan, you should also remember that your contract states that you are an *at will* employee."

Is he threatening to fire me? "Mr. Bundy, my section in the Sprite program was finished three months ago. It's bug free and has operated perfectly since testing began. I really need this time." Deciding not to push any harder, Logan made a strategic retreat. "Three days, Mr. Bundy. I'll come in Thursday and Friday to go over my part of the Sprite program. Again."

Mr. Bundy reluctantly agreed. "Okay. Don't leave town. Make sure my assistant has a current phone number so we can reach you if we have a problem."

Hearing this last comment, Logan was already in the process of hanging up before Bundy could change his mind. "Yes, sir. Thank you, sir."

"Logan, you're not using this time off chasing after that dead girl, are you? I've heard—"

Logan clicked off.

*   *   *

Lanie walked to the window of her apartment. The view was magnificent. In the distance, she could see downtown, LAX, Santa Monica, and beyond that, the ocean. "What did I do to deserve this?" She finished fixing her hair for the third time and set down her brush, half satisfied.

There was a soft knock on her door, and she opened it.

Dolph stood there. "Are you ready, ma'am?"

"Just a second, Dolph." She walked back to her bedside table and picked up her mobile phone. "I'll be out in a moment."

"Yes, ma'am." Dolph turned and went back to the car.

Lanie sat on the edge of the bed and started to dial Dave. She dialed five digits and stopped. *What am I doing? I'm at the biggest moment of my life and here I'm having second thoughts. I've got to take control and make these decisions myself.* She put the phone in her purse and went out to the car.

Lanie didn't want to betray her ignorance of the movie world to Dolph, as she knew he had Buckley's ear, so she sat quietly in the back seat as he drove. In her nervousness, she struggled not to speak. When he headed west on Sunset, she could no longer resist the urge. "Where are we going? Isn't the studio in the other direction?"

"Today we go to the beach, ma'am. Boss's orders."

Lanie was surprised. "The beach?"

"Yes, ma'am."

"I thought we were going to start shooting today, and please don't call me ma'am. You're older than I am."

"Yes, ma'am. I'd guess there are some scenes to be shot at the beach."

"Oh." This puzzled her.

"And yes, Ms. Becca, I am older than you—quite a bit older."

Dolph's deep chuckle rumbled through the limo.

Chapter 48

LIGHT MY FIRE

They lapsed into silence until the ride ended near the Santa Monica Pier. She got out and Dolph showed her to a new trailer in a cordoned off area. The door read, "Ms. Becca Tramell," and below that, "No Entry." Lanie noted that someone had stenciled in a pink trident above her name.

"Do I wait in here, Dolph?"

"I have *no* idea. *You* are the actress, Ms. Tramell." Dolph laughed, again with a deep rumble, and walked away.

Lanie opened the door and entered, gazing around her trailer. The table was arranged with a vase of roses, a bottle of champagne, and a note. She picked up the note and opened it. There was one handwritten line—"Do What Thou Will"—with a scripted California . as signature. Lanie felt a chill when she read this.

She set the note down and continued to explore the trailer. A small refrigerator was filled with fruit, snacks, and cold drinks. There was a small living area with a couch, two comfy chairs, and a big-screen TV on the wall. She had just entered the small bedroom when a soft knock startled her. She heard the outer door open, and a voice called to her, "Ms. Tramell, hello?"

Lanie walked into the living area to see a young woman's head sticking in.

"Hello?" Lanie responded.

"Hi. I'm Tanya Gates. The prince has assigned me as your personal assistant."

"Nice to meet you, Tanya."

"You too. What would you like me to call you?"

"Lanie is fine."

Tanya gave her a strange look. "Excuse me?"

Realizing what she said, Lanie backtracked quickly. "Sorry. That's what my dad and friends used to call me. They said I looked just like Lanie Kazan when I was a kid. Becca would be great." *I've got to be more careful.* "I guess I'll need today's shooting schedule and script."

"I have the schedule right here." Tanya waved a piece of paper. She stepped in and set the schedule down on the table. "No lines today, but I can get you a script if you'd like."

Lanie shook her head. "No, don't bother. Guess I'll be doing stunt work, eh?"

Tanya laughed. "I hardly think so. It's my job to see that you get the next day's schedule each night by 6 p.m., but today's different. I'll put a copy of changes and revisions under your door every morning. Today you have costuming and makeup at 2 p.m. On set at 4 p.m. There is only one scene with you today. Right now, they are filming a scene with Mr. Rollins. I hear it's not going very quickly—or very well."

"Rollins? Rock Rollins the singer?"

Tanya again gave Lanie another odd look. "Of course."

"I never knew he was an actor."

"He's not. In my opinion, he's not much of a singer either."

"Well, I didn't know he was *in* this movie." Lanie took the schedule from Tanya and scanned it, turning it over to read the backside as well.

"Originally, *Nero* was going to be a musical, you know, like *Hair* or *Cats*. The prince hired Rock Rollins to write the score. Well, Rock came up with a couple decent songs. Then Rock decided that he should be Nero and began lobbying the director. Rock was so persistent that Sir Geoffrey—he's the director—was on the verge of firing him."

Lanie looked back at the girl, again not wanting to seem out of the loop but wondering who this "prince" person was. "How did Rollins take that?"

"Not very well. He started a fistfight with Sir Geoffrey in the dining commons. Rock banged up the old man pretty well. Broke his nose before Brennan—he's Nero—stepped in and tossed him out the door."

Lanie giggled nervously.

"The prince didn't think it was funny. It set production back nearly a week."

"Who is this prince you keep mentioning? Prince the singer? Isn't he dead?"

Tanya laughed. "Yes, he is." Then a look of disbelief and fear came over Tanya. "You really don't know?"

"No, I don't. Mr. Buckley hired me. He's not the prince, is he?"

"Becca, Mr. Buckley is a beard—a face. Although I don't think he knows it. Most of them don't. The prince is *the boss*. He is the prince of California, the most powerful of the thirteen princes of North America. I'm surprised that you've gotten this far without knowing him or even knowing about him." Tanya changed the mood abruptly. "You are very *pretty*." Tanya reached over and pushed a strand of Lanie's hair to the side. She opened up a concealed door on a side table and took out a bottle of rum and two glasses.

Lanie was surprised. "No thanks. I'm not thirsty."

Tanya shrugged her shoulders. She put the items back. Lanie saw a change flicker over her assistant. *I must be going nuts. Did I just see her face change?* "Tanya, I need to rest. Come get me at two o'clock, please." Lanie opened the door for Tanya to exit. At that moment, an unearthly scream filled the air and a figure ran down the beach, his back aflame and diving into the ocean.

Tanya grinned. "I think that was Rollins. I wouldn't count on any filming today."

* * *

In spite of Tanya's dire prediction, the show must go on. Later that same afternoon, costuming took five minutes as the designer took a look at Lanie then handed her a tiny bikini and the rest of a harem suit. She swallowed hard as she held out her costume while looking at it.

Makeup was a different story. She was in the chair for nearly an hour as a young man fiddled with her hair. After cutting, teasing, curling,

229

combing, and spraying, he spent another half hour trying to perfect her skin tone. He tried shade after shade of makeup, most of which were indistinguishable to Lanie.

When he was finished, Lanie looked in the mirror. "I think we've got it now," the man said.

Lanie gazed with awe at herself. She felt beautiful for the first time in a long while. *This guy knows his stuff.* "Thank you."

"You're quite welcome. Sorry it took so long. Next time should be a snap."

"What's your name?'

"Krupa."

"Thank you, Mr. Krupa."

"No, just Krupa."

Shooting continued in the absence of Rock Rollins, who had been taken to a nearby hospital with partial thickness burns over his neck, back, and arms. In fact, the director seemed downright jovial as he spoke to Lanie prior to filming. "Okay, Ms. Tramell, just face the camera and dance for about thirty seconds—and please don't mug or be too obvious. Add a hint of mystery. When you see me raise my arm, stop, put on a look of alarm, and begin to run toward the white van over in the parking lot. You'll get used to my methods quickly. Don't expect micromanagement. I normally give my actors minimal direction."

"Do you mean that white van with the Saturn logo on the side?"

"Yes, that *is* the white one. To continue, you probably will not see him, but Brennan will approach you from behind on horseback. He will ride past on your left, and as he does, he'll sweep you up and carry you off into the sunset. I mean, *literally* he will carry you west into the ocean. Somewhere over there." He pointed out toward the water.

This concerned Lanie as she could see six-foot waves breaking just short of the beach.

"Okay." Lanie was having second thoughts about this. "Sir Geoffrey, I've never danced on camera before. What am I supposed to do?"

The director shook his head and looked skyward. "Ay-yi-yi. Wiggle your hips, girl. All women can dance. It's in your DNA. Think about Ali Baba or something Oriental, and just let it *f-l-o-w*."

Lanie stood there fighting her rising panic and frustration and seconds later heard Sir Geoffrey yell, "Action!" She stood frozen in place. She looked at the people watching her and saw Tanya and Dolph. Tanya was laughing and pantomiming a hip-swinging belly dance to encourage Lanie to loosen up. She saw the words "Move it!" form on her lips, and Lanie began a jerky writhing twirl that ended in a hard fall.

Tanya rushed up and helped brush the sand from her face.

"Cut! Cut! Ms. Tramell, loosen up. We're not filming the zombie apocalypse here. Try to at least remain upright."

Lanie began to laugh before realizing he was dead serious. She tried to think of an Asian tune, but all she could come up with was the old snake charmer music from cartoon shows.

"Take two. Action!"

Lanie began a slow, gyrating dance while thinking of a swami playing a flute and a cobra rising from a wicker basket. She thought back to the lissome Brigid Mary Bazlen dancing for Peter Ustinov in the old movie *King of Kings*. Lanie made it twenty seconds before she began to laugh hysterically and lose her rhythm.

"Cut! Cut! Take five, everyone."

Sir Geoffrey walked over to Lanie and put his arm around her shoulder. "Ms. Tramell, or whatever your real name is, I've been in this business long enough to know that you're no actress, and it is plain you're no dancer either, but I never bite the hand that feeds me. I don't know why Mr. Buckley insists that you're the female lead in this music video, but that's good enough for me. With today's special effects and editing techniques, I can make you look like Katharine Hepburn, *but* you have to give me something to work with. I *will* have a decent product, regardless of having to include Rock Rollins. And if we have to do this scene seventy more times, we will. It's up to you. Close your eyes and try to relax. Let the music in, and let it move you. Shall we try once more?"

Lanie closed her eyes and began to relax as the music played. She almost enjoyed the process.

Three takes later, she heard the horseman approaching as she ran. He scooped her up effortlessly and rode hard into the water, where he carefully let her down as a wave blasted her.

The director called, "Cut! Excellent! Or at least good enough."

Lanie's first day of shooting ended.

Chapter 49

GOOD OLD-FASHIONED RESEARCH

Logan arrived at UCLA's Jung research library and went directly to the reference desk. The clerk was a pretty, young woman and just finishing her conversation with an elderly professorial type who was obviously happy with her. He smiled and walked away toward the book stacks. "If you can't find the original manuscript, Dr. Bazyl, come back and I'll help you. I've seen it in there."

He called out a heavily accented, "Thank you, Jane," and walked away.

The young lady at the desk's name tag identified her as "Jane Guff— Reference Librarian." She said, "Good afternoon, sir. How may I help you?"

"Hello. I need information on disappearances in the Yosemite Valley area over the past, say, fifty years. How can I find this efficiently?"

"Then you are not looking at the disappearance of a particular person?"

"No. I'm trying to check out an idea that Yosemite has been a hot spot for disappearances, missing persons, and UFO sightings." Heat reddened Logan's cheeks as he heard his own words.

"Oh, you want UFO abductions?" Ms. Guff tried hard to suppress a creeping grin. "You might be better served at the Cal Tech library. I hear that they keep secret *X-Files* type information stored in their basement. Here. I can give you the secret password." She took a piece of note paper and picked up her pen.

Logan reached out and covered the paper. "No, I'm interested in missing persons—not UFOs. Can you help me or not?"

Ms. Guff broke into a laugh. "I'm sorry, Mr.—"

"Williams. Logan Williams."

"Working here can be pretty boring, Mr. Williams. I get about one laugh per month. Yes, I can and will help you. What you'll need to do is a topical newspaper search. We have an extensive collection of old California newspapers on microfilm, paper, and computer; some date back into the late 1700s. You should be able to find several papers from that region dating back at least to 1900. Most should be in English. I presume you've already contacted the law enforcement agencies for that area?"

Logan was caught up short by the question. "Yes, I have been in touch with the authorities for quite some time—without much cooperation."

Ms. Guff had risen from her chair and moved off in the direction of the computer bank. She typed in search parameters "Newspaper articles. Yosemite region. Missing persons. 1970 to present." The computer immediately filled the screen with references. She hit print on the keyboard and a nearby printer spit out a list of articles meeting the search criteria.

The librarian took the list and scanned it, marking many of the articles with an "M." and others with the letter "P." "There, Mr. Williams, that should get you started. I marked certain articles with an 'M' if they are on microfilm. The ones with a 'P' are only in the original paper copies of the newspaper. We are entering all of the articles into the computer system, but as you can imagine, it's a slow process and with funding being continually cut, well, you know how that goes. Come by my desk later and let me know how you did, or come by anytime if you need help."

Logan sensed a slight blush with her last words. "Thank you very much, Ms. Guff."

"You're welcome. One more thing. I recall listening to a man on a talk show speaking about this very subject. I think he was writing a book, but his attempts to get information from the National Park Service were met with a surprising amount of resistance. I'll let you know if I can remember his name."

"Great. Thanks again."

Ms. Guff smiled and walked back to her desk. Logan headed off toward the periodicals section. Logan had used microfilm readers occasionally during his undergraduate studies so he was already familiar with the process of hunting for the films and using the machine, but he wasn't prepared for what he discovered. He decided to save the newspaper searches for later and to ask Ms. Guff whether he could access the library resources from home when he had finished with the microfilm.

Logan located a film labeled *Yosemite Pioneer Gazette 1972* and searched for the article referenced. He found it quickly and read.

> Fourteen-year-old Diana Wilbanks disappeared last Tuesday while on a camping trip with her family in the foothills of the Yosemite mountains. She had been sitting at a campfire when she decided to go to bed for the night. In the morning when her parents went to her tent to rouse her, it was apparent that she had not slept in her bedroll as it was still tied up. Local law enforcement has been conducting an investigation into this troubling disappearance but so far have not turned up any leads.

Logan looked up and considered the story. *Not much detail, but the basics are there.*

He decided to move on to a second story, also in the *Yosemite Pioneer Gazette.* This one was from the summer of 1973.

> Willa Gentry, a sixteen-year-old girl vacationing with her parents at the Hoof and Mane Dude Ranch, was reported missing Saturday afternoon. She was last seen walking from the chow hall toward the horse barn with a newly hired stable boy. Willa is an accomplished equestrian, having won the Nebraska State Junior Dressage Championship three years in a row. The stable boy told the police he helped her saddle up her mare and then went to the employees' lounge. His alibi has been corroborated by other employees. The mare was found in a nearby pasture grazing near a tree.

The story went on for two more paragraphs before concluding, "Police have no leads in this recent disappearance. The public is encouraged to report any information to the authorities or the Gazette Crime Stoppers' Hotline."

Logan went on through twenty-five similar stories from the area around Camp Sequoia—about one per year. After a time, he realized with some surprise that he had only reached 1998. Some of these disappearances involved boys, but those generally differed in that the family or group was engaged in some activity such as a hike. Most of the girls, either singly or in small groups, simply walked out of their family environment never to be seen again. Six disappearances actually occurred at church camps. Logan was using a map of the Yosemite area from his backpack, marking the spot and a few details of each disappearance in black magic marker.

As he analyzed the map, it became clear the area involved covered about four hundred square miles of rugged territory. This was only about twenty miles in each direction, with the epicenter near Camp Sequoia.

A few of the stories mentioned weird lights or other supposedly otherworldly accompaniments, but for the most part, the persons involved just vanished. One of the stories even postulated that these children were the victims of occult human sacrifice. Logan steepled his fingers and considered this.

Then, shaking his head, he remembered the obsidian blade fragment and all the odd things that had happened recently.

After three hours of looking at old newspaper articles, Logan decided it was time to quit. He was exhausted mentally and physically. His back ached and his eyes were tired. He was also hungry. This somber reading was depressing work and a bit unnerving.

He passed by the reference desk and noticed a different librarian now working. She had gray hair tied up in a bun and was humming to herself. He decided to skip asking about computer access and head over to Panchito's Tex-Mex down the block. A chimichanga would sure hit the spot.

As he exited through the library door, he heard a voice call from behind, "Mr. Williams!" and turned to see Ms. Guff. "Were you able to find any useful information?" She smiled.

"Yes. Thank you. It wasn't fun, but I now believe the stories of all these people vanishing may form a pattern."

"Say, that's it—the name of the book I mentioned. *Vanished.* I still don't remember the author, but I think his first name is David—or Derek. In any case, call me in a day or two and I'll try to have his name for you."

"Thank you. You are very kind. I can also try to look it up online."

Jane Guff smiled shyly. "I'd still like to know what you come up with." She took out her card and handed it to Logan, then turned to walk away. On the back was her handwritten cell phone number.

Chapter 50

THE PRINCE OF CALIFORNIA

The prince of California drummed his fingers on his desk. His back was to the vista of the mountain dropping away to the city of Los Angeles and the ocean in the distance. He sat in his home office in the Mount Olympus neighborhood of the Hollywood Hills. His was one of the prime spots in this exclusive subdivision. Through the floor to ceiling windows, this home afforded him views of the entire Los Angeles basin. However, the prince had not chosen this location for its natural beauty.

When the celestial rebellion began, the Father curtailed the powers of his disobedient servants. Even the King of Darkness himself had to operate within strict boundaries. One of these restricted the knowledge of events in the material realm to that geographic realm while limiting access to the godly dimensions. In their quest for ultimate power, the demonic forces had knowingly defied the Father, bringing on this punishment. While the lower echelons of the demonic forces may not fully understand or accept their ultimate end, they understand the hatred of life that their master nurtured and his ruthless nature so they toed the line.

The prince of California had once been a powerful lieutenant of the Father but had followed his current master, the great deceiver, in betrayal. Throughout his time on earth, the prince had served this master well, rising through the ranks to his current position of prominence. Unlike many of his predecessors, who knew only destruction, the prince used a combination of guile, persuasion, and force in his work with equal skill. He knew when to reward his minions and when to bring the hammer down. It was this combination of brains and brawn that made him the near equal of the accursed archangel.

But the prince also knew how to hide his ambition. He also understood that Lucifer's plan for the end of man's time on earth would ultimately fail, but he clearly saw his master was mad with and for power. The prince had come to realize early on that any plan to cordon off earth from the rest of God's kingdoms was doomed. The Father's wisdom, goodness, and power were limitless. Since Adam surrendered man's right to dominion over the earth to the serpent for a personal will independent of the Father, the forces of darkness had attempted to eradicate humanity's thirst for God. Lucifer himself failed to recognize this as impossible. The prince recognized that God had placed this longing within each person at birth, and it would come to varying degrees of fruition according to the will of the person and their response to the call of the Holy Spirit.

The prince raged internally as he ruminated on this. He understood that the sacrifice of Jesus Christ alone must ultimately lead to the undoing of all of Lucifer's meticulous plans. He looked across the large oak desk at his visitor and carefully guarded his thoughts.

"Yes, you can inform his highness that our—or I should say *his*—plan for the western United States is proceeding on schedule and without a hitch."

"This is good to hear, my brother. He was not pleased with the failures of his servant Miguel last year."

"You don't need to remind me. I was there. And I shouldn't need to remind you that the enemy was empowered by a full cadre of the adversary's henchmen. We were not to resist them. That was a direct order from our leader." The prince considered that the visitor knew of their reduction of powers when a demon wandered from their territory.

"Of course, of course." The demon looked out the window. Small wisps of smoke issued from his nostrils. He paused several seconds and then continued. "It has come to our attention that two of the humans involved in that fiasco are now operating within your domain and Saturn's activities may be compromised."

"Yes, I am aware that they're here, but Saturn remains a secure operation. I've taken steps to neutralize that adversary who was investigating Saturn. In fact, I'm meeting with my supervisor of the building project, Cashwell, after you leave. It seems he may have overlooked the fact that the twin brothers who are involved follow the cursed way and may require some *counseling*. However, Cashwell has succeeded in driving the one off and the other is incapacitated for the time being."

The guest chuckled at this. "I understand, and I expect you have plans to permanently neutralize these meddlers? You should also remember that our leader might not be so understanding."

The prince looked away out the window. He kept his face expressionless as he burned at this chastening. He knew that a direct attack on, or perhaps even contact with, a Christian without their "invitation" would bring his instant destruction. He wondered whether this visitor was hoping for such a lapse on the prince's part. *Someday soon I will eat this arrogant fool.* He looked back at his visitor and saw he had risen to leave.

"Give my regards to his highness," said the prince.

"I shall. I look forward to your upcoming ceremony and the opening of the great door, which will bring legions of our demonic brotherhood through to unite with prospective human agents. Is everything going smoothly?"

"It is. Our military operative in San Francisco has secured the use of several cargo aircraft to fly in our human cargo."

Each laughed at this, but the prince's eyes did not radiate humor.

"Well then, goodbye, my friend." The emissary vanished.

Friend. The prince smirked.

The prince leaned back in his office chair and steepled his fingers, thinking about the upcoming event. It would be spectacular. Too bad there would be no spectators to appreciate his efforts.

As he sat there considering, the prince heard a knock on the door. "Come in."

Cashwell entered. He made his obeisance to the prince and walked toward the desk. He took in the scene through the window as he walked. "Ahhh, such a beautiful day. Humans love this climate and weather to an extreme, although my lord, I've never understood why."

"I'm not interested in a weather report, Cashwell."

Cashwell, stung by the reproach, flushed. *He's upset about something. I hope it's not me.* Cashwell did not fear many things, but the prince of California was one of them. He'd seen the prince annihilate opponents and deal terribly with those who failed him. It wasn't something he wanted to experience. Cashwell recognized a ruthlessness that both inspired terror and had set his suspicions in motion. California had plans beyond his present station. Cashwell was certain of it and wanted to be part of that move. *In any case, Saturn is still secure. I've dealt with the intruder. And the "lawman."* Cashwell smiled at this. *He will soon be leaving empty-handed.*

"Tell me about Saturn." The prince took a deep breath and appeared to relax. "The whole thing."

"Everything is going well. I assume you've read my report about the intruder this past weekend. He had the mark of a follower of the Way, so I couldn't kill him, but I put the fear into him and he's been neutralized effectively. Other than that, our plans proceed undetected as we bribe or threaten those people in important positions, as appropriate. The public goes on their merry way drinking in our swill and gratefully adopting the rudimentary technology we supply. Those who know of us never question our motives, and the rest choose to worship the purported brilliance of their own scientists."

"You see then how they lack the capacity to look ahead and put two and two together."

"Yes, either the capacity or desire, my lord. Our technological offerings only seem to nurture a sense of lassitude among the general population. At least with respect to societal direction. I remember your program surrounding the introduction of the phrase *the me generation* into the American psyche. It seemed quite ambitious at the time; however, looking around, we can now observe the results everywhere."

Cashwell went on to outline the state of affairs for those areas of Saturn Enterprises for which he was responsible: entertainment, drugs, and music. He detailed the activities at the new regional headquarters and hydroponic drug plant. Here Cashwell described his encounter with Dave Maxwell in self-congratulatory terms.

However, the prince was not to be distracted so easily. "Cashwell, you do know that it was not you who neutralized the Maxwells, don't you?"

Cashwell looked stunned. The prince's tone and his use of the plural *Maxwells* caused Cashwell to tremble. "My lord, I don't know what you mean."

"I mean the *Maxwell* which you rousted is one of a set of identical twins, dunderhead, and he is *not* the one who crashed our party in Yosemite Grove. That brother is currently in the hospital after a visit from one of our human operatives. He will not be capable of interfering with our affairs for the foreseeable future. *This* is what has neutralized the intruder, not your parlor tricks."

The prince turned red as he stared intently at Cashwell, who was now trembling.

"My lord, I don't know what to say." Cashwell was nearing terror at his superior's demeanor.

The prince spun in his chair and looked out the window. "Good. I'm not in the mood for excuses. Tell me about your efforts with the girl."

"The drugs have worked on her and we did receive solid information on the lawman, his cohort, and the, uh, Maxwells from her. Our plan using Buckley's ongoing love for his departed Gwen—"

"Gwendolyn serves in our kingdom as we speak."

"Understood, my prince. I've cultivated the expectation of Gwen's return in Buckley, as you originally suggested. However, he continues to follow an incoherent path of new age garbage mysticism and partial truths from the occult. He truly believes that this Lanie Martin contains Gwen's essence."

"Amazing."

"I know, sir, but this is how these humans are. They persist in what they want to believe in spite of the obvious problems and contradictions. In fact, Buckley has now become so enamored with Lanie's ongoing presence that we've been unable to obtain any new information from her for several days now. However, this shouldn't pose a problem since the lawman is scheduled to leave shortly."

"Make sure he does. And soon." The prince leaned across the desk toward Cashwell. "Are things ready for the ceremony?"

"The sacrificial materials are ready, and the other preparations will soon be finished. The doorway will soon be opened, and human homes provided for a new group of *our* kinfolk. We will tear a hole in the sky!"

California let a smirk spread slowly over his face. "Good."

"Sir, any idea when the Dark Lord will finally show himself to the world and allow us to come out into the open?"

"I assume when he decides the time is right. There are still certain pockets of resistance, Cashwell, as *you* should realize."

"My efforts on *your* behalf shall be redoubled."

"Just get rid of the interlopers."

"It shall be done."

"See to it then. I have other pressing matters."

Cashwell understood his time with the prince was over and got up to leave. As he walked out, the prince was staring out the window. He thought to ask the prince if Alaimo had arranged transportation of the human hosts to the ceremony as promised but decided not to press his luck.

Chapter 51

DINNER AT RUSSO'S

Lou and Hank lounged under an umbrella at their hotel pool. The sun shone strong, raising the temperature into the nineties, but a breeze blew down off the mountain to give them a bit of relief.

Lou looked up at the mountain. "Five-letter word. St. Vitus blank."

"Dance."

"Tarzan's Title. Thirteen letters. Fifth is *g*. Not sure about that one. Twelfth is *k*."

"Dunno. King Gunsmoke?"

"Nope." Lou appeared to be counting. "Only twelve letters. I don't know if we're getting anywhere with this investigation. We've known the girl is dead pretty much since the beginning, and I'm concerned that we're getting these young people mixed in over their heads—especially if they do not recognize the spiritual consequences. Maybe it's time to regroup and see what direction they intend to go. In short, I guess we ought to be thinking about getting home, Hank."

"Guess so. Anything you'd like to do while we are out here?"

"Disneyland."

"Disneyland? Lou, you are kidding, right?"

"No, I've always felt like I was missing something in life because we were never able to go when I was a kid. I'd see Uncle Walt on TV every week and dream about going to his magical park."

"You've been to Disney World, haven't you?"

"Yes, I have. Several times."

"Well."

"It's not the same."

"I know. Okay. Disneyland it is. We can fly home then at the end of the week."

"Sounds good. I'll go online and get us tickets."

"For Disneyland or the airlines?"

"I was thinking Disneyland."

"Okay." Hank laughed.

Just then, Logan called and asked if Hank and Lou were interested in dinner at Russo's with himself and Dave. Hank indicated they were. It was decided that Dave would drive and Lou and Hank would leave the Hummer where it was parked at the hotel. On their way to dinner, the discussion remained light with the midwesterners commenting on California's natural beauty. Hank opined that the area around Yosemite had awed him with Lou feeling that the extreme variability of the climate and landforms was staggering. "I haven't felt an earthquake yet, though I guess I can do without it. By the way, how is your brother, Dave?"

"No change. Still asleep."

When they arrived at the restaurant, Logan asked, "Does this place look familiar to either of you?"

Lou answered, "I don't think so."

Hank replied, "Not really. Should it? But I'm guessing it is a set location for a TV show or movie."

Dave laughed. "Correct! Movies and TV shows, usually procedural dramas. I guess TV cops like the ambience—and food. Or at least I hope so."

After ordering their food, the discussion turned serious. Dave surprised the two men with his declaration that he was opting out of the inquiry.

Hank and Lou looked questioningly at each other, then at their dinner companion. Hank asked, "Why?"

"There is just too much on my plate right now. Teaching Sam's class, Lanie getting involved with those psychos, and the realization that Toni has been dead all this time just makes all this seem like an exercise in futility."

"Okay."

"If the police haven't been able to turn anything up so far—" Dave let that thought hang in the air.

Lou looked levelly at Dave. "I'm not trying to change your mind, and there's no judgment here, but is this you or your dad talking?"

Dave's face showed a flare of pink. "Me!" He raised his voice slightly. "Look. I'm sorry I got you mixed up in this. I'll reimburse you for your trip and expenses."

Lou responded calmly, "If that's how you feel about the investigation, we can understand it. In fact, we were going to tell you tonight that Hank and I are thinking about heading home in a few days. As for the money, I think we've already been over this. We came out here on our own nickel and I, for one, have enjoyed our time with you. Besides, we have one final stop to make before we go."

"Where?"

"Disneyland."

They had just finished their meal when Hank abruptly lowered his head and whispered, "Look who's tending bar."

The other three looked and there, mixing a drink in a silver shaker and grinning at them, was the bushy-haired man who had been hit by the bus the other night.

Dave stared open-mouthed at the man. "That man was dead. He had no pulse."

The bartender was now skipping sideways behind the bar, spinning and twirling his shaker overhead as he went, like an insane flamenco dancer. He came to a stop in front of a big man who stood leaning over the bar with his weight resting on both elbows. The bartender took a long, thin, tubular glass from the rack behind him and slammed his fist down in front of the patron, who jumped in apparent surprise. The customer staggered back about three steps and threw his arms out with a yell. He and the bartender engaged in a brief stare-down that ended suddenly with each laughing uproariously and pounding the other on the back.

Lou's table watched in fascination as the bartender held the shaker high above his head. He gave it one final shake and twisted off the top. Into the glass he carefully poured about a tablespoon of an amber liquid that captured and reflected the room's ambient light, breaking it into brilliant beams.

The patron held his glass high above his head and the bartender began to sing in a surprisingly pleasant voice, "The drink o' Tom Bombadil, such a merry fellow! Amberish the essence is-s-s-s, but oh! She'll make you bellow!"

"Not much of a lyricist," remarked Logan.

The patron downed the drink in one gulp and bent over the bar, pounding the surface with his open hand. The customers on each side of the man stared at him. One, a muscular fellow in a USC football jersey, shouted, "I'll have one of whatever that was!" The bartender had already poured from a number of bottles into his shaker and was at it again.

"No, laddie, this one is already spoken for."

"Hey now, my money's as good as anyone's here!"

The bartender reached across the bar and pinched the footballer's neck. "Save it, me boy. Don't involve yourself in this."

The footballer instantly collapsed, hitting his face on the bar on his way to the floor.

The bartender looked up directly at Lou and sang out, "This one's for our Wyatt Earp. It's gar-on-teed to make him burp." He danced over to Lou's table while spinning and shaking the drink above his head. When he was directly in front of Decker, he bent over and grabbed Logan's glass. He poured the remaining lemonade onto the remains of Logan's prime rib dinner plate.

"Hey!" Logan mopped up the runoff with his napkin as it dripped down onto his lap.

"Hey-Hey. Sorry am I." The man spoke now in a crude imitation of Yoda. "Mr. Detective, a little present from Miguel this is. Remember him, do ye?"

"I don't drink." Lou kept his voice calm and thought back to last year's encounters with Miguel, the demonic force behind the Congregation of Light.

"Sure, ya do. Tell that to Garza."

Hank stood up. He put his hand on Lou's shoulder. "I think it's time for us to leave."

Lou reached over and took Hank's hand off. "Hold on, brother. We haven't had dessert."

Dave gaped up at the bartender. "You're dead. I saw you die."

"Maybe that was *my* identical twin. Ye *do* know about twins, don't ye?"

Logan, sensing evil behind this chaos, had been praying since he first saw the bartender. He looked around and saw many of the diners had now changed appearance and become tall, wraithlike, whitish-blond people. They stared at Logan's table with undisguised malice. Some stood and began to move toward the four.

Logan trembled as he tugged on Lou's sleeve.

He opened his mouth to ask if Lou saw this, but Lou anticipated him. "I see them, Logan."

Hank shifted his position so that his back was to Lou. "Dave and Logan, get between us." The young men knew a fight was imminent.

The swinging door from the kitchen suddenly opened and a tall man wearing a gray robe and sandals stepped into the room. He strode directly up to the bartender. "Greetings, rebel. I don't believe you are scheduled to work here tonight, and you seem to be intent on hassling some of the Father's children."

"Stay out of this, slave. Your master allows us freedom within our domain. They're on our turf now. And what's with that cheesy Hollywood robe? Did you come from a toga party?" This brought general laughter from the bar patrons.

The new arrival began to glow intensely. "Perhaps you would prefer a different look?"

Dave blanched as he recognized the face of the man who had pushed him out of the path of the speeding car a few weeks ago.

"It's time for you gentlemen to leave. I'll handle these creeps, but I don't need distractions or it might get messy." The man drew a glowing sword from somewhere and gave the men a serious look.

The four men headed to the door and left. On the street was the large patron from the bar. He attempted to step in front of the four. However, a second glowing man walked up behind him and gave the man a flick that sent him reeling through the door back into the restaurant.

This second stranger said, "This is not your fight. Go now."

As they walked quickly to the car, they could hear two strong male voices singing praise to God from inside the eatery amid the sound of commotion and fighting.

The drive back to Pasadena was quiet. Each was lost in his thoughts of what just happened. Finally, Logan broke the silence. "Who was that man?" Logan asked.

Dave added, "He wasn't a man, was he?"

Hank and Dave answered simultaneously, "No."

They rode the rest of the way back in silence.

At seven the next morning, Dave received a call from the hospital. Sam was fully awake.

Chapter 52

JUNIOR DETECTIVES

Logan sat at the desk in his home office studying the map he'd marked up at the library. He screwed up his face and shook his head, aghast at the sheer number of disappearances of children and otherwise normal young adults in the Yosemite region over the years. Three even appeared to have occurred on or very near Camp Sequoia property. Why hadn't he ever heard about these at camp? He'd been going there since second grade over twenty years ago. Did Mr. Adamson know about these missing persons? Logan decided to call him and ask. He dialed the pastor's phone number at the camp and was informed that the number was not in service. He then called the hospital where Mr. Adamson had been taken. Logan prayed to calm down his anxiety and try to keep his tone nonconfrontational. He was still shaken by last evening's events.

Logan was put through to Mr. Adamson's room and was surprised to hear his voice, cheerful and light as if nothing had even happened. "Hello?"

"Hello, Pastor Adamson? It's Logan Williams. I'm a bit surprised you're still in the hospital."

"Hi, Logan. I'm just a bit slow in recovering. Getting old, I guess. I lost the use of my left side from the injury, but it's slowly coming back. I can hold a cup of water in my left hand for almost five seconds now." Mr.

Adamson chuckled. "I'm over in the rehab wing and will probably be here for a bit yet."

"Well, I'm certainly glad you're getting it back, and soon, I hope. You had us all scared there. The last time I called the hospital was a few days after the assault, and they said you were still unconscious. Things have just been a bit crazy busy here so I haven't had a chance to call back." Logan was uncomfortable at trying to excuse this bit of negligence.

"No, don't worry about it. Praise God and thanks for everything, Logan. The doctors said if you hadn't found me when you did and gotten me to the hospital, I wouldn't be here today."

"It was the Lord's timing, sir. In any case, I have a couple questions I'd like to ask you if you feel up to it."

"Fire away."

"Are you aware that Toni's is not the first disappearance from the campgrounds?"

This question was met by a long silence. "Hello?" Logan continued.

"No, I don't know. I seem to recall Deacon White speaking of a couple of runaways that happened right before he got there in the late eighties."

"Pastor, I don't think they were runaways."

"How so?"

"I've been doing some research at the UCLA library, and I've found over twenty kids gone missing in the Yosemite area from 1972 till 2000. These are not all runaways, Pastor. Many cases are documented in newspaper reports from the area. I think Toni may have been abducted."

"Well, I think everyone including the FBI has considered that angle, Logan."

"Don't you recall our last conversation before you were assaulted? You knew that the FBI was never involved and that the supposed agent we met, Hogan, was not genuine."

"I'm sorry, son. I really don't remember us having a conversation like that. But my memory is a bit foggy. All I remember is that Agent Hogan came to the camp and investigated, and I remember him taking a rock or something."

Logan was frustrated, but it would be no use badgering Mr. Adamson. He prepared to hang up. "Thank you. If you can think of anything else about this, would you please call me?"

"Sure, if I can remember. It was certainly good to hear from you."

The thought occurred to Logan that he had one untapped resource left, Scott Nash. Would Nash even know about these abductions? He decided there was nothing to lose in making the call.

"Hello, Mr. Nash?"

"Yes. Who is this?"

"It's Logan Williams, sir. You know from Los Angeles. We had dinner the night after."

"Of course, I remember. How are you?"

"Fine. I hope I'm not interrupting anything. If you have a minute, I'd like you ask you a couple questions."

"I'm just watching some wrestling on the tube. Wait a minute and let me pause it." There was the sound of Nash mumbling as he hit the buttons on the controls. "How can I help you?"

"Have you ever heard of missing persons cases in the Yosemite area of California?"

"Yeah, I have. As a matter of fact, a good friend of mine has a series of books on clusters of missing persons in national parks and the like. He noted a large concentration of cases in the Lake Tahoe/Yosemite area. Unfortunately, he's out of the country or I'd put you in touch with him. He's in Turkey—out in the boondocks doing research—but maybe I can help. Go ahead."

"Well, Mr. Nash."

"Call me Scott."

"Okay, Scott. I did some research at UCLA on missing persons in the Yosemite area over the past fifty years and I've detected what I think is a cluster on and near the grounds of Camp Sequoia. It appears to me that these were never linked up by the authorities. We think our camper was abducted and killed, possibly as an occult sacrifice."

Logan then went on to describe their trip to Yosemite, Dave's encounter with the Saturn Snake, the man getting hit by the bus, and the events of last night.

"That's a real mouthful son, but I'm not saying you are wrong. Let's say she was abducted. Are you suggesting that her abduction was part of that cluster—not a singular event?"

"Though I can't prove it yet, yes, I think her abduction was part on an ongoing *operation,* for want of a better word."

"Do you think this operation is an organized human trafficking ring or that something deeper might be involved?"

"Like what?"

"Occult or UFO activity?"

"I'm not sure how to answer that. Both are possibilities, I guess. Personally, I don't think I've seen evidence of either, specifically, but what I saw last night was supernatural, no question."

"I remember you saying that you found a part of a ceremonial blade at the site."

"Yes, but we weren't able to confirm that because the phony FBI agent took it."

"Did you see anything that might serve as a sacrificial altar?"

"An altar? You mean like a giant carved stone?"

"No, no. A pile of medium-sized rocks, each a foot or two in diameter, would be more likely."

"Say, we did notice there were a lot of rocks about that size in the clearing, and as I recall, they were lying on top of the grass as if they had been rolled there recently."

"Sounds like they disassembled their altar. You didn't see any blood on the ground."

"No, not there. There was blood on a stone where Sam had hit his head, and I thought there was blood residue on the piece of blade Dave found. There was also a strong odor in the area. Dave recognized this as old blood from his days hunting with his father, but we dismissed this, thinking it was probably from a hunter."

"Maybe or maybe not. Were there any scorch marks on the grass or deep indentations on the ground?"

"No, why?"

"This area has also been a UFO hot spot, but not in the usual manner. People there primarily report beams of colored light appearing to spring up from the ground before noting vehicles in the sky. I guess we can check our *Fortean Life* records and see if any of the dates when UFO reports were filed correlate to your disappearances. I know investigators have made the case that these disappearances are related to a Project Zebulon supposedly run by the US Air Force. However, there is no solid evidence that such a project exists."

"Okay, but I'm not concerned about UFO abductions here. I'm worried about Toni—and now Lanie."

"I get it, but you do recognize we need to look at this in an organized and comprehensive fashion. And what's this about Lanie?"

"Yes, of course I do. Lanie is now working for the other side."

"As a nurse?"

"No, as an actress in a movie or video or something."

"Hmm. Well, you see that if you don't stay organized, you'll continue to swim around in this morass."

"Okay. Can you please check these dates?" Logan then gave Nash ten dates from his investigation at the library.

"I'll call my office first thing in the morning and have my secretary get on it. But let me continue. We can assume that no one from your group or camp saw any lights on the evening of Toni's disappearance."

"Correct. No one mentioned that."

"So we are down to abduction by persons unknown or that she wandered off by herself at some point and got lost."

"The latter doesn't feel right. We have reliable witnesses who have said she left the camp with a young man."

"Okay. Abduction. For what purpose? We know that the incidence of human trafficking has spiked over the past few years, but it can also be a cover for occult activities.

Logan shuddered as the reality of what they were talking about became heavier and more personal. "What can you tell me about this?"

"We know there are numerous practitioners of the occult on the West Coast. As you might expect, they're found in the greatest numbers around San Francisco, LA, Phoenix, Albuquerque, Las Vegas, and other large metropolitan areas. However, there's also activity in deserted and isolated places like the Mojave, Yosemite, and Sedona. It's speculated that these locations also function as portals for demonic activity tied into UFOs. In short, I guess it's possible that your camper was a victim of one of these groups."

"Then I'm not out of my mind?"

"No, on the contrary. Your concerns and surmises are quite legitimate, at least as far as the Fortean community is concerned. There is one thing though I should warn you about. You can't expect help from the police. They have little patience with alternate worldviews. Furthermore, you might be painting a big target on your back by even looking into this."

"The two demon hunters that you recommended are out here with us and I'm sure they're on board that there is some type of occult activity going on."

Nash laughed. "I don't recall referring to them as 'demon hunters,' but you could do much worse for allies."

"The trouble is we're at a standstill. Dave seems to have lost interest, his brother is in a coma, again, and Hank and Lou are heading back home later this week. I just don't know what to do."

"Well, here's one thing you can count on: the 'bad guys' are not going to announce their presence. First, I'd investigate covertly to determine whom or what you are up against. It seems you already are on that road. Also be careful, son. Their powers are real, and they will not hesitate to use them on you. Have you ever heard of Jack Parsons?"

"I know they celebrate a Jack Parsons Day every year at the Jet Propulsion Lab. I assumed he was a bigwig in rocketry. But more than that—no."

"In fact, the joke is that JPL stands for Jack Parsons Lab. He was the real father of American rocketry. Parsons invented the solid rocket fuel that made rocket engines a reality and kick-started our space program. But enough history. Here's where things might be relevant to you. Jack Parsons was also a high priest in the Ordo Temple Orientis."

"You mean Aleister Crowley's occult organization?"

"The same. His religion, if it can be called such, was called Thelema, and it consisted of the prime dictum 'Do what thou wilt.' The practitioners engaged in many occult and evil activities. Jack Parsons was said to have used these forces in his work. In fact, he and his friend L. Ron Hubbard— you know, the founder of Scientology—performed a ritual called the Babylon Working in the Mojave Desert. This was said to have opened a pathway for demonic spirits to enter our world."

Logan sighed deeply. "Do you think that we saw them at the restaurant?"

"From what you've told me, it's a possibility, but I can't say."

"That's really strange. It seems this activity would've disqualified Parsons from government service of any type."

"Not so, Logan. Officially, he is regarded as a kooky genius, but certain people in government knew exactly what he was. They'll accept assistance from any source. Look at Operation Paperclip."

"I see what you mean. My dad said that until he was well into his adult life, he wasn't even aware that Werner Von Braun had been a Nazi."

"And that's exactly the way the government wanted it. Can you see what I'm driving at here?"

"Not sure, but it looks like you can't rely on the government to do the right thing."

"That's right. Logan, I don't know if anything Parsons did in the occult realm was real or efficacious in *our* world, but that's not the issue. *He* believed it was, and thus, his actions reflect that belief."

"So you're saying that even if there is no 'reality' to occult practice, the idea isn't whether or not I believe it but that they believe it and how strongly."

"Exactly. That's where their power lies, so expect them to act accordingly. Be careful, Logan. These people can be *very* dangerous."

"Okay, got it. Thanks a lot for your help."

"You said Sam is in a coma. Is it related to his earlier injury?"

"The doctors don't know, but they don't think so."

"Okay, give Dave my best. I'll be praying for Sam. And ask Lou to give me a call when you see him."

"All right. Good night." Logan leaned forward in his chair and rested his forehead in his palms. Into what exactly had they gotten themselves?

Lord, help us.

Chapter 53

AN EVENING OUT

Benjamin Buckley knocked softly on Lanie's apartment door. There was a brief interval before a voice called, "Who is it?"

"Ben Buckley." He heard the lock being undone and the door opened. Standing there in a UCLA T-shirt and shorts was Lanie.

"Come in." She moved aside to let him enter. He walked down the short hall to the living room and looked about. The sun was setting out over the Pacific and Lanie was listening to Fleetwood Mac. There was a Coke on the coffee table.

"Have a seat, please. Would you like something to drink? Coke? Something stronger?"

"An ice water would be nice. I don't drink alcohol." Benjamin took a seat on the couch. "That's quite a view. I hope the apartment meets with your approval."

Lanie walked to the kitchen. "It's beautiful. And so is the trailer." She put ice into a glass. "I need to ask you, Mr. Buckley, why me?"

He ignored the question. "I hear there was a little excitement on the set yesterday." Buckley gave a short laugh.

"You must mean Rock Rollins." *Why does Rollins being burned cause Mr. Buckley to laugh?* "I think he's going to be okay. Tanya said there were only minor burns and they can cover anything that shows."

Buckley chuckled again and shook his head. He leaned back in his seat and stretched his arms over his head. "It certainly is a beautiful view." He pointed out toward Santa Monica. The lights on the big Ferris wheel were coming on. "That's the pier near where you were filming today." He wanted to prolong his time with Lanie and worried he was already running out of conversation topics. But suddenly he exclaimed, "Say, are you hungry? Why don't we take a drive to Gladstone's or Duke's over on the water and have a nice seafood dinner?"

Lanie smiled and nodded. Although she was famished, she'd become uncomfortable during today's events and looked at Buckley intently. "That sounds wonderful. But how 'bout if you answer my question first?"

Buckley's mouth turned up at the corners. "Okay, Becca. You remind me of someone with whom I was once very close, and you have her spunk."

"I am not Becca Trammell. Mr. Buckley, you don't know anything about me."

"I've known for a long time who you are—Lanie Martin. You were a nursing student and the daughter of Blazer Martin, the erstwhile UCLA football star."

Lanie realized at some level she wasn't surprised by his knowledge. She persisted. "But why me?"

"Get dressed and I'll tell you over some of the best seafood you'll ever taste. Casual is okay. We can sit outside on the deck by the ocean."

"All right." She nodded slowly. "I'll just need a minute."

"Take all the time you need." Benjamin, sensing her unease, stood and gazed out at the ocean in the distance. "There's no rush." He walked around her apartment, noting the lack of personal items. *Oh well. Sad that she won't have time to make this apartment her own.*

Lanie changed into an appropriate outfit. She touched up her hair and makeup. When she came out, Buckley smiled appreciatively. "Lovely." This time, Lanie did not blush. He opened the door and they headed to the car.

They took Sunset Boulevard down to the Pacific Coast Highway. Buckley had the top down on the Lamborghini but was a considerate driver and both he and Lanie enjoyed the evening drive. They passed Doheny and Buckley said, "Do you remember the old Jan and Dean song 'Dead Man's Curve'?"

"I think I heard my grandma play it a few times."

"Grandma? Geez, I know I'm old enough to be your father, but grandma?"

"I didn't mean it like that."

They both laughed and Buckley continued. "Well, Jan Berry, was one of the singers. He sang about this spot up ahead as the real dead man's curve. Less than a year later, he crashed his Corvette into a parked truck. People like to say that it was here. But I don't know. He wasn't killed, but his career pretty much was. In any case, this road is pretty during the day, but at night, it's dark and twisty, and I need to pay attention and drive safely." He laughed.

They reached Gladstone's and took a wooden booth on the deck. The night was warm, and the sky was clear. Small waves broke rhythmically on the shore. The combination of an ocean breeze and the aroma of fresh cooking stimulated Lanie's appetite. They started off with oysters and lemonades while Lanie gazed to the south to watch air traffic in and out of LAX and the lights on the Santa Monica Pier.

Buckley watched her attentively, then cleared his throat. "When I was in college in the seventies, I was engaged to a girl name Gwen. We were at a fraternity party one weekend and one of my frat brothers offered us mescaline. Gwen was drinking and not thinking straight. She took it. She had a bad reaction to whatever the drug really was and died in my arms. I've never gotten over this. And until you came along, I never saw anyone who reminded me of her. You are her reincarnation in looks and, as I've seen in our limited time together, in behavior." He noticed her gaze begin to narrow. "I don't mean this in a creepy sort of way. Look. I realize I'm too old for you and I'm *not* coming on to you. I just think that we can help each other."

"I don't know, Mr. Buckley."

Buckley laughed. "What is there to know? I will continue to pay you for your work in my projects, and you'll continue to be available to me as company, like tonight."

"That's it? No hanky-panky?"

"Hanky-panky? Ha ha. You're so like her. No. No hanky-panky. Let's just try it out for a while until the time is right."

Right for what?

261

The waiter approached and recognized Buckley. "Good evening, sir. A beautiful night to be here at Gladstone's. Will you and the lady be eating dinner with us?"

"Good evening, Paul. Yes, this is just the warm-up." He swung his hand over the oyster shells. "What would you like, Lanie?"

Lanie was a bit nervous about how to play this. "I don't know what's good. Why don't you order for me?"

Paul looked wide-eyed at Buckley, who shrugged and chuckled. "It's *all* delicious. Why don't we try some caviar and Manhattan clam chowder? Then maybe some crab legs and grilled mahi-mahi. That should get us started."

Paul raised his eyebrows and smiled. "Of course. A fine start it is, Mr. Buckley. It's always good to see you, sir." He turned and walked briskly to the kitchen.

Paul returned a few minutes later with servings of caviar and the soup. After this, they dug into the best crab legs Lanie had ever tasted.

The conversation was light and easy and Lanie was enjoying her mahi-mahi. Buckley told her of his youth and gave her a story about his success as a producer and as CEO of BIE Enterprises. She asked how long he'd known Cashwell.

He coughed in surprise when she asked this and stammered out, "I guess I've known him my entire adult life."

Buckley looked up over her head and she turned to see Cashwell approaching, dressed in what looked like a 1950s-style black tuxedo with a top hat and a cane.

He removed his top hat as he addressed Buckley. He then turned to Lanie and said, "Good evening, Ms. Tramell." Cashwell performed a deep bow, sweeping his top hat in front of himself, but he had the hint of a grin when he greeted her.

"Good evening, Mr. Cashwell."

"May I have a word, sir?"

Buckley stood and said to Lanie, "Excuse me. I'll only be a minute."

They walked over to the railing and talked for several minutes. During this time, Lanie noted Buckley becoming agitated. He made a hand gesture that Cashwell duplicated and walked back to the table.

Her phone beeped and a message came through. She looked at the screen. It was from Logan. "Sam's awake. We need to talk."

By the time Buckley sat down, he was collected and smiling again. "Well, no dessert tonight, Gwen—er, Lanie. But this will give me an excuse to bring you back here. The Key lime pie is incredible." In fact, Buckley raised his hand and spoke briefly with Paul, who brought over a fresh Key lime pie for Lanie to take home. "I'd recommend trying it as soon as you can." He laughed happily. "I hope you enjoyed your meal."

"Thank you very much. It was wonderful. I need to get some sleep anyway—after I have a piece of pie. I need to be on the set tomorrow at 6:00 a.m."

"That's partially why Cashwell came here. We've had some unexpected complications with transportation of our cast and have to straighten this out. We need to push back shooting till tomorrow night. We've rented the Olde Topanga Ranch. It will lend an air of *authenticity* to the climactic scene. Dolph will call for you at 2:00 p.m. Traffic's awful that time of day, so it may take a while to get out to the ranch. However, by all means, do get some sleep. I expect tomorrow will be a late night for everyone. You're free as a bird tomorrow morning. Call this number if you need anything or want transportation anywhere." He typed a number into his phone and Lanie's cell phone beeped. "Again, I apologize, but Dolph will drive you home. Apparently, I need to solve this crisis personally." He chuckled and walked Lanie out to the lot where Dolph stood by the limo. "Thank you for a splendid evening. I'll see you tomorrow."

"Thank you, Mr. Buckley, for the fine meal and good company. Good night."

As she got into the big, black Lincoln, Buckley and Cashwell peeled out of the parking lot in the Lamborghini. Lanie lost sight of the sports car speeding north on the PCH.

Buckley pulled out his mobile phone and dialed. "What do you mean you can only get four planes for tomorrow? General Alaimo, the deal was seven. I don't think the prince is going to be very happy."

Chapter 54

THE BEST-LAID PLANS

The Maxwell parents and Dani had left the hospital. Sam and Dave were planning their next morning when Sam was scheduled for discharge.

Sam sat on the side of his hospital bed as Dave told him of his trip to "investigate" the new Saturn Building. "You *saw* the snake then?"

"Yes."

"So I wasn't hallucinating or dreaming about the camp. I can't wait to see that building,"

Dave was staring out the window. "I'm done with this, Sam. Toni is dead and there's no reason for me to pursue this any further. If the cops aren't interested, they aren't interested and nothing I do will bring her back."

Sam saw something in his brother he had never seen before. "What is it, Dave? Why the sudden change?"

His mouth was pressed in a grim expression. "Lanie is with them now."

"What? How is she *with* them? And who are *them?*"

Dave related Lanie's sudden career change and his suspicions about a connection between the Saturn Corporation, Benjamin Buckley, and Toni's disappearance.

Sam shook his head and, reading his twin, offered, "I can see why you're upset, but this isn't just about Lanie."

"Well, not entirely, I guess."

"Dave, you at least owe me a trip down to the building. It sounds like Saturn is planning to use it as a multilevel hydroponic farm for hard-core narcotics. Brilliant!"

"You know about these things?"

"What? Narcotics or hydroponics?" Sam laughed. "Next to nothing about narcotics, and just the basics about hydroponics. But what else could it be? Solar power, poppies. It's off the grid so no one will notice a spike in electric use."

Dave asked Sam, "What do you remember before you were unconscious?"

"There was a knock on my door. It was about 6 a.m. When I opened it, there was an older, bushy-haired guy wearing a delivery man's outfit and I smelled a very strong cinnamon odor. Come to think of it, he may have blown something in my face. He asked for somebody whose name I didn't recognize, then he turned and left. I went back into the apartment and developed a headache. After a bit, I called Logan. Then I began to feel extremely sleepy. I remember trying to wake up throughout the day, but then nothing, and here I am."

Dave scratched his head. "This is all very strange. Someone must see us as a threat, and I don't doubt that they were trying to kill you. *Why it didn't work* is the question."

"Also, *who would do this* is a question."

"I think I know who. Saturn seems to be involved in all of this—possibly from Toni's disappearance and cover-up to overt criminal activities. I think it's time we speak with Agent Hogan at the FBI."

*   *   *

Lanie called Logan on arriving home. "Hello, Logan? You texted me."

"Lanie, you need to get out of there."

"Why? What do you think is going on?"

"Those people are evil. They are planning something. I can feel it. I know it, Lanie."

"You sound like Scott Nash. Look, Logan. These folks may be a bit eccentric, but they're Hollywood types and you have to expect that. I—"

"Yes, I know what you mean, Lanie. But they're *evil*. They have something planned and it's not for your benefit. I think these guys are all occultists and demonic."

"That's just crazy. I was actually having a nice meal with Benjamin when you texted me."

Now he's Benjamin. "Look, Lanie. Dave was almost killed the other day."

Lanie scoffed. "Don't be dramatic, Logan. How? By whom?"

"By Cashwell."

"Cashwell? Now I know you're nuts."

"I'm serious, Lanie. He—" Logan realized that it might not be the smartest thing to bring up Cashwell's indwelling a toy that transformed into the giant snake, so he stopped.

"Well, I'll say it again. If you're not joking, then you sound crazy. Are you reading those conspiracy magazines again?"

"Lanie, I'm dead serious."

"Logan, I'm going to hang up now. I've got to get some sleep. Tomorrow we wrap up shooting and it's apparently a big deal. Benjamin mentioned he rented the Olde Topanga Ranch and that the 'big boss' was going to stop by. Good night, Logan." She disconnected the call.

"Lanie, wait—" Too late. She was gone.

Chapter 55

A LATE NIGHT CALL

"Hello, Scott, it's Lou Decker. Logan told me you wanted me to call. What's up?"

"Hi, Lou. Thanks for calling. I'm concerned about him. I know you and Hank are there in LA looking into things. I guess I just wanted to get your take on what's been going on."

"Well, we've been here nearly ten days and until the other night, everything we had seen pointed to human trafficking."

"But then—"

"That's when the weirdness began, at least for us. Once again, the Saturn Corporation seems to be involved."

"Tell me about it."

Lou described the oddities of their trip to Yosemite. "When we returned to LA, we had dinner at an open-air restaurant in Hollywood. There was a street person paying way too much attention to us. He followed us, or maybe he anticipated our path to the Chinese Theatre, where he drew an excellent chalk portrait of Rock Rollins, the singer, before being run off by security guards. He then stole Dave's wallet and ran out into the street directly in front of a bus, which hit and *killed* him. He had put a threatening note in Dave's wallet."

"Hmm. I noticed that you pronounced the word 'killed' in an unusual manner."

"Yes, well, the same man showed up at the restaurant a couple nights ago. He was tending bar, mixing up some sort of psychedelic drink for patrons, and came to our table where he offered me one. I guzzled it down in one gulp."

"What? You drank it?"

Decker laughed. He turned the phone's speaker on and placed it on the table where Hank could also hear the exchange. "I'm kidding. Just testing to see if you were listening. No, I refused it. Then things got ugly. The restaurant customers all took on the appearance of alien-looking people who appeared none too friendly."

"Describe them."

"Generally, quite tall, thin, and very pale. Their hair was uniformly whitish blond, and it was clear they were not happy with our presence. Then one of the—er, good guys wandered in from the kitchen. He confronted the bartender and the others, who then began to retreat."

"What did you do then?"

"As our guardian suggested, we left *quickly.*"

"The aliens—did they speak?"

"Not to us. They were speaking to each other. It sounded like a foreign language."

"Did they attack you? Was there any physical contact?"

"No. I think they were going to but were afraid of our guardian."

"Did any of them assume any other shape?"

"Like what?"

"A snake or reptile?"

"Not that I saw." Lou looked quizzically at Hank, who shook his head.

"Scott, what were they?" asked Hank.

"Not sure about the bartender, but the rest go by several names: Nordics, reptilians, snake-men. You were fortunate, I think, that your protector showed up when he did."

"This wasn't our group's first encounter with him. Dave identified him as a man who had saved his life a few weeks back."

"I don't think that he was a man."

"Okay, I'll buy that."

"Was he like the entities you had interaction with back in Michigan?"

"More corporeal, if that's the right way to put it. He looked very solid. Like a man. But for once, I was seeing him close up."

Nash was silent on the phone.

Decker finally asked, "Scott? You still there?"

"Just thinking. It seems that you encountered a race of beings who took exception to your presence on their turf. There was a rumored secret project, code-named Zebulon, which has supposedly been around for many years now. It involved the US government attempting to make contact with an off-world race who had shared technology with the Nazis during World War II. As you know, Operation Paperclip brought a group of Nazi rocket scientists to the US to run our rocket program. The government brought over other Nazis who became integrated into areas of American strategic planning and our security services. I think it's inevitable that Nazi occultism contaminated traditional American thinking. As time passed, some came to believe a decision was made to contact these alien beings on behalf of the US government and offer an exchange for their technology."

"What could *we* offer an advanced race?"

"Some say resources. Some say *people.*"

"Sounds like an *X-Files* story line."

"It does. But as I've said, my job is to report. I don't confirm or deny the story. In any case, I am scheduled to be in Los Angeles over the weekend. How about if we get together? That is, if you are still among the living?"

"Not funny, Scott. I'm not sure we'll still be here, but let us know where you'll be staying, and I'll keep in touch from this end, okay?"

The conversation ended, and Hank looked earnestly at Lou. "The US government, really?"

"You heard him Hank. He admits that he doesn't know if this is real or a fairy tale."

"Well, we know those creatures in the restaurant were real enough."

"Sure, we also know the government doesn't tell the public everything it does."

"I understand that, but I don't want to wind up fighting *against* the US government—*our* government."

"Fair enough. I don't either. It's getting hard to tell the players without a scorecard. We'll have to tread softly here. I think I'll turn in. It's supposed to be over ninety degrees tomorrow, and I'm sure we'll do a lot of walking."

"Good night, Lou." They each went to their bedrooms and Lou dialed Lenore. "Honey, it doesn't look like we'll be home until early next week."

"What's going on now?"

Lou brought her up to date on the recent events and Lenny commented, "Where did we go wrong that big corporations like Saturn can do anything they want without consequences?"

"It seems to me that the basic cause is greed, laziness, and sinful nature in general, but I don't think I'm going to have much support for my position these days."

"Probably not. Hey, you and Hank aren't going to try to take on Saturn, are you?"

"No, we came out here to help find a missing girl and we're sticking to that. In any case, tomorrow is our Disneyland trip so things should be fine, but do pray for us, okay?"

"You know I do, Lou. So does Shelley. Tell Hank hi for me."

"Will do. Good night, Lenny. I love you. I miss you."

Chapter 56

CURIOSITY AND THE SNAKE

It was nearing 2 p.m. when Sam was finally discharged. Once in the car, Dave took out Agent Hogan's business card and handed it to Sam. "Go ahead and call him while I drive. Maybe he can meet us at the Saturn Building."

"What should I say? We need your help checking out a giant snake downtown?"

Dave laughed. "Let's just stick to the drug angle, although I might not get too specific about that. We don't want to get shunted off to another agency like the DEA."

Sam dialed and after several rings was sent to voice mail. "Agent Hogan, this is Dave and Sam Maxwell, and we have some important information for you regarding the case I described to you. Would it be possible to meet us today?" Sam left a return phone number and remarked, "He probably has our number already, but—"

They were nearing the Saturn Building when Sam's cell phone rang. "This is Hogan. I understand that you wish to speak with me about a case?"

"Maybe 'case' is too strong a word. We're grad students at Cal Tech and have some information about illegal activities at the Saturn Building that will interest the Bureau."

"Saturn isn't my case. Can you hold on a minute?" Hogan's line went silent, and Sam waited for nearly five minutes before the agent came back on. "I'm not sure what's going on with Saturn, but I see the Bureau has made inquiries at our national level. I do remember meeting you at the convention a while back, and I'm still waiting for an email from you, Dave." Hogan laughed. "Okay, how about if we meet at the Saturn Building about 4 p.m.?"

"Great, thank you."

"See you then." Hogan hung up.

Sam smiled as he looked at Dave. "Four p.m. at the Saturn Building. We have an hour, so how about an In-N-Out Burger? There's one on Sunset Boulevard right on the way."

"Sounds good. I could use a double-double protein style."

The time was nearing 4 p.m. when they finished their burgers. They pulled up to the Saturn Building behind a black Suburban and when the driver got out, Dave said, "That's Hogan." He rolled down his window and called to the FBI agent, who walked toward their car as they exited.

"Am I seeing double? No, now I remember. Your brother had been injured when I talked to one of you before. For some reason it didn't sink in that you were twins."

"We get that a lot, and I don't recall mentioning it." Dave introduced Sam. They walked over to the empty bus shelter and sat on the bench.

"What is it you want me to see at this building?"

"We believe Saturn is running a drug operation here."

"Go on."

Sam gestured to the building. "We're both science grad students at Cal Tech and noted that there's an unusual electrical distribution system from their high-efficiency solar panels on the roof. There are multiple conductor lines to each floor from about the fifth on up. There is also a system of pipes we believe carry water in large amounts to each floor."

"I'm neither an electrician nor a plumber, but there doesn't seem to be anything illegal about this so far."

"There is if the facility is using a grow-light hydroponic scheme to grow opium poppies."

Hogan took out a handkerchief and wiped his forehead. A small smile played at the corner of his mouth. "Opium poppies?"

"I saw them bringing in truckloads of the young plants." Dave took out his cell phone and showed Hogan several photos he'd taken of the operation. "I was shooed away from the property by their—uh, security."

Hogan lost his smile as he examined the pictures then looked directly at the young men. "This is a serious accusation." He gazed up at the building and was lost in thought for a minute. "Let's take a walk."

They crossed the street and walked along the side of the building to where Dave had peeked in and encountered the snake. The missing and broken boards had been replaced, and looking in through a small slit, they couldn't see any trucks or activity outside. Sam explained the gist of hydroponic growing systems as they walked.

They looked over the fence and Dave pointed out to Hogan the unusual distribution of cables coming down from the roof. He speculated that these powered the fans, pumps, and grow lights. "Honestly, all of this could be done in any location because the solar array takes them off the grid."

Sam chimed in, "A botany professor estimated that a set-up this size could produce over a billion dollars' worth of product per year."

Hogan looked sharply at Dave. "But you don't know for sure. Tell you what. I need to pay a visit to this building. I'll go in and badge the desk clerk. It'll be interesting to see what cooperation I get. I want to thank you two for your assistance."

"Don't you want us to go in with you?" Sam asked.

"No. You have no official standing in this matter. Plus on the outside chance that they decide to play rough, I don't want to have to worry about protecting you."

Dave Maxwell looked away at hearing this. This wasn't what he expected or wanted, and he was ready to argue.

Sam saw him about to speak and took Dave by the arm. "Okay, Agent Hogan. Good luck. Please let us know if we can do anything else." Sam then pulled his brother toward the car as Hogan trotted up to the front entrance to the building. "Get in the car, Dave."

They positioned their car so as to be able to watch Hogan's attempt.

Agent Hogan took out a business card and ripped it in half. He pocketed one half and looked for a mailbox. Hogan took the other half and jammed it up under the bottom of a bar supporting the letter *S* in the building name Saturn and the wall. He then tried the door. It was locked, so Hogan rapped on the door repeatedly until a security guard appeared in the window of the door. The agent flashed his ID, and the guard swung the door open.

Sam and Dave saw the two men speak briefly but could hear nothing. After a moment of conversation, the guard smiled and ushered Hogan into the building. They walked around a corner inside and out of the young men's view.

Dave started the car and Sam turned to him. "What now? Shouldn't we wait till he comes out? The guard didn't seem too concerned with Agent Hogan's visit."

"You heard Hogan. We're done here. Let's get a move on it. The doctors want you to rest. You've got your look at the building and I'd like to get home before dark." Traffic was already becoming congested with rush hour in full swing.

*   *   *

Inside the building, Hogan spoke to the guard. "I've been sent by the Bureau to check into complaints about unsafe working conditions. I thought I'd just stop in informally and clear things up."

The guard, a tall, black-haired man, regarded Hogan with a look of amusement. No Saturn employee or contractor would dare complain about anything—especially with the amount of cash Saturn was paying. And since when did the FBI investigate working conditions? "I'll be glad to take you anywhere in the building, except the executive offices, which contain sensitive proprietary information. However, you must leave your phone and any camera equipment here. If you wish to take them or enter corporate offices, then I'm afraid you'll need a court order before we can proceed."

Hogan took out his phone and laid it on the desk. "No camera other than my phone. I don't think I need any access to the executive offices. Do you?"

The guard shrugged. He had picked up a metal detecting wand and was running it over Hogan. His firearm tripped the sensor, and as Hogan went to remove it, the guard said, "Not necessary. You're good. Shall we proceed?"

"Thanks. I'd like to keep this on friendly terms," Hogan said.

The guard flashed a smile.

The two men walked toward a bank of elevators. The guard pressed a sensor and an elevator door opened. "Where to?"

Hogan answered, "Let's try floors two and three. We can go on from there if I have any concerns."

"Very good." The guard's lips tightened.

The door closed and the elevator rose quickly to the second floor, where the door opened and the men stepped out. "This is an administrative area. Basically, bookkeeping for phone service and cable operations."

The guard followed Hogan as he wound through rows and rows of business cubicles, each having a brand-new desk complete with computer, monitor, and phone. "We're in the process of getting ready to open."

"Doesn't look very dangerous to me."

"I don't think we've had anyone injured yet."

Both men chuckled and reentered the lift.

When the elevator stopped at the third floor, Hogan stuck his head out. "Looks like another admin section."

"That's right."

"Okay. Let's just go up to ten and call it a day."

The guard pushed the close-door button, and they rode up to ten. Hogan did not see the guard's lips tighten.

When they arrived, the door opened and the men stepped out. They were in a short hallway with a heavy, metal door opposite. The guard held his badge to a lighted box and the door swung open. Hogan stepped in and walked about twenty feet. His face tightened as he realized that the Maxwells were spot-on. Each floor appeared to be divided into three levels with steel grating forming a walkway for the upper two. A maze of pipes and wires connected rows of steel tubs holding medium-sized poppy plants on each level. Numerous grow lights and fans were arrayed above each tank.

Hogan stepped forward and turned on the guard who had stopped just inside the door. "This doesn't look like an administrative floor to me. You've got quite an operation going here, kind of like a super FTD."

"Let's drop the theatrics, Agent Hogan." The guard had pulled a small automatic pistol from a pocket and aimed it at Hogan. "Hands above your head. See that bracket behind you on the wall?" Hogan glanced back to see a small bracket below a shelf about twenty-five feet away. The guard fired and the bracket flew from the wall. "Just so you don't get any ideas, Agent."

"Oh, I think I've seen enough," Hogan deadpanned.

"What? You don't want to see all 150 growing levels?" A machine kicked on and the water in the growing tanks started to flow. It had a golden tinge to it. The pump ran for less than a minute then shut down. The next moment, the grow lights snapped on to full brightness, blinding Hogan. He gasped.

The guard said, "Pretty nifty, eh? Fully automated. Minimal maintenance. Maximum profit. We are truly trendsetters here at Saturn."

"What do you figure to take from this?" Hogan trembled slightly.

"We estimate between 1.2 and 1.4 billion, with a *b*, per annum. This is just our prototype. We figure with improved technology the costs should go down and the yields go up. Personally, I think 2 billion isn't unreachable. Multiply that times four facilities in LA, and fifty or more nationwide, and I think you can see why we won't be inviting the FBI in for a tour."

Hogan's vision had cleared somewhat as his eyes struggled to adjust to the light, but he was certain the guard had changed appearance. He was now wearing a business suit and was pale and balding. However, he still had the gun pointed squarely at Hogan.

"You know that if you kill an FBI agent, the whole American law enforcement apparatus will pursue you until—"

"Until when? They get bored or reassigned. I'm not worried, my friend. We have enough juice with the government to shut down any investigation we choose. I'm not sure who or what turned you on to us, but I'm running short on time here. I need to be in the hills for a special event and you know how traffic can be this time of day, so I'll bid you goodbye."

Hogan's eyes widened as he watched the man transform into a large snake. He drew his pistol to fire, but the snake was lightning quick and fastened onto Hogan's gun hand. There was incredible pain and Hogan dropped his weapon. The snake withdrew and struck again, this time biting Hogan on the neck. The effects of the venom were instantaneous. Hogan's vision faded and he gasped for air as his legs struggled to hold him upright. A final bite on Hogan's forehead sealed the deal as the FBI agent collapsed dead on the floor.

The snake's tongue darted in and out as he controlled his hunger and assumed his Cashwell form once again. He scooped the dead man as if Hogan were a newborn baby and walked back to the elevator. When the lift reached the main floor, Cashwell dropped the agent on the ground and pocketed Hogan's cell phone. Then he went into a small alcove where he recovered his briefcase. Cashwell set the alarm and cursed to himself, thinking of this delay. He carried Hogan out the back door of the facility and dumped his body unceremoniously into the Dumpster. Cashwell withdrew and crushed the phone in his hand and tossed it in with the agent. "I'll let our maintenance men dispose of him."

Chapter 57

THE SCOUT

Logan lay on a flat rock overlooking the Olde Topanga Ranch. A crow cawed in the branches of the gnarled Joshua tree that stood above him; however, neither the shadows of the tree nor bird offered relief from the blistering sun. Logan peered through his binoculars at the old western movie set below, his view occasionally obscured by dust kicked up from breezes moving through the valley. He had arrived just prior to dawn to find a scene already alive with activity. Many of the western buildings on the movie ranch had now been fronted by facades depicting imperial Rome, and work continued by riggers and carpenters. Logan thought he could identify the senate forum and a small amphitheater he assumed would become the Colosseum with proper CGI effects. Perspiration soaked his shirt, which stuck to his back as he lay there watching for any sign of Lanie. So far, he had seen none.

Logan rolled over onto his back and stared up at the deep-blue sky. He reached over and picked up a pebble and made a half-hearted toss at the bird. It ruffled its feathers and dropped a load near Logan's head before cawing loudly and lifting off to join three of its brethren flying south. Logan had read in a Carlos Casteneda book that a murder of crows flying south indicated that death was near. A shiver raced down his spine as he recalled this, but the birds suddenly veered eastward. Logan briefly considered asking Hank if this were a general Indian belief or unique to the Yaqui nation of Mexico that Casteneda was living among and studying. *This heat is making me crazy.*

Logan sat up and retrieved the large plastic bottle of water he'd brought with him this morning. He made a sour face when he found only about four ounces of tepid water left. Logan chugged it down and scooted back from the edge of the rock. Logan stood, took off his Dodgers cap, and stretched. He tried to brush the dust from his clothes without much success.

Logan noted a military cargo plane flying low over his head. It disappeared behind the ridgeline bordering the valley to his left. This was the third plane he'd seen this morning execute a similar landing. *Now that's odd. I don't know of any airbase around here, but maybe they are doing some kind of drill. Camp Pendleton is somewhat nearby.*

He needed to get out of the sun for a bit as his surveillance had so far proven a waste of time and the skin on his arms was turning a bright pink. A glance at his watch showed him it was now after two in the afternoon.

He walked the quarter mile to where he'd parked his car along a dirt ranch road and opened the vehicle. A blast of hot air hit him, making him feel like he had stuck his head into an oven. He reached in, inserted his key, and turned on the AC full blast. Logan popped open the trunk and grabbed a bottle of water from the case he stored there for emergencies. It was hot enough to be undrinkable so he put it back. *Well, this seemed like an emergency to me.* He then opened the back windows and sat down alongside the car, trying to find a bit of shade. Ten minutes later, he rechecked the temperature inside his car and found it bearable. He got in and headed for the party store on the road up from the ocean, at the corner of the PCH he'd passed coming in.

He was in luck. It was a Circle K with a variety of beachgoer items for sale. The store even had a shaded area with two picnic tables on the side. He decided to wait here a bit to cool down and have lunch. He went inside the air-conditioned store and purchased a six-pack of ice-cold, bottled water, a small Styrofoam cooler, a bag of ice, a tube of aloe lotion, some sunscreen, a section of plastic tarp, a roll of duct tape, and a cheap beach towel with "UCLA—Home of the Bruins" and a grinning bear printed on it. After stowing this gear in the backseat of his car, he went back in and bought a couple pieces of pizza and a bag of chips. Logan walked over to the Freezie machine and laughed when he saw a photo taped to the dispenser. It showed a vaguely familiar actor bent under the nozzle with the words "No Wheezing the Juice!" scrawled on it. He drew a large frozen Coke and then took his lunch to a picnic table.

The beauty of the view from the tables caught him off-guard. Looking back up to the ridgeline over which he'd come, cultivated green foliage covered the rolling landscape, in marked contrast to the scrub desert where he'd lain all day. To the right and left were homes—many large, some very large, and others gigantic. Downhill he gazed at the deep blue of the ocean. The homes here were built on the hillside to take advantage of this panoramic ocean view. He could see an island miles out from the shore. *Catalina Island?*

He sipped his Coke. Relaxing there, he thought it odd that he'd grown up around Hollywood yet knew so little about how movies were made. *I wonder if* Wanted Dead or Alive *or* The Wild Bunch *was filmed at the ranch back in the day.* He made it a point to look it up online later.

He was walking his trash to the barrel when a limo turning off the PCH sped by. Logan caught a glimpse of Lanie's profile through the half-open back window as the vehicle continued uphill. He dashed to his car and started it. He was ready to patch out in pursuit but realized he wasn't going to confront her so he slowed his pace.

He had time to kill before his friends would arrive as back up, so Logan drove across the ridgeline hoping to appease his curiosity about the aircraft he'd seen. When he reached a vantage point, the airplanes had gone. Large field tents lined a makeshift runway, but instead of military personnel, many civilians wandered in and out of the tents, each dressed in a robe. *Must be extras for the film. But why bring them in military planes?*

Logan drove back to his lookout perch above the ranch, parking about a hundred feet back from his perch. He grabbed the towel and his binoculars and walked to his spot on the outcrop. He spread the towel, lay down, and scoped the ranch. The limo was just pulling onto the property behind the old western buildings. Buckley came out from a trailer nearby, approached the car, opened the rear passenger door, and helped Lanie out. They exchanged smiles and words and walked toward the trailer where an unknown woman opened the door, and they all went inside.

Logan sat up and sat still. *What am I doing here? I feel like a voyeur spying on Lanie. This may be her big break and here I am, relying on hints from a conspiracy writer, trying to ruin it.* The sun was at its highest point in the sky now, and the heat was stifling. He heard a crow caw in the distance down over the forum set and used his binoculars to glance at the area again. Most of the workers from earlier were gone. In fact, the place was almost empty. This time he noticed that between the Colosseum and senate forum sets was a small, roped-off section with a pile of rocks. A lump formed in his throat. *An altar! Just like Nash described.*

He scanned back to the limo and saw the driver he now identified as Dolph, Buckley's doorman, removing a satchel from the trunk. Dolph carried it toward the altar and set it on a waist-high flat stone near the altar. Logan watched as Dolph took a red cloth from the satchel and draped it over the stone. He then took out a long, glistening black blade and laid it on the cloth. Now Logan's heart began to race. The blade bore eerie resemblance to the stone fragment from the clearing.

This done, Dolph took the satchel back to the car, got in, and drove away. Logan was hyperventilating, and sweat was pouring off him. He turned and walked back to his car in a swoon. He shouldn't have come here alone. Clearly, they were dealing with a level of evil he'd never encountered.

*   *   *

Hank looked out over the crowd and sighed. "It is definitely hot today. I feel like I've walked ten miles."

Lou checked his computer watch. He punched a button. "Eleven point three. But I think a mile of that was from the parking lot to the gate."

Hank chuckled. "Who wants to ride a tram? Especially when we're here, we can ride the exciting WEDway or Disney PeopleMover as I guess they call it now. Just the ride for the middle aged."

"I read that they once tried to change that ride into something with more zip. They sped it up considerably and called it Rocket Rods or some such."

"Why is it back to being slow now?"

"They didn't bother to change the track and since it was flat, the cars kept jumping from the rails and stopping the ride. They also found the speed was damaging the integrity of the support posts."

Hank laughed and pointed at a child running by. "I wonder if I can get one of those 'Paging Tom Morrow' shirts in my size."

Lou screwed up his face in a smile. "It's Disneyland, Hank."

The ride rolled into the station, where they exited and rode down the moving sidewalk to ground level. "Hey, wanna ride Mr. Toad again?"

Lou laughed. "No thanks. Twice is enough for me. You know they took that ride out at Disney World?'

"No, why? Was the theology too messed up for the Floridians?"

Mr. Toad's Wild Ride was a freaky throwback that seemed to the men to have been invented by some carny worker rather than Walt himself. Guests were treated to a "wild ride" in one of Mr. Toad's antique cars through a series of unDisney-like vignettes, including passage through a wild bar scene. The ride culminated with the riders ostensibly being killed in a head-on crash with a train and being sent directly to hell, where they were presumably tormented by animatronic devils indefinitely. Good family fun.

"Who knows? Walt was dead when they removed it, so I'd guess it was a financial rather than artistic decision."

Lou's cell phone rang. "Hey, Logan, what's up?"

"I'm in the mountains above the Olde Topanga Ranch. You know, where they used to make old westerns. I need you and Hank. I think they're going to kill Lanie tonight."

Lou stopped short. "What makes you think that?"

"They've got a stone altar set up, and I just saw that bouncer guy from Buckley's place lay out a ceremonial knife right there beside it."

"Are you sure these aren't just movie props?"

Logan looked at the phone in disbelief. "Lou, these items don't fit in with what they are filming here."

"Did you call the police?"

"Yes. They thought I was crazy. When I told them where I was, the officer laughed and said, 'I'll watch for the movie on the big screen.' When I threatened to call Ike, the Channel Twelve Troubleshooter, they agreed to send a car out. A patrol car arrived after a few minutes. I could see down below that the director or someone took him around the set, pointing things out. While they did this, a worker came out and took the blade and knocked down the altar. They shook hands and the cop got in his car and left. The worker then rebuilt the altar and replaced the dagger."

Hank asked, "Is this the ranch where Charles Manson and his family of killers holed up back in the day?"

"No."

Lou raised his eyebrows and shook his head. "You know we're at Disneyland so it'll be a while before we can get there." The rides now suddenly lost their appeal and the endless sound of "It's a Small World" playing over the loudspeakers took on a vaguely sinister tone.

Hank raised an eyebrow and leaned over, trying to listen in on Lou's conversation. Lou finished up his call with Logan. Lou shook his head at his brother-in-law to let him know that their day of fun was being cut short.

Logan outlined the best route across the city and sent them a pin with his location.

Lou confirmed what Hank suspected. "Vacation's over." He outlined the situation as they fast-walked to the parking lot tram line. They headed downtown on I-5 through surprisingly light traffic. En route, Hank searched on his phone browser for a gun shop. When he found one along their route, he called to make sure it was open for business.

A male voice answered, "Gun shop." Hank asked his questions, confirming the location, and hung up. Hank knew Lou had his nine-millimeter locked in its case in the trunk, but he felt the need for a weapon of some kind as well. They had turned onto the Santa Monica Freeway and were headed west now. "There is a gun shop up ahead in Culver City. Exit at your next opportunity and head north."

Lou exited, and they went only a short distance when Hank called out, "There it is, on the right."

Lou pulled to a stop in front of the store, and they walked in. A customer was testing the feel of a shotgun, but otherwise the store was empty. Lou approached a wall rack of ammunition. He found the nine-millimeter Luger display and pulled two boxes containing a total of fifty rounds of ammo. Lou carried it over to the counter. Hank had gone over to the edged weapon section and was examining items in the display case.

A muscular man wearing wraparound sunglasses came out of the back room. He walked over to Hank. "Can I help you?"

Hank noted the red tattoos inked on the man's upper arms. "Yes. I'd like to see *that* tomahawk please." Hank pointed.

The man opened the display case, removed it, and handed it to Hank. "Good choice. Should do the job."

Hank hefted the tomahawk, noting its perfect balance and that the grip wrapped in quality leather. He held it up to the light and examined the blade edge and neck of the weapon closely. "I've used one before." He smiled. "I'll need some sharpening tools as well." Hank bent back over the case and found a bayonet and three throwing knives. "I'll take these too."

The proprietor bent over and retrieved a stone, oil, and cloth from a space below the display box.

Hank moved on to a clothing rack and selected a desert camo pullover and pants. He tried on a lightweight pair of desert boots. "I needed these anyway," he said to Lou. Grabbing tins of tan and black face paint, Hank walked it all to the cash register where the man rang up the purchases.

Lou paid with his credit card, and the man looked closely at him. "Cop?"

"Detective. Retired."

The man looked at Hank and narrowed his eyes a bit. "Ranger?"

"Nope. Marines. Force Recon. Iraq."

"Corps. Vietnam." The man tossed Hank a belt holster for the weapons. "On me."

"Thank you." Hank and the man exchanged nods and the faintest of smiles.

As Hank and Lou turned to leave, the man called, "Good hunting, brother. Semper fi."

"Semper fi," Hank replied.

Chapter 58

COME AND SEE THE SHOW

Lou pulled in next to two dusty cars on the ridge above the desert movie set. Exiting his vehicle, he approached Logan, Dave, and Sam. He grinned in surprise to see the latter two and then smiled broadly as he greeted them. "Gentlemen."

Logan turned on his side, staring up at Lou. "Where's Hank?"

"He'll be along. I dropped him off below. He's doing a little recon."

Logan and Sam exchanged looks, but Dave held Lou's gaze. "I know I've been a pain in the neck with my indecision and attempts to run things, but I'm through with that. I'm totally out of my depth with all of this, but I'm all in now and I'll rely on your and Hank's direction."

Lou nodded and gave a small smile. "And the Lord's."

The sun had gone down, and twilight was fading as they sat down again on Logan's plastic tarp, passing around bottles of water. Logan spoke quietly to keep the sound of their voices from carrying in the night air. He described what he had seen in the afternoon: the airplanes and the tents with the strangely garbed crowd. He also related his conversation with Scott Nash. The three others listened quietly.

Dave then related his and Sam's experiences with Agent Hogan at the Saturn Building earlier in the day. When Dave finished, Logan suddenly jumped and let out an exclamation of surprise.

Sam whispered, "Shh, Logan. Your voice carries."

Behind Sam, Hank reached down and tapped him on the shoulder. He spun and jumped back as well.

Hank chuckled, standing there in camo with his face and hands painted. He looked deadly.

Hank sat down cross-legged and spoke barely above a whisper. "The good news is that they, whoever they are, do not seem to expect any visitors. I found three guards. Two are at the gate, which they now have chained and padlocked. The third is roaming. The two at the gate are carrying clubs. The roamer appears unarmed. All have walkie-talkies."

Lou peered at Hank. "Did you hear Logan and Dave?"

"Yes, I was standing there for a while." Hank laughed, and the three young men looked at each other. "The guards do not seem to be trained up. From their positioning and posture, they appear to be putting in time. One odd thing is they all look alike: tall and thin, very pale, and with longish, white hair."

"Like Cashwell? Or like the guys at the restaurant?"

"The latter. I remember Cashwell as balding."

Logan interrupted. "They sound like the Nordic reptile-men or whatever Nash called them. He suggested that they were capable of assuming dangerous forms."

"Nordic reptile-men? Like the Swedish bikini team?" Sam laughed.

Dave thumped his twin on the back. "It's not a joke, Sam. We both know about the snakes, and remember I've seen what they can do up close."

Sam, chastened, lowered his head, still laughing to himself.

Lou looked at Hank. "Maybe they aren't relying on guns."

Hank shrugged. "And this is assuming I've made them all. I don't know what to make of the throng in the valley beyond that hill." He indicated the ridgeline with his chin then sat down with his back against the Joshua tree and took out his tomahawk and bayonet. Retrieving his sharpening tools, he went to work on the blades. "Logan, before it began to get dark, did you notice anything unusual about the ground where the altar sits?"

"No, the altar was already there when I got back from lunch. Why?"

"Don't know. There is a slight convexity to the ground under the altar. It almost appears to have a metallic sheen."

"Does that mean anything?"

"Again, I don't know."

Logan scratched his head. "What is our plan?"

Lou responded, "Plan? We wait and see what they're going to do." He glanced at Hank, who nodded his agreement.

As the darkness thickened, a man could be seen below walking around the altar, placing torches in the ground and lighting them. He then disappeared through a gate in the senate wall into the livery stable of the western set.

Hank stood up. "I'm going down there now. Be quiet, and keep your eyes peeled. Put a hand up if you are in danger. I'll be watching." He vanished into the night.

The workman returned and this time placed four thin, metallic pyramids at the cardinal compass points about ten feet from the altar.

"What are we supposed to do now?"

"Patience, Sam," Lou whispered.

A klieg light snapped on above the forum set and a cameraman was visible in a chair with a large movie camera, on a rising boom platform, aimed at the altar.

"Looks like the show is about to start." Lou whispered a silent prayer as the three young men situated themselves, fidgeting with nervous anticipation.

The barn door of the stable swung open. A second light appeared in a window below the steeple in the western town church, and a second camera moved forward out of the opening. Music emanated from the area of the altar, a slow droning melody with a heavy beat. Through the door of the stable came a man wearing a blue robe with the hood down. He was leaping and gyrating in a wild dance as if a parody of David before the Ark of the Covenant.

Logan whispered to his friends, "That's Rock Rollins. I'd recognize him anywhere."

Behind Rollins, a line of black-hooded figures emerged. They followed him in a bizarre shuffle, dragging one foot and stomping the ground with the other while holding onto the shoulder of the man ahead with their right hand. They murmured a dissonant tune along with Rollins. Only a few of the words could be distinguished, including "light of the earth, fallen from the sky." And Rollins bellowed out what sounded like "Oh mighty spirit, slither this way. Your word is power all shall obey!"

"What in the world is that about?" Sam muttered.

Lou shrugged.

Logan's anxiety rose. "They are getting ready to sacrifice Lanie."

Sam and Dave both looked at Logan.

Dave said sharply, "Knock off that craziness." He pulled his knees under him, muscles tense.

Lou set a hand on his shoulder. "Easy now, Dave." It was still unclear whether this was all part of an elaborate film take, but the deep unease in his gut told Lou they were witnessing something much more. He stared harder at the procession. The marchers formed a circle around the altar and the music stopped. A long line of white-robed people became visible, cresting the ridgeline and coming up from the valley beyond the stable.

Rollins stepped into the middle of the circle. He picked up a Stratocaster guitar from where it had been stashed behind the altar. In the still, deathly quiet, he began to strum softly. He sang out in a quavering baritone, "Come, oh come, on wings of steel. Come, oh spirit. Take the wheel."

Sam laughed. "Geez, these goofs are really into it. Who would pay to see this trash?"

Logan elbowed Sam. "People who watch snuff films. I'm telling you we need to do something. They're going to *kill* Lanie."

Lou felt confident Logan was not overreaching in his estimation of what they were witnessing, yet he knew they needed to wait for the Hank's signal or some prompting from the Holy Spirit. Adrenaline rushed through his veins, and he prayed for the Lord's guidance with more fervor. Lou gestured for quiet. "Shhh." He saw a movement in the camera light beyond the set. It flashed quickly between two of the town buildings. Prompted by something unseen, Lou pulled up to standing and crept about seventy-five away, hoping for a better angle. Hanging back from the young men in the dark next to a tree, he soon identified the movement as Hank.

Rollins crooned on for a brief time then suddenly stopped. He placed his guitar on the altar and threw back his robe onto the ground. His body reflected sweat and oil, and he wore only a blue, fuzzy loincloth. As he stood there in the glare of the camera lights, he threw his arms out above his head and cried, "Come, oh winged serpent. Oh prince of the west,

292

receive your due." He then began a shimmying and shaking dance around the altar.

This was too much for Sam. He tried to stifle his laughter, but Dave shook him and covered his mouth.

"Looks like Grover's uncle is having a seizure," Logan observed, inciting another round of laughter.

Suddenly behind Logan a voice asked, "Enjoying the show, boys?" Cashwell was standing there above them, flanked by the two ersatz FBI agents, Hogan and Page, holding assault rifles. They pointed at the three young men and Cashwell continued. "May I see your tickets? Oh, I forgot. *You don't need no stinkin' tickets.* You belong in the VIP section. Let's go down and get a better view of the action. Heck, the prince might even give you a small role in the production. A brief one, but a role nonetheless."

Cashwell jerked his chin forward and the two riflemen motioned with their barrels for the three young men to proceed down the mountainside on a path next to the flat, rocky overhang where they had sat.

Logan and Dave each raised an arm in the air as they walked. Sam raised two.

Lou watched from behind the tree and a clump of brush about a hundred feet away, thankful he'd listened to that inner voice directing him to move. This alone had saved him. As he watched his friends being marched off, he felt and heard a loud whoosh of air above. Lou sensed a dark form fly overhead. He looked up to see what looked like a very large bird crossing in front of the moon, circle the set, and come to rest on the church steeple. When the creature landed, Lou could see it was no bird. It was a dragon! Its color was a mix of pale and royal blue, and it was nearly twice as big as Miguel's dragon form had been in Michigan. He'd seen this creature before, carrying the dying Brother Love out over Lake Michigan and then dropping him into the drink.

Lou's heart pounded with fear and anger. He knelt down and prayed, wishing he could communicate with Hank.

The dragon dipped his head forward and opened his huge mouth. Great flames and a roar of thunder issued forth. The sulfurous stink of brimstone filled the valley. The creature then lowered his gaze to the proceedings below, his giant eyes glistening in the klieg lights. Smoke curled from his nostrils. His smile showed great teeth set in a mirthless grin.

The door of the trailer burst open and out marched Buckley and a woman Lou didn't recognize. She was holding Buckley's shoulder and forcing him onward. Lanie's assistant, Tanya, appeared taller than a normal human being and walked with long, jerky strides on outsized legs, swaying as if she were a poorly done Claymation cartoon. Her trunk and arms bulged with grotesquely outsized muscles. Her head was gigantic with long, scraggly, black hair. Lou thought she might be wearing some kind of crude costume, but he couldn't tell in the dark from this distance.

Tanya roughly pushed Buckley to the altar, and then she suddenly turned and loped unsteadily away into the livery where she disappeared. Buckley was the only normal-appearing person present.

At that moment, an ornate litter emerged from a side building, carried by four Nordics. Lanie sat enthroned upon it. She smiled and waved to the crowd of neophytes who now filled the route to the altar. Lanie wore a sparkling gold and silver gown covered with jewels reflecting the camera lights, and a headdress fashioned in the likeness of a pontiff's miter with a snake head attached to the peak. Like a deranged Miss California, she stood and blew kisses. Lanie swayed back and forth unsteadily as her conveyance plodded toward the altar. She passed the concentric rows of initiates who circled the altar and her litter entered the circle of torches.

The Nordics lowered their poles to the ground and Lanie stepped off the litter, stumbling. Rollins caught her, preventing her from falling on her face. He swung her around the altar in a clumsy waltz to camouflage her misstep from the cameras. This provoked a rumbling laugh followed by a low growl from the steeple above. More smoke issued from the beast's nostrils.

Lou followed Cashwell and his gunsels down from the overlook, hanging back about twenty yards.

"Okay, that's far enough," Cashwell ordered.

The three men trembled and glanced at each other as they regarded the creature atop the steeple.

Sam turned to his colleagues and said, "Is that what I—" before Cashwell barked, "No talking! Eyes forward!"

"Hogan" jabbed Sam sharply in the back with the barrel of his rifle. Cashwell then walked out into the circle of torches. He yelled over his shoulder, "Be ready to bring them to the altar on my cue." A Nordic helped Cashwell don a red-hooded robe. Buckley stood next to the table, drenched in sweat and shaking. He looked around frantically. A Nordic wrapped Buckley in a white robe. Lanie stepped out of her gold and silver gown and let it fall into the dust. She wore only her tiny dancing bikini. Buckley grabbed a white gown from the table and wrapped Lanie in it. He stood protectively next to her as Cashwell put a hand on their heads.

On the hillside, Lou felt a tap on the shoulder and turned to see Hank with his hand up to his lips. He pointed to the guards and indicated to Lou that he should hit "Agent Hogan" on the head with his pistol. Hank then held up his tomahawk and pantomimed hitting "Page" with the flat of his weapon's head.

Hank mouthed a quick prayer and they moved forward as one.

Both strikes rang true, and the phony FBI men dropped to the ground.

When Lou reached out to Sam to let him know the captors were neutralized, Hank grabbed his hand to prevent him touching Sam. Hank shook his head vigorously and whispered, "Don't. We don't want any disruption that would tip the others off that their guards are down."

Chapter 59

OPEN THE DOOR

An odd, rhythmic drumbeat and baseline rang through the valley and built-in volume. Sam found the tune familiar but it was rendered in a minor key and played in a manner designed to inspire fear.

Cashwell nodded to Buckley and intoned, "Benjamin, it's now time to give you your reward for services rendered. Honestly, I've enjoyed our time together. I want you to know this reward comes directly from the prince."

The platform camera moved in on the altar. Rollins had picked up his guitar and began to strum along with the drumbeat. He continued to stare up at the giant dragon with terror and visibly shook as he hopped around wildly while unsuccessfully playing in time. The dragon opened its mouth and roared. Fire and smoke issued forth, and it was all Rollins could do to not pass out.

Hank crawled to the front of the three trembling young men and indicated they should kneel in a huddle. "Gentlemen, we need prayer cover. Don't look at or think about that demon. Just pray, and stay here. Lou and I need to handle this."

With a nod from Cashwell, Rollins swung his guitar up in the air and smashed it over Buckley's noggin. Buckley went down in a heap. Four black-robed assistants left the circle. They lifted Buckley by his extremities and laid the unconscious man on the altar faceup toward the rapidly darkening sky. The drumbeat grew in intensity as the torches threw a flickering light over the circle of hooded figures who once again started their thump-shuffle chant around the altar. The clouds thickened and roiled. Lightning crackled within rapidly forming thunderheads.

Rock Rollins stood nearby, trembling and mewling, frozen with fear. He tried to sing but all that came out was a discordant version of an undecipherable rip-off of an old Knack tune.

Cashwell stepped up onto a rock alongside the altar and raised his hands above his head.

Lanie appeared to be ensorcelled or drugged. She stood next to the altar, swaying and waving her arms overhead in ecstasy.

The marching and music ceased suddenly, and Cashwell bellowed, "Come forth!"

From the livery burst Tanya. She was now in full ogre form, glowing gold and green, her arms outspread. She stalked slowly toward the altar. Lou could now see she was definitely not wearing a costume. She bellowed as she entered the circle and was answered by a colossal roar from the beast on the steeple. She stomped several times around the scene while roaring out her power, then stopped in front of the altar.

Cashwell bowed low at her approach and four Nordic supplicants picked up Lanie, who didn't protest, and laid her atop Buckley facedown. Buckley awakened and struggled to push Lanie off. He yelled when he saw Cashwell raise the ceremonial knife.

Crying out in an unknown tongue, Cashwell stretched to lift the obsidian blade high above his head and began his stab down into the pair of offerings.

Rock Rollins had bolted from the circle up the path past the three captives. He did not see Hank and brushed him as Hank threw his tomahawk.

There was a whirring sound in the air. The weapon whizzed by Tanya's head and struck Cashwell's arm just above the elbow. Cashwell howled in agony as the knife dropped onto Lanie's back—point down.

Lightning bolts now crisscrossed the sky, and blue light began to flicker within the four pyramids. The knife had stuck, pinning Lanie to Buckley. Cashwell slumped over, driving the point home with his chest wall. Blood mingled from the two victims and rolled down the altar onto the ground, flowing through troughs to bathe the bases of the pyramids, sending blue light leaching from their pinnacles. A deafening, crackling roar rent the night as a brilliant blue beam merged over the altar and lanced up into the sky. The clouds vanished in the glow and forms could be seen moving above. The inner row of the initiates began to radiate an identical blue.

Hank pulled his bayonet and rushed Cashwell to finish him off, though it appeared to be too late for Lanie and Buckley.

A bright light grew in intensity beside Lou as Tanya stepped toward Hank, roaring and flexing with rage. Lou stepped forward and fired a half dozen rounds into the chest of the ogre to send it stumbling backward. The shining form took the shape of a muscular man brandishing a gleaming sword and moved forward with Lou. Lou had seen this man before. He looked on in wonder as Tanya, now wounded, cowered before the light. The being leapt forward and struck the neck of the creature, severing its head.

Monstrous forms began to take shape above the altar within the light beam, but the glowing man turned and sliced the beam with his sword, extinguishing it and causing the demons to vanish.

The prince of California vaulted from the steeple, his great dragon form hovering in the air above. He roared with rage as the angel in its gleaming robe rose into the air to meet him.

Lou now recognized him as the guardian from the restaurant. The protector floated in the air, increasing to a size nearly equal to the dragon. His sword glowed with ever-changing colors of the rainbow and he spoke with authority to the dragon. "It's finished. Back off and leave. If you move to strike these, the Lord's children, you will meet your doom here and now."

The dragon, seething with rage, responded, "You don't frighten me! You have no right to barge into our territory and threaten us! You know the rules!" In his fit of anger, the prince drooled a fiery molten liquid and brandished his talon.

"I will not repeat myself. Do you question the Lord's authority?" The man's blade began to hum and pulse with a blazing intensity as he spoke.

The dragon wheeled and glared down at the confusion below. "The girl and man are mine, as is the high priest."

The bright spirit moved toward the monster. "Take your priest if you can. Leave the others. You too know the rules."

The dragon opened his talons and began to drop toward Cashwell; however, he halted when he saw Cashwell changing into his giant snake form. The dragon laughed and a loud rattle filled the air as the snake squared off with Hank.

The glowing man now landed beside Hank. He smiled and handed Hank his sword. "Trust the Lord."

The snake struck at Hank, but Hank moved aside, brandishing the sword and avoiding the strike.

Logan, Sam, and Dave had all run to the altar, and after pulling the blade from Lanie, they lifted her off Buckley. She was unconscious and appeared mortally wounded. Buckley, now freed, rolled off the altar, jumped down, and grabbed the tomahawk from the ground. As he bent over, blood seeped from his abdomen. He quickly lurched toward the snake from behind and delivered a blow to the back of its head. The snake howled and turned, biting Buckley ferociously on the leg.

Buckley screamed and went down.

This was the moment. The snake had been distracted by Buckley and Hank quickly moved in, raising his sword. He brought it down with all his strength, decapitating the monster. The snake's head opened its mouth in a silent scream while the body wriggled its final throes.

The glowing man reached out, and Hank handed him his sword. "Praise God."

Hank closed his eyes briefly then turned to the man. "When—"

But the man had moved away. Hank opened his mouth and let loose a joyous laugh from the depth of his soul.

Above in the air, the dragon roared again, this time even more enraged. He drew in a great breath. He arched his back and spewed torrents of fire, bathing the valley in a sea of flame. The bright angel blocked the fire from touching each of the men. Hank bent over Buckley to shield him. The entire area was now a hellish chaos with dead Nordics lying on the ground aflame. Other Nordics and many of the initiates ran about in pain and terror, on fire and waving their arms. The set buildings had burst into flame. Everything was engulfed in giant plumes of fire. The carcasses of

Tanya and Cashwell burned with unrestrained fury. Over the hills ran those initiates who survived to this point.

The heat was nearly unbearable as Dave knelt down, cradling Lanie's head in his arms. Tears welled in his eyes. He'd seen the blade plunge through her body and knew she couldn't survive. Devastated he'd been unable to do more, he lifted up a desperate, fervent prayer. Just then, she moved, coughed, and seemed to be coming awake. Logan watched in puzzlement. "What in the—"

Logan leaned over them, staring in wonder. "Dave, you saw she was stabbed through the chest, but she isn't bleeding or having any trouble breathing."

Dave carefully moved the shoulder of the gown off the back of her shoulder to find no visible wound, only a bold, red, linear scar on her back. He looked up at Logan and smiled sadly. "I'm sorry I doubted you, Logan."

Chapter 60

THE FINAL CURTAIN

The great dragon crested the mountain and flew off to the southwest.

Ten feet away, Buckley writhed and rolled on the ground in considerable pain from both the snakebite and where the knife had run through Lanie and penetrated his abdomen.

Sam scanned the chaotic scene. "We can't just leave Buckley."

"You're right. We need to get him some medical attention. Sam, can you bring the car down here?"

Sam ran up the hill and retrieved the Hummer.

Lou kneeled over Buckley and exposed his abdomen. There was blood oozing from the stab wound. Hank brought over a section of the toga from a dead neophyte and cut two large sections—one he folded into a pad and the second into a long strip. He tied the makeshift bandage to Buckley's midsection. "There, that should do for now. We need to get him to a hospital, Lou. Who knows what that beast's venom will do to him?" Sam assisted Hank in laying Buckley on the back seat. Blood loss and the venom were causing Buckley to move in and out of consciousness. During a semilucid moment, he asked, "Are you taking me to the police?"

Hank answered, "No. UCLA Medical Center."

Buckley raised his brows, a relieved smile playing over his face. He nodded, "Thank you," and then passed out again.

Lou, still coming down off the adrenaline, looked at the young men and Lanie. "You guys okay?"

He heard a collective, mumbled yes.

Dave and Logan walked Lanie up the path to their car. By the time they reached the top, the exertion had cleared her head. The sky had begun clearing, but it was still difficult to breathe with the heat and smoke rising up out of the valley. Her jaw tightened as she turned to look back at the conflagration below. Her gown showed large bloodstains front and back. It clung to her, and sweat dripped in tiny rivulets.

She was wide-eyed as she watched the buildings engulfed in the firestorm. Smoke and ash drifted up and over them, causing Lanie to cough. She looked up at Logan. "What happened?"

Logan replied, "You wouldn't believe me if I told you."

Lanie then looked at Dave with a sad smile. "Is Benjamin dead?"

Dave stared straight ahead and refused to meet her gaze.

"No," Logan replied. "Not yet anyway. Lou and Hank are taking him to the hospital."

Her expression did not change. "Are you all right, Dave?"

"Yeah, why shouldn't I be?"

"I think you two need to talk." Logan led Sam away by the elbow. "Come on, Sam." Logan got into his car and Sam walked around and got in on the passenger side.

"See you at home, Dave." Sam waved.

Dave nodded in reply. He opened the car door for Lanie and then walked to the back of his car, where he stopped momentarily. He stood sweaty and soot stained, leaning against the trunk and gazing out over the burning valley. Bloodstains marred the front of his shirt.

Sirens could be heard in the distance. Lanie opened the door and got out. She walked quietly to the back and stood next to Dave. Neither one spoke for several minutes.

Lanie broke the silence. "I know what you must think of me, but I was only trying to make something of my life."

Dave's jaw tightened, but he did not respond.

Lanie continued. "I can see you don't want to talk to me, so I guess you can either drive me home or I'll start walking." Lanie turned to go.

Dave reached out and caught her arm. "I won't lie. I think you made a poor choice. Trading in a career helping people—and you were very good at it—for the promise of what? Money? Fame? I don't care about you and Buckley, but it hurts that you thought so little of me that you didn't even consider talking to me. I cared for you, Lanie. No, I loved you and thought we might have a future, but—"

Lanie hung her head and began to cry softly. "There never was a 'Buckley and me.' He straight up told me that I—I reminded him of his dead fiancée and he was trying in some way to make up for her death. He felt responsible for it."

"That doesn't sound like much of a disclaimer."

"Once I took the apartment, he—or they—kept me busy every minute. Today, I started noticing odd things. I couldn't explain them, but I got scared, Dave. Logan told me they were planning to kill me. I laughed it off, but his words scared me. All of this ritual stuff. When I arrived here, I felt a poke in my neck, and I remember waking up with you holding me."

"You did *not* wake up. You were dead, Lanie."

Lanie stared at Dave. "That's nothing to joke about."

"I'm not joking. You were dead. You had no pulse and weren't breathing. That's what Logan meant when he said you wouldn't believe what he might tell you."

"Dave, you see me here in front of you. I'm clearly *not* dead. If I were, I wouldn't be here."

"This is your blood on my shirt, Lanie. I can't explain it. There was an *angel,* I guess. He helped us. Or we'd all be dead."

Lanie looked away and began to cry harder. Dave pulled her close.

"Why are you making fun of me. You know I care about you." She did not see Dave roll his eyes and shake his head in confusion.

"I'm not making fun of you. Look. You can ask any of the others and they'll tell you the same thing. Did you see that Buckley was stabbed in the stomach?"

"No, I don't think so."

"Well, he was. And the blade went through your heart and into him."

Lanie shook her head, denial and anger flaring in her eyes, and she shouted, *"Dave, why are you making this up?"*

"See for yourself." He took her to the side of the car and tilted the mirror so that she could see her upper back. Her breath came in a gasp when she saw the deep, red scar. "I suggest that you look for the corresponding mark on your chest wall. That wasn't there before, was it?"

She fell against Dave's chest and was wracked with sobs.

* * *

Lou and Hank decided to wait at the hospital to see how Buckley fared. They sat in the ER waiting room while he was administered rattlesnake antivenin. The ER doctor came out and asked Lou and Hank a few questions about how the injuries occurred. Lou told him that they were on a camping trip and Buckley was cutting up some potatoes when a rattlesnake bit him and he accidentally fell on his knife. The doctor raised his eyebrow. "That makes a lot more sense than the story he told the nurses about a dragon and being a victim of ritual sacrifice. Your friend has quite an imagination."

"Yes, he sure does. He's a Hollywood producer, you know."

The doctor hesitated for a moment. "I guess that, or the envenomation, explains it." He smiled, but he did not look convinced. "The abdominal wound penetrated into his belly so he'll be going to surgery in a few minutes. We'll know more after the surgeons get a look inside, but the snakebite shouldn't cause any more issues." He looked at Hank's outfit and shook his head. "What were you making? A Rambo film?"

Hank laughed. "No, I was just doing some recon." The doctor looked confused.

Then he shrugged his shoulders and walked away. "Go get some rest. Your friend will probably sleep till the morning after his surgery."

Lou and Hank took the advice of the doctor and headed back to their hotel. Along the way, they bantered, trying to ease the residual nervousness.

"You know, Hank, you do look pretty intimidating."

"Why, thank you, brother. Did the doc mention anything about calling the police?"

"No. He seemed pretty confused—or maybe amused—by the whole thing. I'm sure he has bigger fish to fry here in LA with their knife and gun club."

"Good. The police should have enough on their plate trying to figure out what happened at the ranch without worrying about us."

Lou flipped on the radio. They listened to a news report about a large fire near Malibu. The Old Topanga Movie Ranch was burning. The authorities stated there were casualties, but no identifications have been made. It was thought that a freak dry lightning storm had ignited the movie set, but more information would follow when it became available. "Hmmm. Wonder what they will make of Cashwell's skeleton and the giant or whatever she was?"

"Movie props?"

Hank chuckled. He called Logan for an update, and they were surprised that Lanie was alive.

"Wasn't she stabbed through the heart?" Lou asked.

"It looked like it to me. Last I saw, she was lying there motionless and Dave was cradling her head."

"Wow." They lapsed into an easy silence for the remainder of the ride.

*   *   *

At seven in the morning, Hank had a strange dream. He was out fishing on Lake Superior. The waves were hitting the boat with a peculiar frequency that was getting him seasick. He gripped the gunnels and held on.

"Hank! Wake up." Lou stood in the bedroom doorway.

Hank felt his bed undulating under him. And then it stopped. "Did you feel that? I think that was an earthquake."

Hank flipped on the radio next to his bed. "We are receiving reports of two simultaneous tremors this morning. The epicenter of one was near El Cajon. That measured out at five point seven. The second was just west of LA and just east of Malibu near the site of last night's fire. That one measured out at five point nine. There are reports of property and road damage coming in from around the Malibu region, so be careful out there and stay tuned to KLLC for the latest updates and all your favorite oldies. Now here's the title tune from Rock Rollins's new CD soundtrack, *Nero*."

Lou laughed and walked out to the kitchenette. He poured himself a cup of coffee, and a second one for Hank as he wandered in.

"Thanks," Hank said, taking the cup. "Guess you can take earthquake off your bucket list. You wouldn't believe the dream I was having."

"Were you being chased by a snake?"

"No nothing like that." He laughed.

They decided to skip breakfast and head over to the hospital. When they entered Buckley's room, he looked confused. "Can I help you?" he asked. "Are you the police?"

Lou laughed. "Not anymore. I'm Lou Decker, and this is Hank Cloud."

"We brought you to the hospital last night," Hank added.

Buckley's look of confusion intensified. Then recognition dawned in his eyes. "Thank you." Buckley looked down at his sheets. His eyes teared up. "Is the girl dead?"

"No. As far as we know, she's fine."

"I assumed she was dead. How could she survive being stabbed through the chest? It had to have hit her heart."

"There was a lot of intervention last night, Mr. Buckley. Otherwise, none of us would have made it," Lou said. "I think you have some serious life path choices ahead of you now."

Buckley looked Lou in the eye. "I've done horrible things, Mr. Decker. I don't think I have any choices left, except where to wait until the prince or his agents come for me."

Hank stared back at Buckley. "We've all done horrible things. I've killed more men than I can remember. Each one was a living soul, but Jesus Christ has made atonement for our sins—all of them. You need to accept God's forgiveness." Hank then went through the God's plan of salvation with Buckley. "And you saw firsthand that my side's medicine dwarfs that of your old prince."

Buckley sighed as he looked up at Hank and Lou. Tears flowed, and sadness lined his face.